MAFIYA

MAFIYA

CHARLIE STELLA

PEGASUS BOOKS
NEW YORK

MAFIYA

Pegasus Books LLC
45 Wall Street, Suite 1021
New York, NY 10005

Library of Congress Cataloging-in-Publication Data is available.

ISBN: 978-1-933648-65-1

10 9 8 7 8 6 5 4 3 2 1

Interior design by Maria Fernandez

Printed in the United States of America
Distributed by Consortium

For Peter Skutches,
our Maestro,
with all our love
Ann Marie & Charlie

"For these be the days of vengence,
that all things which are written may be fullfilled."

LUKE 21:22

MAFIYA

Prologue

IT WAS AGNES Lynn's fourteenth birthday the first time she caught her mother with another man. The pool party was in full swing when Dolores Lynn sent her husband to pick up the birthday cake. A few minutes later Dolores's boss arrived. Agnes watched her mother lead her boss inside the house. Ten minutes later she found them in the basement bathroom, her mother on her knees giving her boss head.

Agnes was sworn to secrecy that day. Although she would never tell her father what she had seen, her mother tried to explain why it had happened.

"I know you can't understand it now," Dolores had told her daughter, "but I needed something for work and now I have it. You'll understand when you're older, I promise."

Agnes spent the rest of the party in her room feigning illness. She spent the rest of her life hating her mother.

One month after her fifteenth birthday it happened again. Agnes and an older girlfriend were driving around an empty parking lot at Jones Beach when they spotted a BMW convertible behind a stack of replacement boardwalk lumber.

They drove to within yards of the car when both girls saw a pair of women's legs sticking up out of the backseat. Agnes's friend leaned on the horn as both girls giggled wildly. The couple in the convertible scrambled for cover. The car backed out from behind the lumber, and Agnes found herself staring at her mother. She stopped laughing when she realized the legs she had seen a moment ago belonged to the same woman.

The incident at Jones Beach was never mentioned, but Agnes's hatred for her mother turned visceral.

Life at home turned especially ugly during Agnes's last year of high school. The more estranged mother and daughter became, the less respect Agnes had for her father. When a late-night argument between her parents revealed Francis Lynn's knowledge of his wife's infidelity, Agnes could no longer restrain her anger. She confronted him the very next day.

"I won't divorce your mother," he had told her.

"Why the hell not? She obviously doesn't love you."

"She doesn't have to," he had said. "I love her."

The fact that her father was a willing participant in a faithless marriage was devastating to Agnes. Whatever love she had for him turned to disdain. Her disgust for his obsequiousness not only ended their relationship, it also ruined her ability to respect other men.

She learned how to manipulate them instead. She used boys her own age to experiment with sex; although she remained a virgin until she was seventeen, Agnes became expert at wielding sexual power to control men.

During the spring of her senior year she became involved with a local bartender, who took her on a weekend junket to Las Vegas. Two weeks later she was roaming the Strip and absorbing all the potential Sin City offered a young girl with a game plan. Within a week after her high school graduation, Agnes left her parents and New York for good.

She took a job dancing at a strip club in downtown Las Vegas. One month into her new job, after she had finished for the night, her father was waiting for her outside the club.

"I didn't think I'd ever see you again," she told him.

"I can't believe you're doing this," he said.

"This, Daddy?"

He had motioned toward the strip club then, unable to bring himself to look at it. "Stripping," he'd said. "Why?"

"I make two hundred dollars a night," Agnes told him, "sometimes more. It isn't so bad. All I do is dance."

He had tears in his eyes. "What did I do that was so wrong?" he'd asked.

Agnes had wanted to hug him and cry and beg him to stop her and maybe even save her from the anger that was fueling her steady downfall. She shifted her weight to one leg instead.

"If you don't know by now . . . ," she had said, letting her thought trail off.

Francis Lynn wore his defeat like a favorite overcoat. He

sniffled before turning away and heading for the limousine he'd had waiting to take them both back to the airport. When he looked back at his daughter one last time, Agnes turned her back to him.

One year later, a few days after she turned nineteen, Agnes would turn her first trick. It would take ten years before she turned her last one.

Chapter 1

"WHAT ARE JASON tabs?" the attorney asked.

Agnes glanced over her shoulder before moving her chair a little to the left of where he was standing on her right.

"A program glitch," she told him. "When you adjust an outline numbering scheme, the program drops a tab in the format line and the text adjusts to it, usually too close to the number. You have to remember to clear tabs when you're finished working inside the numbering scheme."

He didn't get it. "Why do they call them Jason tabs?"

"Like the Jason movies?" Agnes said. He shook his head. "You can't kill them. They keep coming back."

He still didn't get it. He squinted at her.

"It's not a problem," she said. "I'll go through the documents."

"Can I watch?"

It had been a mostly dead morning. Agnes had volunteered to clean the document just to pass the time, except now he was finding excuses to hang around her desk. Agnes wasn't interested. She gave him a polite smile.

"I'd rather you didn't," she said. "I can show you what to do, how to do it, but I'd rather you didn't stand over me like this."

He leaned forward. She could feel him close to her ear. He reached forward to point, and his arm touched her hair.

Agnes used to tell her tricks, *"No kissing, no touching, and if you want straight head, keep your fingers out of my hair."*

"God damn it!" she yelled.

She shoved her chair back away from the desk and slammed into the attorney's legs.

He took a few steps back and turned pale. "I'm sorry," he said. "I didn't mean to . . . ."

Agnes used a controlled breathing exercise to calm herself. She stared at the blank video screen on the desk in front of hers until she said, "Why don't I type out the instructions for you?"

It was a tense moment. The attorney looked from Agnes to his secretary and back. His telephone line rang and spared him further embarrassment.

"I'll get that," he said on his way back to his office.

"Good for you," his secretary whispered at Agnes.

Her name was Lorelei Beauregard. She was a southern woman around the same age as Agnes. She sat at the station to

Agnes's left. There were two more stations directly in front of them that made up the cluster of four. Two of the regular secretaries were out sick. Agnes was there to help out with the overload. She had worked with Lorelei a few times over the past month.

"He's a sleaze," Agnes said.

Lorelei waved a hand. "Oh, honey, they all are."

"I tried to warn him."

"Yes, you did. And then you ran him over. I love it."

Agnes managed a smile when Lorelei chuckled.

"I know he's been calling for you specifically," Lorelei said. "I heard him place the order myself. 'Can you send me that blond woman? Agnes, I think her name is.'"

"I know what he's up to," Agnes said. "Makes my skin crawl. I was here two weeks ago when his wife and daughters were waiting for over an hour out here while he was on the phone in his office."

"Don't you hate that, when he makes them wait? He tried hitting on me the first day I was hired, but I think my tattoo turned him off. He actually put a hand on my shoulder and asked me how it was going. That's when I show him this."

Lorelei bent her right arm to flex her muscles. A red rose with a dagger through the center blossomed.

"Two thoughts came to mind when he leaned over me like that," Agnes said. "The other was elbowing him in the balls."

"My word," said Lorelei through a chuckle. "Now that would've been something else to see."

"I don't want you to think I'm some crazy woman," Agnes said, "but I have this thing about being touched like that, suddenly I mean, when it's a surprise."

"No need to explain, darlin'. The man was wrong. And I suspect he won't be doing it again."

"Or calling me back in for work."

It was a genuine concern. Lately there had been less and less work in the word processing centers she temped for. Agnes had welcomed the desk assignment today.

"He usually leaves that for me, calling in temps," Lorelei said. She was picking up a document at one of the printers behind Agnes's desk. "He's about two weeks from a closing, so we'll be busy the next few weeks. Don't you worry, sugar. If it's up to me, you're the first one I'll call."

Agnes turned to Lorelei and reached out to take her hand. "Thanks," she said. "I appreciate it."

Lorelei squeezed Agnes's hand before letting go. "Us girls have to look out for one another," she said. "With all the talk of outsourcing and whatnot, we better. I know of at least half a dozen firms farming their work out to India already."

The lack of steady work had become a growing concern. Agnes had noticed the younger attorneys were very well versed in many of the software programs law firms used. Between the attorneys doing their own work and the out-sourcing of word processing many of the firms had turned to, the writing on the wall was becoming all too clear: word pro-cessing was an industry on the wane. It was only a matter of time before she'd have to change professions one more time in her life.

"I'll tell you what my father used to tell me," Agnes said. "'There are some things you can do something about and some things you can't.' I'm thinking outsourcing is both. We know its coming, and we better be prepared for it."

Lorelei nodded her approval. "Sounds about right to me," she said, "although secretaries should be somewhat immune."

Agnes pointed toward the attorney's office. "I'll bet that makes him happy."

The women had bonded a few weeks earlier after working an entire week together for another attorney. Today Agnes was thinking about exchanging numbers with Lorelei and maybe going out for drinks after work some night.

Lorelei pointed to the attorney's office. "He keeps *Playboy* magazines in one of his desk drawers. No big deal except the one I saw the other night was opened to the centerfold. Another blonde, by the way, although I could hardly tell from the way she shaved a little heart around it. I suppose he opens the drawer every so often when he needs a thrill."

The thought of the attorney ogling over women, even pictures of women, repulsed Agnes.

"It'll be hard not to laugh in his face when he turns on the charm again," she said.

"I think you wounded his charm, darlin'," Lorelei said. "I doubt he comes back out until he's had a few." She leaned over to whisper again. "He's got a bottle of Johnny Walker in there he takes nips at for courage."

Another gutless wonder, Agnes thought. She wondered if he was a partner. Her father had been one at his firm. "How ironic is that?" she whispered to herself.

Lorelei excused herself to use the ladies' room. It was close to noon and she would be leaving for lunch soon. Agnes used her time alone to think about her father's advice again. She wondered if she was doomed by her past or if she would ever be able to get beyond it.

Lately, Agnes had been thinking about her father more and more.

"*Who loves you more than anybody?*" Francis Lynn would ask before sweeping her into his arms.

"*You, Daddy!*" Agnes would reply. Then she would squeeze and kiss him and ask: "*And who loves you the most?*"

"*Agnes does!*"

The attorney stepped out of his office, looked at Agnes, and quickly turned toward Lorelei's desk. When he saw she wasn't there, he stepped back inside his office and closed the door.

The interruption to her memories was a subtle reminder that her father's love had proved less weight than circumstance, and that all she would ever have were the cherry-picked memories from before she'd lost all respect for him.

She glimpsed at the desk blotter calendar and realized it was going on sixteen years since she'd last seen him. A phone call brought her back. Agnes answered the phone, but was too late.

"I got it!" the attorney yelled from his office.

Agnes was proud of herself for backing the bully off earlier, but she also knew that she hadn't been in control of the situation; his touching her hair had triggered a violent reaction.

"I'm going to head out to lunch a little early, sugar," Lorelei said. She had returned to her desk for her purse. "Gonna meet my beau for Indian food. I'll be back before one. I know you said you were meeting a friend, so I'll make sure and be back in time."

"Go ahead," Agnes said. "Don't worry about me. You enjoy yourself."

Agnes smiled at Lorelei's enthusiasm about seeing her boyfriend. Except for a puppy love crush or two when she was a very young girl, Agnes didn't know what it was like to be in love. Today she was two weeks from her thirty-fifth birthday. She wondered when, if at all, she ever would know.

Chapter 2

THE ENTRANCE TO Battery Park alongside the Staten Island Ferry was crowded with smokers when Agnes went to meet her friend. It was a cold but sunny January afternoon. Except for an occasional gust, the wind off the tip of Lower Manhattan was relatively calm. Agnes spotted her friend crossing the park from one of the State Street entrances near the Statue of Liberty Museum.

Rachel Wilson was a light-skinned black woman. At five six, one hundred twenty-six pounds, she appeared stocky in the heavy white sweater she was wearing under a black leather coat. Her short, brown leather skirt matched her thigh-high boots. She modeled both for Agnes by placing a foot on the edge of a bench.

"At least they match," Agnes said.

"Especially the hair and the boots," Rachel said. She performed an exaggerated, slow-motion pirouette.

Both women wore sunglasses. They leaned into each other and embraced. Agnes gave her friend an extra squeeze. Rachel had been holding onto a pretzel. She broke it in half to share with Agnes.

"I do like the wig," Agnes told her.

Rachel turned her back to a sudden gust of wind. Agnes preferred the cold and wore her down jacket unzipped at her chest. She was two inches shorter than Rachel and a few pounds heavier. Her short blond hair was uncovered.

"You better get used to it," Rachel said. "I have a job requires I shave my head. Most of it anyway."

"That doesn't sound good. I hope it pays a lot, you're even considering it."

"It pays more than I can afford to ignore, except the guy's an Arab. I already took care of his business twice before. For twelve hundred bucks, I might add. Half the tuition I owe the preschool for Kiesha, so I was grateful for the opportunity. The Arab thing bothers me a little bit, the way they are with women, but I can't afford to ignore this job. Can't afford to be too picky, not now."

Agnes said, "You trying to convince me or yourself?"

Rachel frowned.

"You're gonna stay in the business, you better profile," Agnes said. "A guy doesn't feel right, whatever the reason, you walk away."

They had first met in Las Vegas, where they both worked for the same escort service. They became friends the night they were paired up to work a private party for a group of Tokyo investors visiting Sin City.

Ten years later Rachel was still hooking while bringing up two kids. Agnes had tried to help her friend quit the business a few times since Rachel returned to New York, but the economics of single parenthood continued to be an obstacle for the thirty-year-old mother of two.

Rachel said, "I know, I know. Except he has a big-ass boat parked not far from here on the East River. Liked me to wear boots while I handled him."

"You know the rules," Agnes said. "If it doesn't feel right, it isn't."

"He's offering to pay the tuition plus. I figure my hair'll grow back. The tuition money isn't there otherwise."

Agnes remained silent.

"I'm just saying," Rachel said. "I didn't take it yet, the job. I am thinking about it, though. I'm thinking hard."

Agnes was uncomfortable discussing Rachel's business. Every self-help book she had ever read advised against having a relationship of any kind with somebody still in the life. Agnes knew it was sound advice, except this was her best friend. Agnes was godmother to both of Rachel's children and had been in the delivery room when they were born.

She said, "Don't tell me, this came from Nelson? I can't believe he has those kinds of contacts."

"Please," Rachel said, "some people are looking to move Nelson out. What he claims."

Agnes waited for more.

"Russians," Rachel said.

"Oh, that's great," said Agnes with deliberate sarcasm. "The Russian mob is known to provide the women they exploit excellent benefits, especially when they can't turn them out anymore."

"I'm talking about paying the tuitions in full here. One night, everything paid for."

"Overnight?"

"If I have to, why not? I can think about therapy the day after."

"Except the money will always be too easy," Agnes said. "If you do this job, pay for the tuitions or whatever, you'll always know it's there for you."

"As something to fall back on? If you're telling me my options are that or my kids going to public schools, I guess it will always be something to fall back on, yeah, you're right."

It was a touchy subject. Agnes knew to go easy. "So long as you're looking good, you can fall back on it," she said. "Ten, fifteen years from now what happens?"

Rachel huffed. "Sorry, but starting a personal crusade right now won't pay the tuitions this semester. And my ex can barely afford to buy himself lunch. He's trying, don't get me wrong. He's staying out of trouble and working two jobs, but the money just isn't there. I don't have the office skills you do, and I don't have the time to get them, okay?"

"You don't need office skills to get out," Agnes said. "You need to make a decision. After that, if need be, you need a gun. Besides, I've told you this before, I can lend you the money for the tuition."

Rachel didn't like the idea of borrowing money she might

not be able to pay back. Agnes felt she needed to keep the offer alive in case her friend was looking for a way out.

"Well?" Agnes said.

Rachel set her hands on her hips. "And how'm I supposed to pay you back?" she asked. "What, typing lessons until I can word process? Then what? How do I pay my bills, next semester's tuition, and then pay you back at the same time? And don't forget that I have a record. How's that going to work for me on an interview someday, six months for prostitution?"

Agnes hung tough. "That's an excuse and you know it."

"I know I can afford to feed my kids, pay my rent, and pay their tuitions hooking, that's what I know," Rachel said.

"And what if I make it a gift to my godchildren? I love them and I love you, and what the hell am I doing with it anyway? It's not like I'll have kids anytime soon."

Rachel was clearly annoyed now. "Cut me some slack here, okay? I came to see how you're doing and to chitchat, maybe invite you to dinner. I didn't come here to argue. I'm not taking charity, Agnes, so enough with that."

Agnes took a long, deep breath. She decided to accept the olive branch. "Dinner when?"

"One of the football playoff dates coming up. Next weekend or the one after. I can take a day off, they all home watching football."

An uncomfortable pause ensued. Agnes felt guilty for pushing too hard. She took one of Rachel's hands.

"Dinner is fine."

"You want to bring someone? Maybe that badass you met."

"Calm your jets," Agnes said. "I like the man, that's all. I'm not anywhere near what you're thinking."

She had been seeing a former cop she had met in a bookstore a few months ago. A brief exchange over a Steven Sidor thriller led to coffee, then a lunch, and after that a dinner. Agnes hadn't thought of it as dating. The relationship was still in its infancy. She liked the man, but it was impossible for her to imagine having sex yet.

"And how you know what I'm thinking?" Rachel asked.

"Nothing happened," Agnes said. "I'm attracted to the man. We're going fishing in the morning, you can believe it, but we're a long way from anything happening. I am, anyway."

Rachel shifted her sunglasses up onto her forehead. "Fishing?"

"Please, I'm a nervous wreck about it. I was trying to think of ways to escape it, but I had promised him last week, and tomorrow he's going to wake me up early and I'll be on a boat on the ocean in the middle of January."

"Fishing for what?"

"I don't know."

"You must like him then, you going on the ocean in this weather."

"Look, he's a nice guy so far, but that's it. I'll let you know if anything develops. I promise."

"What's he do again?"

"Private investigations. He's a former cop."

"Former cop because?"

"I don't know. I didn't ask."

"Well, can you ask him to come to dinner?"

"Yes, okay, but let's change the subject."

"Yeah, sure," Rachel said, "soon as it gets interesting." She turned her back to a gust of cold wind and asked, "Okay, so how's work?"

"I had a little incident this morning."

"Another touching thing?"

Rachel was aware of a few incidents in Agnes's past. Once, when a homeless man had grabbed her around the neck, Agnes had gone wild with rage fighting him off. Luckily, Rachel had been there to stop her before the police arrived.

"Some attorney," Agnes said. "He's been trying to hit on me. I tried to warn him to back off, but he thought he was being cute, I guess."

"What happened?"

"He leaned over my shoulder to get close."

"And?"

"I tried to run him over with the chair."

Rachel's eyes opened wide. "No way."

"It wasn't that bad," Agnes said. "I just reacted, you know."

"You panic?"

"I guess so, a little."

"What he do?"

"Oh, ran into his office and stayed there. He's pissed off and probably won't request me again, but who cares. His secretary is a doll, though, and she said she'd call me anyway."

Rachel took one of Agnes's hands. "My girl," she said.

Agnes squeezed Rachel's hand. "How are the kids?"

Rachel shuffled closer to Agnes on the bench. "Roger's mom has been a big help," she said. "Roger, too, but he's still giving me shit about . . . well, you know."

Agnes offered Rachel a cigarette.

"No, thanks," Rachel said. "My CFO is a stickler for clean breath. I'm his secretary. I have to be polite and clean and innocent until he starts to touch me under my skirt.

Then I'm overcome by his touch and he tells me to take it out and rub it."

She stopped to stroke the air with a fist. "The only time the routine varies is when he's rushed for time or we can't use his office," she continued. "Then it's up to the Waldorf and it costs him more, so he actually wants to fuck me. Not that it lasts any longer, but then I have to shower and waste an extra half hour or so."

"And time is money," said Agnes facetiously.

"Luckily, he still goes off like a rocket soon as I play with his balls."

Agnes remembered the routine. It made her uneasy.

"Spit, shine, and jiggle their balls," Rachel said. "I believe it was you first taught me that one."

It was a technique hookers used to get their johns to ejaculate. An old pro had taught it to Agnes early on in her Las Vegas years. She would wet her fingers and massage the testicles. Some johns couldn't hold back. It was one way of making quick work of a trick.

Agnes closed her eyes tight in an attempt to block the image now.

"Forget the Arab," Rachel said, "it's the guys like this one keep me stuck in the life. How do I turn down a quick two hundred like this? Where do I make it up? Two hundred bucks for a five-minute hand job."

Agnes was still fighting ghosts. She remained silent.

"I know you want to help," Rachel said. "And I'm grateful for it. You know I am."

Agnes covered her mouth with both hands to stop herself from saying the wrong thing. She knew their conversation was over when Rachel looked at her watch again.

"I'll call you about dinner," Rachel said.

They exchanged a tight hug before getting up off the bench. They exchanged another hug before Rachel used a breath spray and kissed Agnes on the cheek.

"Be careful," Agnes said.

Rachel left the park and headed north on Water Street. Agnes watched until her friend disappeared into the flow of people traffic. As she turned to head back to work, she felt a sudden chill from a gust of wind blowing off the water. Agnes turned again to search for Rachel, but her friend was gone.

She felt another sudden chill. This time it unnerved her.

Chapter 3

IT WAS TWO THIRTY when Rachel was leaving the office building lobby after her afternoon appointment. She was surprised by her pimp, Nelson Freeman, and the two white men standing on either side of him. One of them was tall and bald; the other, stocky and bearded.

"Here's the lady of the hour now," Freeman said.

Rachel looked at the two men she didn't recognize. "Who're they?"

"Your new bosses."

"Excuse me?"

"I am Yuri," the bald man said. He had a Russian accent. "This is Sergei."

Rachel turned to Freeman. "They're my bosses, says who?"

"Mr. Fahd," the bald man said. "You remember him, eh? He's wants you for big job today." He turned and pointed at a Mercedes parked across State Street. "He's waiting there in car."

Rachel looked at the Mercedes before turning to Freeman again. "You said it was tomorrow night."

"Don't act surprised," Freeman said. "I mentioned it more than once, some Russian boys taking over."

"Is mutual arrangement," the bald man said. "Nelson says he is going to retire. I make job for you."

"You might think to ask first," Rachel said.

"Of course, but Mr. Fahd is waiting for you now. He says he doubles the price he's offer you."

"Doubles what? How much?"

The bald man shrugged. "I don't know what price is. Whatever you and Mr. Fahd negotiate last time, eh? He says to tell you he doubles it today."

"He's talking about a lot of money," Rachel said.

"Mr. Fahd is rich man. You see his boat?"

"That where we going?"

The bald man shrugged again. "Is between you and Mr. Fahd," he said.

Rachel turned to Freeman again. "This for real?" she asked. "You retiring?"

Freeman thumbed over his shoulder. "Soon as you pay me for the job upstairs."

"That was none of your business."

The bald man pulled out his wallet. "How much?" he asked Freeman.

"Half what she got paid," the pimp said. "That was our deal."

The bald man turned to Rachel. "How much I should give him?"

"Two cents," Rachel said.

The bald man smiled. He fingered a hundred-dollar bill from his wallet and handed it to Freeman. The pimp was suddenly reluctant to take it.

The bald man said, "Go 'head, what you want, eh?"

He put the money in one of Freeman's hands when the pimp hesitated. "Good luck with retirement," he said.

Freeman nodded before glancing at Rachel and leaving.

"Okay, Mr. Fahd is waiting," the bald man told her. "What you say? He says double whatever you discuss with him last time."

Rachel looked at the two men who were supposed to be her new bosses.

"Yeah, okay for now," she said. "But we need to talk about my working for you in the future."

"No problem," the bald man said. "Whatever you says."

•—•

The hairdresser, Leonid Fetisov, had finished shaving most of Rachel's hair and had begun to apply blond streaks to what was left. They were in a basement apartment in Brighton Beach. Rachel had been unconscious for a few hours. She remembered having the drink in the back of the Mercedes and the drive along the Gowanus Parkway through

Brooklyn, but then she had passed out. The last thing she remembered was seeing a very blurry Verrazano Narrows bridge.

Now she was groggy and felt a pain in the back of her head. "Where are we?" she asked.

"Brighton Beach," Fetisov said. "In Brooklyn, near Coney Island." His effeminate voice had a Russian accent.

"Who are you?"

"Lenny," he said. "Leonid, but you can call me Lenny."

"Oh, my God!" Rachel gasped. She saw herself in the small mirror hanging on the wall in front of her. "What are you doing?"

"Yuri says to shave off. Don't worry, grows back fast. How you like streaks?"

He went to the mirror and picked it off the wall. He showed her both sides of her head, where the strands of streaked hair ran down behind her ears.

Rachel tried to turn in the chair. She was restrained by a Velcro strap. "What is this?" she said. "What's going on?"

Fetisov ignored the question. "You like streaks?"

Rachel tried to pull the Velcro strap off. "Why am I tied? Where is my bag? Where are my watch and phone?"

"You have phone call before. Two calls. Yuri has phone."

Rachel remembered the bald man and then the Arab. "Where is he? Where's Fahd?"

"Who?" asked Fetisov. He rehung the mirror.

"Fahd, the fat guy," Rachel said. "The Arab. And the bald guy, where is he?"

"Probably getting drunk upstairs." He motioned at her to turn in the chair. "Go right."

Rachel shook her head. "Wait a minute," she said. "Stop!"

"I am told come here and take care of hair," Fetisov said. "I don't ask question. You know who Yuri is, what you're doing here?"

Rachel shook her head again. Heavy footsteps could be heard on a stairway directly outside the room. The bald man from the car poked his head inside the doorway.

"Are finished?" he asked.

"What am I doing in Brighton Beach?" Rachel asked him. "What's going on?"

The bald man glared at Fetisov. He said, "Big focking mouth, Brighton Beach."

Fetisov stuttered.

"Shut up," the bald man said.

"What's going on?" Rachel asked.

"Job," the bald man said. "You are here for job. Mr. Fahd."

Rachel motioned at the Velcro strap. "What happened to me? Why am I tied?"

"You drink too much champagne. Let faggot finish hair."

Rachel shuffled in a try to get out of the chair. The bald man pushed the hairdresser out of his way to stop her.

"Let faggot finish," he said, louder this time.

"What's going on?" Rachel yelled. "Where's my bag? What are you doing?"

The bald man turned to Fetisov again. "Big focking mouth, eh?"

"I need to call my kids," Rachel said.

"I get for you later," the bald man said. "Phone is upstairs. Now let faggot fix hair."

Rachel looked to the hairdresser. "No," she said.

She began to struggle again. The bald man stepped in front of the chair. He smacked her hard across her face.

"Let faggot do hair!" he yelled.

Rachel was stunned from the smack. She tilted her head back slowly and sat still.

Chapter 4

THE THIRD RING woke her. Agnes rolled across the bed to answer the phone. She rubbed her eyes before searching for the digital clock. She wasn't sure she was reading the time right and leaned over to pick the clock up. It read 4:58.

Jack Russo was proving to be a man of his word. He had said he'd give her a wake-up call at five o'clock, and here it was, two minutes early.

"Oh, God, I think I just fell asleep," she said.

"Think how well you'll sleep when we get back," he told her.

Agnes yawned. "Huh?"

"Nothing," Jack said. "Do you want me to pick you up?"

"No, no, that's okay. I'll get up."

"Promise?"

"Promise."

"Okay. I'll meet you at the marina in forty-five minutes. Still have the directions?"

"Yeah, I think so."

They hung up. Agnes turned over and fell back asleep. Ten minutes later the telephone rang again. This time she jumped out of bed and splashed water on her face before answering the seventh ring.

"I'm up, I'm up," she said.

"Good girl," Jack said. "Don't forget to wear shitty clothes. Just in case we actually catch a fish."

This time Agnes moved quickly to get dressed. She had laid out layers of the nastiest clothes she could find, on Jack's advice, the night before.

"I'm not so sure I won't get sick," she remembered telling him. "How far out do they go?"

"Pretty far," Jack had said. "It's a six-hour trip. Figure one out and one back, the rest of the time fishing."

"Six hours is a long time if you're sick, Jack."

"They go out early, I think, about seven, seven thirty. We're sick by eight thirty, tossing our cookies by nine. Then we lay out on the top deck and wish for death another two, three hours until we get help walking off the boat."

"You make it sound so appealing."

"It's what happened to me the first time I went," he had told her. "I felt like I was on a boat for another two days after I got off."

"Did you really throw up?"

"No, but only because I didn't have anything in me. I wished to hell I did, though. It was horrible, truly horrible."

Agnes had smiled at Jack's candor about being sick.

Then he had said, "Come on, what do you say?"

"Isn't it a little cold on the water this time of year?"

"It's freezing."

It wasn't the best way to spend a day off from work, but Agnes knew she had wanted to go. "Why the hell not?" she had told him.

Now that it was time to go, she wasn't so sure it was a good idea.

She saw there were messages on her answering machine. Two were from temporary agencies requesting her to work. The third was from Rachel's ex-husband. He was ranting about Rachel not picking up the kids the night before. Agnes decided to ignore the call when she heard the liquor in Roger's slurred speech.

She called Rachel's cell phone instead and left a voice message.

"It's Agnes. Roger called and said you didn't pick up the kids. He sounded drunk, so I didn't call him back. I'll wait to hear from you. I'll be out most of the day fishing. Yes, I'm going fishing. I'll call again tonight when I'm back. If I don't hear from you by then, I'll call the police."

It was a security message they had developed when they were hooking in Las Vegas. Leaving a message about calling the police was one way for working girls to protect one another. As much as they didn't want to involve the law, if one of them wasn't in contact with the other after working a job, they had agreed that leaving a message about calling the police was the smart thing to do. When enough time passed after a warning call, they had both agreed to call the police for real.

Agnes hung up and was on her way in less than half an hour. The drive from her apartment in Staten Island to the Raritan Marina in Perth Amboy was a twenty-minute trip without traffic. She stopped at a Dunkin' Donuts on Woodrow Road for an extra-large cup of light coffee with three Sweet'N-Lows. She let the coffee cool until she was crossing the bridge from Staten Island to New Jersey. Perth Amboy was the first exit.

She remembered the directions Jack had given her and found the Raritan Marina without trouble. He was waving to her as she pulled into the parking lot. He was dressed in gray sweat pants and a red hooded sweatshirt. Agnes checked the time. It was six fifteen in the morning. Jack was smiling ear to ear.

"Jesus Christ, you're a morning person," she told him.

Jack held up a large lunchbox. "Ham and cheese, tuna on toast, and peanut butter and jelly. The thermos is filled with black coffee, leaded."

Agnes stretched through a yawn once she was out of her car. She saw Staten Island across the Arthur Kill and pointed to it.

"That where I live?"

Jack pointed to some of the large luxury homes across the water. "That's the money end, but Staten Island doesn't look too bad from Perth Amboy. Almost habitable."

Agnes followed him to a bench, where she stretched her legs again. "Where's the fishing boat?"

He thumbed to his right. "The *Sea Pigeon IV*," he said. "Seventy-five feet long."

Agnes closed one eye. "What happened to the first three?"

"Good question. I'll ask the captain."

They had another twenty-five minutes before the boat left the marina. Jack examined her outfit and approved of the galoshes and paint-stained sweatshirt jacket.

"I got us two spots up front," he told her. "I already filled the mates in on our rookie status. I slipped one guy a twenty, and he said he'd keep an eye on us."

"Is it really gonna be that bad?"

"Potentially."

"You're scaring me, Jack. I've never done this before."

"Are you wearing layers? It's gonna get a lot colder once we're on the water."

"Trust me, I'm layered. Is this boat heated?"

"Absolutely. But not where we're fishing from around the deck. We'll catch whatever wind there is full on."

"There anything else I need to know?"

"I'm assuming you can swim."

⋅◆⋅

Yuri Timkin answered his cell phone while a few of his men arranged furniture around a mattress they had set on the floor.

"Nobody is starting anything," he told his stepbrother in Russian, clearly annoyed with the interruption.

"Last night I got a call from the Italians in Manhattan," said Viktor Timkin, also speaking Russian. "What's going on with you and some pimp in Harlem?"

"Business," Yuri said. "What's wrong with that? I'm doing business with him."

"What kind of business? I don't need trouble now, not with the Italians. I have a deal with the West Side, eh?"

Yuri was insulted. "I made a deal, too."

"What deal? Tell me about it."

"With the Arab," Yuri said.

"Fahd? You went to a pimp in the city for Fahd?"

"I made a deal with the pimp," Yuri said. He turned away from the phone and saw one of his men was injecting heroin into one of the prostitute's arms. "Not too much," he yelled. He held two fingers half an inch apart. "Just a little for now."

"What?" Viktor said.

"What is it?" Yuri asked his stepbrother. "What do you want from me, Viktor?"

"You went to a pimp belongs to the West Side," Viktor said. "I don't need any headaches now. What was the deal you made? Why are they calling me?"

"To break balls, I don't know."

"Yuri? Why is the West Side calling me about some fucking pimp?"

Yuri was shaking his head. "I bought a woman for the Arab," he said, "from one of their pimps."

"What do you mean, you bought her?"

"I bought her. From the pimp, Viktor. I paid him, so I don't know why he's crying now. Fahd likes her. He's been with her before."

"I don't understand."

"She's a whore, Viktor, what do you think what for?"

"Don't fuck with me, Yuri. What do you mean you bought her?"

Yuri was annoyed. "For a party, Viktor, okay? A fucking party."

"What party? You made trouble with the Italians for a party? Don't bullshit me."

Yuri had had enough. "Fuck the Italians," he said.

"Careful what you say, idiot."

Yuri's jaw tightened. "What is the problem, Viktor? The pimp wants the girl back? Fine, I'll bring her tomorrow. I'll give them more money. Okay?"

"The pimp is with West Side. Understand?"

"Yes, yes, I know, I know."

A long pause followed. Yuri finally said, "Anything else, Viktor? I'm busy."

"No bullshit," Viktor said in English.

Yuri didn't respond.

"You hear me, Yuri?" Viktor said. "Don't bullshit me."

"It's a fucking party," Yuri said, and then he hung up.

He noticed the heroin was taking effect on the black woman faster than it had the night before. He instructed his men to move her to the mattress and to bring in the two actors.

Chapter 5

"THIS ISN'T SO bad," Jack told Agnes.

They had stayed inside the cabin during the trip to the fishing spot. Now that they were anchored, the boat rocked just enough to upset their stomachs. They took their fishing positions and tried to stand straight.

"I feel like I'm drunk," Agnes said.

Jack bounced off the boat's railing. "Yeah, me, too," he said, "except it doesn't feel half as good."

One of the deckhands was passing out bait. Jack caught a whiff of the slimy fish and turned away.

Agnes chuckled. "What's the matter, captain, feel like you're gonna upchuck your breakfast?"

Jack waved her off. "Don't kid around about that. I'm not good at hurling. I start now and I won't stop until we're on land again."

"Oh, great," Agnes said. "Just remember this was your idea."

"You're an independent woman," he said. "You didn't have to listen to me."

The deckhand saw the two of them were looking pale and told them where the buckets were inside the main cabin.

"Unless you wanna chum for the rest of the charter," he added. "Then just lean over and let go."

It was all Jack could take. He leaned over the rail.

"Jesus Christ," said Agnes, dropping her fishing pole. "Where's the bathroom?" she asked the deckhand.

"Other side of the wall you're leaning on," he said. "But please try and aim for the bowl."

Agnes was on her way.

Jack continued hurling over the side.

•◆•

They were taking a break from filming. Both actors were washing up at the sink. The woman was unconscious on the mattress. Yuri's Arab client was upstairs taking a nap with a young Russian girl of sixteen. Yuri had witnessed the Arab tipping hundred-dollar bills through the night into the morning.

A few minutes after eight o'clock one of Yuri's men rushed down the basement stairs. Konstantin Grusov, a curly-haired man with a Ph.D. in computer software engineering from

Moscow University, told his boss that one of the callers on the black woman's cell phone had mentioned the police.

"Her husband?" Yuri asked.

"No, it was a woman. The husband called, too, last night. There were two calls from him. The last call was from a woman, probably another whore. She mentioned calling the police if the whore doesn't call her back."

"She knows where the black bitch is?"

"I can't tell, Yuri. Maybe. She expects to hear from her, or she says she's going to call the police."

"We know who the woman is?"

"The digital display said Agnes."

"Maybe if the black one talks to her?" Yuri asked.

Grusov shook his head. "She's fucked up. She isn't handling the heroin. She threw up before."

"Maybe she tells us who Agnes is."

"Maybe, but we can get that information without her, no problem."

"Okay," Yuri said. "Find out about the woman who called. Who she is and where she lives."

"No problem. In the meantime, the actors are coming back in the early afternoon."

Yuri chuckled. "Actors?"

"What they call themselves."

Yuri grabbed his crotch. "They're a pair of faggots with big dicks, eh?"

Grusov chuckled.

Yuri said, "Get Sergei for a card game, the three of us."

"What about Fahd?"

"Fat Arab has girl upstairs, no? Let him play whoremaster."

"He's sleeping now."

"Let him sleep, the fat pig."

"He gave away a lot of money last night."

"He'll give away more today. Let him sleep. Go get Sergei. Put away your computer for two hours. We'll play poker until the slob wakes up. Then we make his fucking film, get the rest of the money, and maybe go to Atlantic City."

"Okay," Grusov said. He headed up the basement stairs.

Yuri turned to the mattress on the floor and saw the black woman was still unconscious.

"Okay, lady," he whispered, "don't make trouble now, eh?"

•◆•

When Rachel opened her eyes, a bright light blinded her. She was groggy and had to force herself to move. A sharp pain throbbed in her head. Her mouth was dry when she tried to speak.

"Good morning," she heard a man with an accent say.

A glass of water appeared below the light. She reached for it. A bearded man held the glass. He smiled.

"Take," he said.

Rachel saw another hand with three pills in its palm.

"Is aspirin," another man said. "Take."

Rachel took the pills without examining them. She washed them down with the water, then gagged on the last gulp and began to choke. When she caught her breath again, she finished drinking the water. The bald man from earlier took the glass from her.

"Where am I?" she asked.

"Who Agnes is?" the bald man asked.

"Huh?"

"Who Agnes is? She calls cell phone."

Rachel couldn't process what he was saying. "Where am I?" she asked again.

"Brooklyn."

She shaded her eyes from the bright light. "Where in Brooklyn?"

"Coney Island. You are good girl we take you on rides later."

She heard laughing from somewhere behind the bright light. She tried to remember what had happened. She had been strapped in a chair while her head was shaved. She touched her head now and felt it was bald except for some long strands.

"Where's Nelson?" she asked. She remembered her pimp and the two Russian men across from Battery Park.

"Agnes calls you," the bald man said. "You want to talk?"

"Agnes called?"

"You talk to her. You are already make five thousand dollar."

"Huh?"

"You make five thousand dollar. We call your friend Agnes, and you tell her you're busy making more money, eh?"

Rachel tried to see who was in the room. "Where's Agnes?"

"She calls telephone. We call her back, eh?"

Rachel realized that she was naked except for her thigh-high boots. "What's going on?"

"You make movie," the bald man said. "You are star."

It was then Rachel realized what the bright light was. She struggled to her knees as she turned her back to the light.

She felt a pain in her rectum and lower back. She looked up and noticed the silhouettes on the far side of the room. Two men stood stroking themselves.

"Relax," the bald man said, "almost is big finish."

Rachel rolled onto her side, curled into a fetal position, and began to sob.

The bald man said, "Save crying for camera. Big finish will hurt like motherfocker."

Chapter 6

NEITHER OF THEM caught a fish, but they shared being violently sick within two hours of their departure from the Raritan Marina. Although the *Sea Pigeon IV* barely rocked on the calm waters, the swaying motion coupled with the lack of a horizon brought on the mal de mer quickly. Once they were nauseous there was nothing to do but wait out the return trip to the dock.

When they were back at the marina, Agnes vomited one last time before getting off the boat. The fishermen on the trip applauded. Agnes shot them the bird.

"You okay?" Jack asked her.

Agnes was wiping her mouth with a paper towel.

"I'm sick, you dumb shit," she said. "And I don't think I can drive."

"You probably can't. Neither can I."

"So, now what?"

"I live about four blocks from here. We can probably make it if we don't fall into the water."

"You have a bathroom?"

"Of course."

She grabbed onto one of his arms and said, "Let's go."

A few hours later, Agnes managed to sleep on Jack's couch through most of the afternoon before a pair of bad dreams disturbed her rest.

They were recurring nightmares. One had to do with turning tricks in the middle of the Las Vegas airport behind a row of slot machines. She was afraid of getting caught in the act of prostitution while her father, dressed as a security guard, patrolled the walkways.

She remembered calling to him in the dream, then ducking down to hide. It was a dream Agnes had trouble understanding. It should have been her unfaithful mother turning tricks in the dream while her father unknowingly patrolled. It had always upset her that she saw herself instead.

She was sweating on the couch when she awoke. She wet her lips and could see Jack asleep in the recliner across from her. She forced herself back to sleep and eventually dreamed about the man who had tried to kill her.

Agnes had just finished working a bachelor party at a suite in the Tropicana. She was supposed to meet a friend at an apartment in the Green Valley section of Las Vegas. When she arrived at the condo, Agnes noticed the front door was opened. She rang the bell a few times before walking inside.

She called her friend's name as she walked through the apartment and was attacked in the hallway between the living room and bedroom. The man was obese and dirty. He pinned her to the floor inside the bedroom by sitting on her chest. She could see her girlfriend's reflection in the wall mirror across the room. She had been strangled with a scarf. Her body was left sitting up; her head slumped against the wall.

Agnes knew her friend had kept a small handgun between the mattress and the box spring. As the obese man tore at her clothes, she reached under the mattress for the gun. Then she felt a sharp slap across her face that nearly knocked her unconscious and she momentarily lost her hearing.

When the obese man shifted his weight onto her stomach, Agnes couldn't breathe. Everything seemed to be moving in slow motion until she gradually gained her hearing back. The obese man's touching her had repulsed Agnes enough to spur a surge of energy that freed her right arm from under his knee.

He had already unbuckled his pants and begun to pull them down when she reached out and grabbed his testicles. She squeezed as hard as she could until the obese man buckled forward and rolled off of her.

Now she drifted in and out of the dream. It became a series of snapshots. She saw the gun in her hand. She saw herself chasing the obese man in the hallway. She saw herself shoot at his back. She saw him bounce off a wall into the kitchen table and fall to the floor. She saw him struggling to get up a moment before she shot him in the back a second time.

He lay on his stomach and tried to look up. He pled for his life. He said he couldn't move his legs. Agnes saw herself kneel down and curse him through clenched teeth. He begged for an ambulance a moment before she shot him in the back of the head.

·◆·

"You okay?" Jack asked.

Agnes was sweating. He wiped her head with a wet cloth.

"Sit up," he told her, then helped her.

Agnes was still groggy from being sick. She took the cloth from Jack and wiped her face a few more times.

"Jesus Christ," she said. "That was a great idea, going fishing, Jack."

"You were pretty sick," he said.

"Tell me about it."

"I made chicken soup."

"Something smells."

"I'll pour you a cup, but just sip it."

"I don't think I have a choice."

He went to the kitchen. A minute later he returned with a towel draped around one arm. He carried a cup of soup and a dry dish towel in his hands.

"Just sip it," he said.

"Thanks," Agnes said.

He sat in his recliner facing her. "I think you were having nightmares."

"I was."

"Who's Becker?"

Agnes nearly choked on her soup. She coughed her way out of it. "Excuse me. What?"

"Becker. I know he was a motherfucker, because you called him that, but who was he?"

Agnes focused on the soup.

"An ex-boyfriend?" Jack asked.

She ignored his question.

"Ex-husband?"

She sipped at the soup.

"Hey, Agnes?"

She avoided looking at him.

Jack said, "I'm trying to understand here. You were pretty upset in your sleep."

He crouched down beside her, then reached for her hand. Agnes pulled away. "I don't want to talk about it."

"Obviously."

"Please, Jack."

"Okay."

He wasn't getting it. She asked him to back off.

"Excuse me for trying to help," he said. He stood up and went back to his chair.

They sat in silence while Agnes ate the soup. When she set the bowl down, she could feel Jack was still staring at her.

"Well, what the fuck?" he said. "Who was this Becker guy?"

Agnes said, "A man I killed in Las Vegas."

•◆•

Two men lifted the chair Rachel was tied to and moved it out of the way. She tried to scream through the gag. She choked for trying.

They had tacked plastic along the walls in one corner. The mattress had been tossed flush into the same corner. Another layer of plastic was tossed on top of the mattress before a white comforter covered everything.

Rachel's heart was racing from panic. They untied her from the chair but left her hands and feet bound. They moved her to the mattress and then replaced the gag in her mouth with one that tasted of alcohol. She quickly felt dizzy.

She turned her head to one side and pleaded with her eyes. A handheld camera was shoved inches from her face. She sobbed hard until she saw the knife one of the men in the background was holding. It was a large hunting knife with a serrated edge.

"Is good, no?" she heard the bald man ask someone. "Look at her face. Is scared."

"Terrified," she heard a man with a British accent say. She saw it was the Arab, Fahd.

"Where do I stay?" the man holding the camera asked.

"There is good," the bald man said. "Or blood spills on clothes."

Rachel did her best to scream through the gag and basement walls out to the street, where someone might hear her. She felt lightheaded from trying to scream.

"She's wonderful," the Arab said. "Brilliant, really."

When they finally removed the gag from her mouth, Rachel did her best to catch her breath to scream again. She could feel her vocal cords vibrating, but there was no sound.

The man holding the camera was wearing a clear plastic poncho. He moved in close. Another man, this one wearing a mask, waved the hunting knife from side to side as he came toward her. She struggled to keep him away, but her attempts were futile. She could hear them laughing at her.

She was rolled onto her stomach as the man with the knife straddled her back. As he leaned in closer, she tried to kick him. He laughed at her and she tried to turn onto her side. She tried to sweep one of his legs with both her legs. It didn't work.

She could feel the man drop to the mattress. She tried looking over her right shoulder and was stopped by a sharp pain piercing the back of her right thigh. She screamed again as she felt the pain moving up her leg toward her buttocks. This time her scream filled the room. She went into shock when she felt the blade scraping bone.

•◆•

When Agnes told him she had killed a man in Las Vegas, Jack thought he might've heard wrong. He was anxious to know more, but a few moments after telling him, Agnes had dashed into the bathroom again. He stood at the open door as she vomited into the toilet bowl.

When she was finished, she looked as bad as she had been on the boat. Jack ushered her into his bedroom and let her sleep there.

He spent the next half hour arranging his workweek on the computer. His private investigation business had taken off over the last two years. Most jobs involved investigative work on insurance claims and spying on cheating spouses. Although he hadn't planned on staying in the business long-term, Jack had come to enjoy the freedom the work offered. He preferred making his own hours and being his own boss.

He had an insurance surveillance job later in the evening. He was loading a handheld camcorder with film when Agnes appeared in his living room again.

This time Jack was direct and to the point.

"You killed a man, why?" he asked.

It was then Agnes opened up and told him about her past life in Las Vegas, how she was still adjusting to her new life, and how nervous she had been about accepting a friendly date to go fishing. She told him what had happened in her friend's condo the night she had killed a man who turned out to be a roving serial killer. Then she told him how it wasn't her friend's murder that had turned her against the life.

"I was a zombie," she said. "It was like being dead inside. Nobody mattered. It was a lack of emotion I had about life in general that scared me, the indifference. I had no attachment to anyone except for one friend, and she was a hooker, too. She still is, but even with her it involved business more than anything real while I was in the life. I woke up one day and realized I was alone."

"Parents?" Jack asked.

"I was close to my father once, but that was a long time ago." Jack waited for more.

"My mother and I never got along," she said. "Can I have some cold water?" she asked before he could pry.

He went to the kitchen and poured her a glass of ice water from the refrigerator.

When he brought it to her, he said, "You obviously needed to tell someone. Why not a therapist?"

Agnes told him about a few therapists and psychiatrists she had gone to over the past few years. "In the end, I don't trust them," she said. "I went to a few once I left the business. Except for some commonsense advice I could've gotten from a crossing guard, it was all bullshit."

"I'm not a big fan of therapists myself," he told her. "What about friends?"

"My best friend is a prostitute," Agnes said. "I've been trying to get her to leave the life for a few years now. She's a divorced mother with two kids and private school tuitions she can't afford without hooking."

"Jesus Christ, what the hell does she tell her kids?" Jack asked. "I mean, she might think her reasons for hooking are noble, but how the hell does she explain it down the road?"

"She says she can't afford to think about down the road. It's a common form of denial for women in the life."

"Fuck that."

"She's a good person, Jack. Don't judge her."

"She may be a good person, but she's a lousy mother."

"You don't know that."

"I don't, huh? We live in America, Agnes. She doesn't have to hook. I don't care what you say. Not if she has kids."

Agnes became defensive. "I'm trying to get her to stop, but Rachel feels she can't until she can afford it. And she is a good mother. She loves her kids more than you can understand."

Jack became sarcastic. "Yeah, well, Rachel needs a fuckin' reality check, okay? Her kids are the ones who'll have to deal with her denial down the road."

"Or they can grow up with a father who can't get his act together either," Agnes said. "Roger just did time himself,

Rachel's ex-husband. Rachel is doing this for her kids because it's an immediate fix. I know it's the wrong way to approach it, but I'm not in her position. Neither are you."

Jack waved the conversation off. He said, "You know what, this is too much for me right now. In fact, I might need a therapist after this."

"Excuse me?"

"You give a guy a lot to swallow."

"Excuse me again? Don't ask questions you can't handle the answers to, mister."

Jack listed off his fingers. "You whacked a guy and you used to turn tricks. Your best friend still turns tricks. It's not the same as 'I once ran over a dog and I used to have a drinking problem.'"

"Fuck you, Jack."

"Oh, lighten up. I'm just being honest. I was a cop, for Christ's sake. I know what that life is about."

"Yeah, well, then you can be a little more sensitive about it."

"Sensitive? You used to turn tricks, for Christ's sake."

Agnes stared hard at him a moment. "I don't need this," she said, and then she got up off the couch. "I'm out of here."

Jack blocked her path. Agnes stood toe to toe with him.

"So you killed this Becker in self-defense, right?"

Agnes stared at him.

"Right?"

"He killed my friend and three other women they knew about," she said.

"And he tried to kill you."

Agnes closed her eyes and saw herself poised over Becker's wounded body a moment before she leaned over and shot him in the back of the head.

"He had his chance," she said.

"Huh?"

"Get out of my way," Agnes said.

"Or what, you'll shoot me?"

They stood staring at each other until Jack smiled.

Agnes said, "This isn't funny."

Jack turned sideways in front of her. "You think I lost weight today? Fishing, I mean."

"Don't be an asshole."

"You know, you're cute when you're about to whack someone."

Agnes started to smile. Jack saw it and said, "Let loose, lady. It'll do you good."

She punched him hard in the solar plexus. He doubled over, then dropped to his knees and held his stomach.

Agnes gathered her things in the meantime. When she was ready to leave, she returned to the living room and looked down at Jack. He had rolled onto his back on the floor.

"I guess we don't have sex this date," he said.

"I'm not ready for sex yet, Jack. I doubt I'd let you hold my hand."

"Yeah, I noticed that, too. What's that story?"

"I guess it's good that everything is a joke to you."

Jack waved it off. "Serious. You've pulled away from me more than once. Why?"

"I have issues, okay? It has to do with my past. It's something I'm trying to get over."

"Letting someone touch you?"

"If I'm not ready for it, yes."

Jack paused a moment.

"It's taken me five years to date someone," Agnes said.

"At least you picked me."

"Was that supposed to be funny?"

"Sorry."

"Just let me go now, okay. We'll talk about it again another time."

"Promise you won't beat me up."

"Did it hurt?"

"Yes."

"Good."

"I was about to apologize for being so insensitive."

"You can't help yourself, can you?"

"I like you, Agnes. Or I would've run for the hills already."

She pointed at his stomach and said, "You need to work on your abs."

Jack looked down at his stomach.

"Take off ten pounds while you're at it."

"Anything else?"

"Keep your dates on dry ground."

"Will do."

"Now, walk me to my car."

"Or?"

"See what I mean? You can't help yourself."

Chapter 7

VIKTOR TIMKIN WAS born in 1958 in St. Petersburg, Russia. He had two university degrees from Moscow University—one in accounting and the other in engineering. After immigrating to Israel in 1983, Timkin became a leader in the Russian underworld there. Five years later he took a position with a satellite organization based in Brighton Beach, Brooklyn. Three years after that he was running the Russian mob in New York.

The last two days had been troubling for Viktor. He had learned of pending indictments against two of his top lieutenants, one of whom had disappeared and was feared to have joined the witness protection program. To add to an already bad day, his pain-in-the-ass stepbrother had started something with the strongest Italian crime family in New York. It had something to do with a Harlem pimp under the protection of a captain with the Vignieri crime family.

He was watching CNN on the television in his home office and contemplating his recent troubles when the doorbell rang. He turned the television off before checking a security screen. He frowned at the sight of his stepbrother waiting in the vestibule downstairs. Viktor glowered at the screen when Yuri gave the camera the finger.

"Idiot," Viktor said.

He poured himself a cup of black coffee before unlocking the apartment door. He waved off his two bodyguards standing watch in the hall and left the door open a crack. He took his seat behind his desk and sat staring at the blank television screen when Yuri knocked.

"It's open," Viktor said. He spoke in Russian.

Yuri let himself into the parlor. He was disheveled and smelled of alcohol. He carried a shoe box under one arm. He nodded once at his stepbrother, crossed into the living room, and set the shoe box on the desk. Viktor ignored it.

"Fat Tony Gangi wants to know why you bothered some pimp for one of his girls," Viktor said.

"I bought her," Yuri replied, also in Russian. "What I told you yesterday on the phone. And I didn't bother anybody. I paid good money for her."

"I still don't know what you mean. Why did you buy her?"

Yuri waved the question off. "It was business," he said. "The pimp agreed to it. He took the money."

"Yeah, and then the pimp complained to the wiseguy he's with, one of Gangi's men, a made man with the Vignieri family, a fucking captain."

Yuri held up three fingers. "I gave him money for the girl three different times," he said. "This last time I bought her. I paid five thousand dollars. She works for me after that. The pimp didn't complain when he took the money. Maybe the wiseguy is bullshitting Gangi."

"You still didn't answer me, Yuri. Yesterday you say you bought her for Fahd. Why?"

This time Yuri avoided his stepbrother's eyes. "Fahd wanted her, eh? He had her two other times. Good money he paid. I bought her from the pimp to sell to Fahd."

Viktor was persistent. "What do you mean sell to Fahd?"

"He's a pervert, Viktor, you know that," Yuri said. "He wanted the black woman. I bought her for him." He pointed to the shoe box. "That's what he paid, in there."

Viktor looked at the shoe box.

"There's forty thousand dollars," Yuri said. "She cost me five thousand, what I gave the pimp. She cost you nothing."

Viktor felt his jaw tightening. His eyes became narrow slits when he looked at his stepbrother again.

Yuri was tall, thin, bald, and much less educated than Viktor. At thirty-five years of age he had been an American citizen for just over ten years. He had already served two years for an assault that occurred the night he went to a Yankee bat-day baseball game and assaulted a Red Sox fan.

"What did Fahd pay all that money for?" Viktor asked.

Yuri hesitated.

"For what?" Viktor repeated. "What did Fahd pay you for?"

"A film," Yuri mumbled.

Viktor held a hand to his right ear. "For what?"

"Fahd wanted the black woman for a film."

Viktor bit his lower lip.

"He wanted the black bitch and I got her," said Yuri, more defiantly now. He pointed to the shoe box again. "Fifty thousand dollars for one film, for one black whore. I kept ten for myself, Viktor, another five goes to pimp. Fucking shit I kept."

Viktor slammed the desk with a fist. "You stupid motherfocker," he yelled in English. "You stupid cocksucker, motherfocker!"

"What?" Yuri said. He shifted uncomfortably in his chair. "What's the big fucking deal?"

"Where is she?" said Viktor, speaking Russian again.

Yuri turned away from his stepbrother.

Viktor slammed the desk again. "Where is the black woman?"

"Gone," Yuri said. "She's gone."

"Fahd paid you to kill her?"

Yuri took a deep breath. He let it out slowly.

Viktor leaned both hands on the desk. "A snuff film, Yuri? This is what you did for Fahd?"

Yuri avoided direct eye contact again. He spoke while waving his hands. "It was short, Viktor, an hour, an hour and a half."

Viktor was seething. Yuri had been a liability since he was released from prison two years ago. Now he was telling Viktor that he had gone ahead and arranged a snuff film for a perverted Arab who had money to burn. And the imbecile was proud of himself for charging a multimillionaire fifty thousand dollars.

The thought process he went through was automatic. Aalam al Fahd was a Saudi weapons dealer and a sexual deviant. He had also been a cash cow Viktor had cultivated since the day he took control of the Russian crime family in New York. Fahd had provided Timkin with weapons he was able to sell off to other organized crime families for great profit and to maintain peace, but a snuff film was a potential disaster he couldn't afford to be associated with.

He continued to stare at his stepbrother. "Who was there?" he asked. "When you made this stupid fucking film, who was there?"

Yuri took in and then let out a deep breath.

"Who?" Viktor yelled.

"Oleg, Sergei, Vitaly, Konstantin, and the two faggots, what Fahd wanted. The actors were gone before she died."

Viktor swallowed hard. "Who else?" he asked.

Yuri was confused. "What?"

"Who else knows about this film? What about the pimp you made the deal with?"

"The pimp doesn't know shit," Yuri said. "And I should shoot him in the head for making a complaint. He took the money."

Viktor was still waiting.

"Nobody else knows," said Yuri, squirming in his chair again. "The woman had a couple of calls on her cell phone, from her husband, another from some whore."

"What about the husband?"

"He was waiting for her to pick up their kids. She didn't pick them up. Konstantin got the numbers from her cell phone."

"Asshole," Viktor mumbled.

"What do you want from me, Viktor? I made business."

"Who was the woman who called? What did she want?"

"I have her name," Yuri said. "Probably another whore. Konstantin got her information from the phone number. What's she going to do, Viktor? Nothing. She doesn't know shit. She can't tell the police anything."

Viktor's head snapped. "Police?"

"She left a message saying she was going to call the police if the black whore didn't call her back. It's bullshit. Whore talk."

Viktor slammed the desk with both hands. "God damn you, Yuri!"

Yuri sat up in the chair.

"Give me the woman's name," Viktor said.

Yuri fished inside his shirt pocket for the piece of paper with the woman's information. He set it on the edge of the desk. "There."

Viktor rubbed his face in an attempt to compose himself. "Who else was there?"

"Nobody," said Yuri, defensively now. "Fahd and me, Oleg, Sergei, Vitaly, Konstantin, and the two faggots."

"Who was there when you killed the woman?"

Yuri waved one hand. "Faggots were gone," he said. "Oleg used the camera. Sergei killed the woman and helped clean up. Then he took her body to dump off his boat. Vitaly drove the faggots back to Manhattan."

"The body is gone? The woman?"

"Sergei took her on his boat."

Viktor nodded.

"What's the problem?" Yuri asked. He flipped the top of

the shoe box off to show his stepbrother the money. "There's forty thousand dollars there."

"Fahd is worth millions of dollars, you idiot," Viktor said. "He gets us weapons to sell the Italians, the Albanians, Chinese, and the Dominicans. We have business with the Italians now, with the Vignieri family, for a piece of Coney Island. Gangi is offering us a chance for big money."

Yuri didn't like having to deal with the Italians. He scowled at the mention of them.

"Fahd is a like a bank for us," Viktor said. "He's our best source for weapons. We make a lot of money from him. We keep the peace, eh?"

Yuri pointed to the cash again. "There's profit right there," he said. "Forty thousand for a five-thousand investment."

"You're a fucking imbecile," Viktor said. "You get in trouble over dumb shit all the time. A fucking baseball game two years ago. I told you no snuff films for Fahd six months ago. Ten fucking times I told you. The women are to keep Fahd happy, not for him to kill."

Yuri moved up on his chair. "Fahd asked me for this," he said. "He wanted this, not me."

"And how many times did I tell you not to do it? Yesterday I told you. No fucking bullshit with Fahd. Remember? And you hung up on me, eh?"

Yuri pointed to the money one more time. "He showed me that. Fifty thousand in cash. I brought you forty."

Viktor smacked the shoe box off the desk. "Idiot!" he yelled.

Yuri sat back in his chair again.

Viktor counted off his fingers. "Oleg, Sergei, Vitaly,

Konstantin, the two faggots, and you and Fahd," he said, holding up eight fingers. "Who is good for business and who is a pain in the ass?"

Yuri spread his arms out. "It was one time," he said. "Okay, no more." He wiped his hands a few times for emphasis. "If Fahd asks again, I'll tell him, no, sorry, my brother doesn't like easy money."

"Easy money, eh?"

"I'm sorry, Viktor. What else you want me to say?"

"You're sure the pimp doesn't know this was a snuff film? Gangi called me yesterday."

"The pimp doesn't know anything," said Yuri dismissively. "All he knows is some Arab wants to see her again. That's all."

Viktor opened one of his desk drawers. "You always make a big fucking mess," he said. "Always."

"I'll fix it," Yuri said. "I promise."

"No," said Viktor, pulling a Glock from the drawer and pointing it at his stepbrother. "This time I'll fix it."

• ◆ •

The body had been stuffed into a burlap bag along with towels they had used to soak up the blood. Two twenty-five-pound weights were added to keep the bag from drifting off the bottom. It was then wrapped with a white sheet and tossed into the back of a car trunk. At the Sheepshead Bay Marina the bag was removed from the trunk and loaded onto a boat owned by the man who had murdered Rachel Wilson.

It was a frigid night. On the water, the wind was cutting. Instead of taking the body beyond the reach of the currents crisscrossing Jamaica Bay, it was dropped into thirty-two feet of water a quarter mile from the Brooklyn coast.

The burlap bag wasn't secured and the currents were strong below the surface. The weights inside the bag pulled it off the body a few feet from the bottom. A weakfish examined one of the blood-soaked towels as the dead body ascended to within five feet of the surface.

It tumbled in slow motion as if at play. Intestines began to unravel through an open stomach wound. Suspended like a macabre leash, they floated out ahead of the body.

A strong current took Rachel Wilson's body from just beyond Floyd Bennett Field, under the Marine Park Bridge, to less than fifty yards off Plum Beach, where it lodged against an old piling. A low tide kept it from washing ashore.

Chapter 8

AGNES SLEPT THROUGH the night once she was home. She spent the morning running errands. When she returned home, she found a phone message from the temporary agency she worked for. They had a second-shift job working with Lorelei that would last through the evening. Agnes called to accept the assignment. She needed to keep herself busy.

Word processing was something Agnes had taught herself during her last year of hooking. She had bought a computer and taught herself how to type with a software program. When she could type fast enough, she took a class on basic word processing. Three months later she took a few tests from different temporary agencies in Las Vegas. Although she failed the first few, Agnes had learned enough from the tests to pass the next few she took. A few weeks later she was offered her first temporary position. After working weekends for one month on a word processing assignment, she left prostitution behind her for good.

Now she took a long shower and ignored the phone when it rang. She stepped under the hot water and let it cascade over her face until it stung. She adjusted the water, turned her back to the spray, and closed her eyes. She thought about Jack and wondered how awkward it had been for him when she mentioned her past. Had she scared him off? Had she tried to?

She didn't know for sure why she had told him about herself, except she knew she didn't want to lie to Jack. Now she wasn't so sure she shouldn't have.

She blocked him from her mind and finished her shower. While dressing, Agnes noticed her answering machine had registered four calls. She hoped one of them was from Rachel and ran through the caller ID. None were from her friend, but there were two numbers she didn't recognize.

Agnes picked up the phone to call Jack, then stopped herself. It was a defense mechanism she had learned from self-help books. Acting impulsively about anything was something she needed to curb. Jack was the first man to put her to the test.

As she gathered her things to leave, Agnes noticed the photo of Rachel with her two kids on her dresser bureau. The faces of Rachel's children stopped her. She had taken the picture the day her friend was leaving the hospital in Las Vegas after giving birth to her son. Rachel was holding her baby boy while standing behind her daughter in the picture.

Agnes called Rachel's apartment and her cell phone to leave messages. Then she called Rachel's ex-husband and was concerned when she learned her friend still hadn't been in contact with anyone.

"She was supposed to pick up the kids from my place and she never showed," Roger Wilson said. "Never even called. My mother's got them now. I'm here to help her out, but I go back to work tonight. You know where the fuck she is?"

Agnes was concerned. "Sorry, Roger, I don't, no."

A long moment of silence followed.

Agnes said, "Did you try her service?"

"I tried the service. Bitch there said she wasn't working. Not for them."

Rachel sometimes used an escort service separate from the jobs she took through her pimp. Roger was aware of both and disapproved wholeheartedly. Hooking remained one of many sticking points between the divorced couple. Had he not served two years for an assault after their second child was born, he would have been able to take custody of his children from his ex-wife.

"What about Nelson?" she asked.

"I don't call her pimp. I won't call him."

"I have the number."

"Then you can do me a favor and tell her to let her kids know what the hell is going on."

Another awkward silence followed.

Agnes said, "Roger?"

"You fucking people," he said before he hung up.

Agnes couldn't blame him for being angry, but she resented his last remark. She had left the life and Roger knew it.

Still, something was wrong. Rachel hadn't picked up her kids or contacted them. Agnes called her friend's cell phone again and was surprised when a man answered.

"Who this is?" he said with an Eastern European accent.

"Is Rachel there?"

"This is Agnes?"

"Yes, can I speak to Rachel?"

"She's busy."

"Put her on, please."

"She's busy. She calls you back."

"I need to talk—"

"Bye-bye," the man said, and then he hung up.

Agnes called the number back, but this time nobody answered. She looked at the time and saw it was getting late. She called Rachel's pimp, Nelson Freeman. She had taken his address and telephone number for the sake of just such an emergency.

"Who the hell is it?" Freeman answered on the fourth ring.

"I'm a friend of Rachel Wilson."

"You got a name?"

"Agnes. Agnes Lynn."

"Huh? Oh, yeah, I know you. You the one she talking to in Battery Park the other day. You the ex-ho or somethin', the one trying to turn her, right?"

"She didn't come home," said Agnes, ignoring Freeman's Q&A.

"Huh?"

"Rachel didn't come home. Her ex-husband called to ask where she was."

"And how'm I supposed to know that?"

"Wasn't she working for you?"

"Not anymore she's not."

"What's that supposed to mean?"

"Hey, who the fuck you think you talking to?"

"I'm just trying to find Rachel before the police get involved."

"That a threat, bitch?"

"Jesus Christ, quit the macho routine already."

"Sure," Freeman said. "How's this?"

Agnes cursed under her breath when the line went dead. She redialed the pimp's number and composed herself when he answered after eleven rings.

"You ask politely, I might answer your questions," he said with a much calmer voice.

Very softly, very deliberately, Agnes said, "Rachel didn't come home. Her kids and ex-husband are concerned. They'll probably go to the police next. I'm just trying to find her."

The pimp didn't answer.

"Hello?" Agnes said.

"Rachel been traded," Freeman finally said. "Don't work for me no more. I don't know where she is. Only thing I know is the private job she tried to hide from me she went to after she talked to you. Maybe you pimping her, too. Maybe the cops want to know about that."

"Do you have a way of contacting her?"

"Yeah, sure. Wave a fifty off a corner someplace."

Agnes heard the click before she could ask another question. This time she didn't bother to redial the number.

Jack picked up a large coffee at a delicatessen on Smith Street in Perth Amboy and drove to the address in Woodbridge where he was sure he'd find the claimant of a debilitating back injury working out at a gym. The man was thirty-one years old and had run the New York City marathon the past three years. He was supposed to have injured his back after being rear-ended by a post office truck at a stoplight on Hyland Boulevard in Staten Island.

Jack had already learned the driver of the post office truck worked out at the same gym. The two men were obviously friends, but he was only there to investigate the genius suing the federal government and filing for permanent disability.

Jack sat in his car on the street fronting the gym's parking lot. He sipped his coffee and wondered about Agnes Lynn and how the hell he might be falling for a former hooker. She was something special, he knew that much, but there was no denying her previous life had been a jolt to his better judgment.

It was hard getting beyond what she had described. Then again, until she had told him, he never would have guessed.

The story about her best friend was a little scary, too. The fact Agnes was still in touch with the world she claimed to have left bothered him. Jack couldn't imagine socializing with a mother who turned tricks to send her kids to a private school.

Then he thought about his own situation and felt a little more humble. His ex-wife was on her fifth or sixth boyfriend since they had divorced. She was slinging plates as a waitress, working days and partying most nights, but she had Jack to count on for support and to help with their son. What if they had had the same options as Rachel Wilson and her ex-convict husband?

It reminded him of a lesson his mother had taught him a long time ago. "There but for the grace of God go all of us," she used to say whenever someone said something derogatory about a person down on their luck.

Jack wasn't religious, but he still understood the sentiment well enough to check himself every now and then. Agnes had a point. Who the hell was he to pass judgment on some woman trying to raise her kids?

He was shaking his head at his own thoughts when he spotted the man he was there to watch step outside the gym with two other men. The three of them were dressed in jogging outfits. They did some stretching in front of the gym before heading off across the parking lot out onto Main Street. Jack mounted his video recorder onto the dashboard and adjusted the lens.

"Sometimes it's just this easy," he said.

He let them get half a block ahead before trailing them for a solid fifteen minutes. When it was obvious they were going on a long run, Jack turned off the camera and headed back home.

He was thinking he might give Agnes a call and apologize for being so self-righteous the day before. When he spotted a florist on his way home, he decided he'd bring her flowers instead.

•◆•

Ten hours after killing his stepbrother, Viktor Timkin told his enforcer, Pavel Chenkov, about the deal he had made with the

Vignieri crime family and why Yuri Timkin's entire crew would also have to be executed.

The two men conversed in Russian in the parlor, where Yuri's body remained wrapped in an oriental rug on the hardwood floor.

"I should've done that the day he came out of prison," Timkin said. "Tony Gangi is offering us Coney Island, except for the baseball stadium, if we take out three guys with the Corelli family."

Chenkov was average height, one hundred ninety pounds, most of it muscle. He had short blond hair and ice blue eyes. He stepped around Yuri's body to sit across from his boss.

"So that Joe LaRocca becomes the new boss?" he asked.

Timkin nodded. "We take out LaRocca's competition, the one who got out of jail last month, and Coney Island is ours."

Chenkov chuckled. "He has nothing to lose, LaRocca. Marino has most of Coney Island now. LaRocca has him killed and becomes boss and gives away what wasn't his anyway."

"And we benefit," Timkin said. "It's the kind of math we can live with, no?"

"Marino has a crew, too," Chenkov said. "What about them?"

"Why Gangi wants us to take three of them out together. The other two are Marino's muscle. Gangi says once the three of them are gone, the rest of his crew won't make trouble."

"If Gangi speaks for the Vignieri family, this is great news."

Timkin lit a cigarette. "Gangi is running the Vignieri family for two years now," he said. "Officially he's the underboss, but everybody knows he's making the decisions."

"And he comes to us because he needs to appear neutral, eh?"

"He needs to keep the other families from taking sides.

They'll know Vignieri sanctioned it as soon as LaRocca takes over. Gangi claims the other families will be grateful they didn't have to get involved."

"And what about the Albanians Marino was muscling? They'll want something from this, no?"

"They'll want to be left alone with their own people," Timkin said. "Costs us nothing. And it's a good excuse to call on Fahd again. He has guns, the Hungarian model we can leave at the scene. Let the police think what they want. I'll let the Albanians do it through us. It will appear sanctioned that way. Nobody makes trouble."

"This is great news," Chenkov said. "We extend our reach the length of the boardwalk now."

Timkin waved a finger. "And with plans for a water park, Pasha, what I'm thinking," he said. "A water park where the old Steeplechase was. We put up the water rides and then put our own people there to run it."

"When do we take care of the three guys?"

"Tomorrow, the day after. Soon, because Gangi says it could go the other way if the people we're taking out strike first and kill LaRocca."

"Gangi is a careful man."

"And smart. He knows his business. Why he's using us instead of his own. And the same as LaRocca, what he's conceding doesn't belong to him. LaRocca doesn't need it. This way he becomes boss, probably what he wanted all his life."

"And your idiot stepbrother almost blows the entire deal with a fucking snuff film."

"Please, don't remind me," Timkin said. "Like I said, I should have killed him years ago, but now is now."

"What happened with the pimp?"

"Fahd told Yuri he wanted a black woman. Yuri knew some Harlem pimp from a card game he used to sit in on on the West Side. He gets the black woman for Fahd from the pimp. Then Fahd wants to see her again. Yuri makes a deal with the pimp and Fahd wanted her for his film. Yuri tells the pimp he's buying her."

"Buying her?"

"Probably the pimp agreed because he was afraid of Yuri," Timkin said. "He told Yuri okay, and then he went to his guy, a made guy with the Vignieri family. The made guy goes to Gangi and Gangi calls me. I call Yuri and ask him what it's about, and the idiot tells me it was for a party. He lies to me over the phone like he always lies. He doesn't tell me what he's doing with the black woman, or I would have stopped him, eh? Instead, he makes a big mess and we have to clean it."

"What about the pimp?"

"I'll have to compensate the wiseguy for the pimp. In the meantime I'll blame his murder on Yuri. I'll say it was personal or some other bullshit."

"This is going to cost us, Viktor, killing the pimp. If he's with Vignieri, I mean."

"He's just another nigger, eh? Vignieri knows this. We'll have to pay compensation. Big deal. The problem is this stupid film. If it ever goes public, we'll lose more than Coney Island. You and I will have to get on a jet back to Russia, Pasha. Even Vignieri would turn on us. And if the strongest family turns, the rest will follow. We'd be at war with the Italians on one side, and the law wouldn't let us breathe on the other. Nobody will tolerate a snuff film. Nobody."

Chenkov smirked. "So Yuri goes and makes one."

"The idiot. I wish I could kill him again."

Chenkov looked down at the rolled rug on the floor. "I'll have him cremated tonight," he said. "Any special place you want to spread his ashes?"

"Flush him down the toilet after you take a shit," Timkin said. "He's not worth the extra tank of water."

"When Yuri's crew is found, there will be an investigation."

"I want them found. If they ever put the snuff film together with Yuri, we save face by killing his crew. We have to make mess to clean mess, eh? Let the police and the FBI think it's a war. I have a sit-down tonight again with the Vignieri people. We can't have any bullshit problems now. The one who started this mess with the black woman, Fahd, he can bring the FBI to our door, too. He's a pervert, eh? He has the film, he's making copies."

Chenkov lit a Marlboro.

"In the meantime, we clean up the mess Yuri started," Timkin said. "This piece of shit on the floor and his crew. And anybody else who knows about the black bitch."

Timkin stopped when he remembered something. "You find the woman?" he asked as he looked for the card Yuri had given him earlier. He squinted to read the name scribbled in his stepbrother's handwriting. "Agnes Lynn?"

"I send my people to address on Staten Island," Chenkov said.

"Good. Once we clean this up, the film never happened."

"My guys are out there," Chenkov said. "I'm sending two after the pimp. The rest will take care of Yuri's crew."

Timkin raised a finger. "Why Yuri's crew has to turn up somewhere public. Because his crazy bastard crew decided to be cowboys and killed that pimp for no good reason, understand?"

Chenkov set his pack of cigarettes back on the desk.

"What about our man with NYPD?" Timkin asked. "The Irish cop."

"I'll call," Chenkov said. "He'll go to where the pimp is."

"Okay, but we still have to get the woman," Timkin said. "Maybe she worked for the pimp, too. Maybe she already knows about this fucking mess. She has to go, Pasha."

"We'll find her," Chenkov said.

"And the black bitch's family, the one Yuri killed. What do we know about them?"

"What you told me on the phone. So far the husband didn't call the police. He's probably embarrassed she's a whore."

"Fucking idiot, Yuri was. Fucking snuff film."

"Where is her body?" Chenkov asked. "I can burn it with Yuri."

Timkin thumbed at the window over his shoulder. "Yuri says Sergei took her out on his boat."

Chenkov chuckled. "Sergei? He has a twenty-foot piece of shit. In this weather? He couldn't get two miles from the dock. I hope he bagged her with something strong to keep her on the bottom."

Timkin scratched at his head. "Please, Pasha, don't tell me anything else to ruin my day, eh?"

Chenkov looked to the bundle on the floor. "You should call the funeral parlor," he said. "They'll take the idiot out like he's a heart attack victim. I'll bring some women come to mourn and make a big show."

"Good," Timkin said, "something exciting for the FBI to film."

"Before they think to investigate the body, Yuri is flushed down the toilet."

"Okay, go and find this other bitch," Timkin said, "before the trouble Yuri made with his fucking film is all over the CNN. Those bastards, they get something like this, a snuff film, they make more trouble than the FBI."

Chenkov read the name again. "Agnes Lynn," he said. "We'll find her. And then she disappears, too."

Chapter 9

AGNES WAS CONCERNED about her friend. When they met at Battery Park, Rachel had mentioned possibly working overnight, but she wasn't the type to ignore her kids. The fact she hadn't called home yet was not normal.

Agnes saw she was running late and ignored the remaining messages on her answering machine. She decided she would call Rachel again later. If she couldn't reach her friend then, she might have to call the police after all.

She left for work a few minutes after five o'clock. If traffic on the Staten Island Expressway was light, she had just enough time to make it to downtown Manhattan before her shift started. Agnes had made the same trip in less than forty minutes a few times when the traffic cooperated.

She was close to the expressway when she realized she'd forgotten her CD player back at the apartment. Music was something Agnes needed to work through the night. She made a quick U-turn and headed back home. When her cell phone rang, she answered it without looking at the number.

"Hello?"

"Agnes Lynn?"

It was the same man she had spoken to earlier.

"Speaking," Agnes said. "Who's this?"

"Where you are?" he asked.

"Who is this?"

"Where you are?"

"One more time," she said. "Who is this?"

"Where you are, lady?"

Agnes hung up.

Her cell phone rang less than thirty seconds later. She saw Rachel's name on the digital display and her heart began to race.

"Who the fuck is this?" Agnes answered.

"Friend of friend."

It was the same voice. "Where's Rachel?"

"Where you are?"

"On my way to the police."

"Girlfriend is working late," the man said.

"Put her on."

"She's working. She calls you back."

The connection ended as Agnes was turning the corner onto the street where she lived. A double-parked car was blocking the space she usually used. When she looked up the walk to her front door, she saw two men standing there. She was about to lean on her horn when one of the men kicked the door open.

Agnes hit the gas pedal and sped away from the condo complex. She did her best to compose herself as she drove back toward Route 440. She saw the sign up ahead for north and south and panicked about which way to go.

•◆•

Pavel Chenkov was thinking about his young Ukrainian girl-friend as he drove through Staten Island. It had been more than a week since he had spent time with the fourteen-year-old, who lived with her aunt and uncle in Brighton Beach. If he had time today, he was thinking, he'd stop by and pick her up.

He was heading to the address one of his men had managed to get through Agnes Lynn's telephone records. With any luck the woman was already dead.

As he turned off the Staten Island Expressway at the Hyland Boulevard exit, Chenkov could see traffic was backed up.

"Shit," he said.

He called one of the men he had sent to kill the woman and was further frustrated when he learned she hadn't been home.

"Did you go inside the apartment and check?" he asked.

"Yes, she is gone to work. We have telephone messages."

"You know where?"

"We have agency number."

"Okay, good."

"There are other numbers, Pasha."

"What numbers?"

"The black woman's husband and the one in Harlem. Some other numbers, too. I wrote them down."

"Okay, meet me in Brooklyn at the hotel. We'll leave from there."

Chenkov wasn't happy his men had missed the woman, but at least now they would know where to look for her. He still might get the job done and have time for his girlfriend, he was thinking.

Then he thought about how the young girl's creamy white skin showed the welts he liked to leave from pinching her, and the gangster grew excited.

"Okay, Agnes Lynn," he said, "don't ruin my fucking night, eh?"

•◆•

Jack had picked up a bouquet of yellow roses and then a bottle of white wine on his way home. He intended to give Agnes a call and maybe hook up later in the day for dinner or a drink or whatever excuse he could use to apologize.

He knew he had stepped out of bounds when he criticized her best friend. Agnes had been very defensive of the woman hooking to raise her two kids. He probably shouldn't have been so judgmental about the situation, except it was something he still couldn't fathom—how a woman raising kids could have sex with strangers for cash.

Then again, he knew former colleagues on the police force who would have sex with hookers in exchange for not arresting them. There was also an incident in his past he wished he could forget; when he spent a long drunken night with a Puerto Rican hooker in old San Juan while on a bachelor party vacation.

Who was worse, he had often wondered, the hooker or the john?

Jack knew one thing for sure: he couldn't stop thinking about Agnes and he wanted to see her again. He took a quick shower and got dressed. He would call and ask her out. If she was still angry, he'd just show up with the flowers and wine anyway.

What did he have to lose?

His cell phone rang before he could dial her number. It was his ex-wife with bad news. Their son had been hit by a car.

·◆·

Agnes called the police and reported the incident she had witnessed at her apartment while she drove to Manhattan. When the desk sergeant requested she go to the precinct, Agnes declined. She was too frightened to return to Staten Island now. She would be safe at work in less than half an hour.

There was also Rachel to consider. Her friend had gone to work an overnight—maybe for Russians, maybe for some Arab. Rachel hadn't been heard from since. The phone calls from her friend's cell phone worried Agnes the most. The man she had spoken to definitely sounded Russian.

Rachel might be in trouble, but Agnes wasn't sure what she could do about it. If the men at her apartment were Russian, there was a chance they were looking for her now, too.

The man on the phone had kept asking her, "*Where you are?*"

Agnes felt her heart race again. She took deep breaths to calm herself. She needed to know Rachel was okay.

She was close to the Battery Tunnel when her cell phone rang one more time. She checked the number before answering and was glad to see it was Jack calling.

"Jack?"

"Agnes, my son was hit by a car," he told her. "I'm on my way to Brooklyn now."

His news caught her off guard. "Jesus, Jack, is he okay?"

"One of his legs was broken. That's all I know. It was a compound fracture. My ex is at the hospital with him now. I have to call her back when I get off with you. Can I call you later?"

"Of course, sure," she said. "I'll be at work, so call my cell."

"Okay, thanks," Jack said, and then he was gone.

Agnes swallowed hard. She started to call the police again when she entered the tunnel. The satellite connection was gone.

Chapter 10

JACK MADE IT to the emergency room a few minutes after his son was asleep in recovery. He met with his ex-wife and frowned at the sight of her latest boyfriend, a young-looking guy with a long, blond ponytail.

"Is he okay?" Jack asked.

Lisa Russo introduced her boyfriend before answering the question. "This is Paul," she said. "Paul, Jack is my ex."

"Nice to meet you," Paul said.

Jack ignored the man. "Is my son okay?"

"He's going to need a few months to recover," Lisa said.

"And he'll have a rod and some pins in his leg the rest of his life. It was a bad break."

"Fuck," Jack said.

"He's going to need a lot of therapy. The orthopedic surgeon said years of it."

"They cut him?"

"Both sides of his leg."

"God damn it. Is he okay?"

"Calm down, Jack. Yes, he'll be fine. He's going to be in pain for a few days, probably longer than that, but they'll keep him on morphine until he comes home."

"How many pins?"

"Sixteen."

"Jesus Christ."

"And there's a rod and two plates."

"Plates? What kind of plates?"

"I don't know, Jack. To hold everything together, I guess."

"How'd this happen?"

"I wasn't there, but his friends claim Nicholas was playing two-hand touch and had just caught a pass when some car turned the corner."

"Was the guy speeding? What the cops say?"

"They have him down at the precinct."

Jack turned red. "They arrest him? Was he drunk, the prick?"

"Easy does it," Lisa said. "The guy wasn't drunk, Jack. He was turning the corner a little fast is what I was told, but that was from the kids. I don't know what happened exactly. There's no one to blame here. It sounded like an accident. Nicholas was running toward the corner, and the car turned into him. His friend said he went up over the hood of the car."

Jack felt his jaw locking.

"Look, there's no use in making yourself crazy," Lisa said. "The doctor said he has to sleep through the night, and then he'll be on morphine the next few days before they release him. He's going to be okay."

For all her wildness, Lisa was a good mother. She was being the levelheaded one now, and Jack was grateful for it.

"I'm sorry," he said. "I hate feeling helpless."

"I know you do, but this one is out of your hands. You don't get to be a control freak with this."

It had been their biggest marital issue. Jack enjoyed taking control. Lisa was too independent to let him.

"Okay," he said. "Can I see him?"

"Not tonight, no. Tomorrow afternoon. He'll still be out in the morning. I'm just waiting on a last checkup."

"Then I'll wait with you."

"It isn't a contest, Jack."

"I know that. I need to be here, too."

Lisa nodded.

"You want a soda?" Jack asked.

"No, thanks."

"You, Paul?"

"No, I'm fine."

"Okay," Jack said.

Paul excused himself to use the bathroom. When they were alone, Lisa said, "Thanks for asking him."

"He seems okay," Jack said. He waited a moment and added, "A little young, maybe. What's he do?"

"None of your business."

"Nicholas says he's jealous of me. That true?"

"Paul doesn't like to hear your name so often, that's all. Your name comes up a lot when I curse. He's confused is all."

"That's probably his age."

"Enough."

"Sorry," Jack said. "You have the cop's name? The one told you about the driver?"

She gave him the number.

"Thanks," he said.

"Once we hear what's what," Lisa said, "you should go home and get some rest."

"Yeah, right," Jack said, "just like you will."

•◆•

Once she was out of the Brooklyn Battery Tunnel, Agnes decided to call the police back from her job rather than from the street. She walked the few blocks from the garage to One New York Plaza with her head down to avoid the wind. A strong gust slowed a small group of people heading for the Staten Island Ferry as they scurried across Whitehall Street. Agnes felt relief when she was inside the lobby.

A few minutes later she logged onto the law firm's network. She called her agency to let them know she was there, but that she might have to leave early. Then she called Rachel's cell number again, heard the recorded message, and hung up. Agnes was about to call the police back when her cell phone rang first.

It was an unfamiliar phone number. She answered the call without speaking.

"Ms. Lynn, this is Detective George White."

Agnes hesitated.

"Ms. Lynn?"

"Yes."

"I understand your apartment was broken into earlier this evening," the detective said.

"Yes, it was," said Agnes, somewhat relieved. "I already called the police where I live."

"Yes, ma'am, I know, but we'll need you to fill out a report."

"Actually, detective, I'm at work right now."

"And where is that, ma'am?"

One of the attorney telephone lines rang. "Excuse me a second," Agnes told the detective. She answered the other call before transferring it.

"I'm sorry," she told the detective when she picked up again. "What did you say?"

"Where do you work, ma'am? I can stop by and take the report myself."

"Oh, okay, fine," Agnes said. She gave him the building's address. Another line rang. She excused herself one more time.

"Look, detective, it's hectic here right now. Can I call you back?"

"That's not a problem, ma'am. Let me give you my direct number."

Agnes put him on hold one more time to handle another call before taking his number. When the attorney lines were clear again, she told the detective about a missing friend.

"How long, ma'am?"

"Two days. At least two."

"And her name?"

Agnes was taken aback a moment. She hadn't mentioned her friend was a woman.

"Ma'am?" the detective said.

The attorney Agnes was working for opened his door and waved at her to come into his office. Frustrated at the interruption, Agnes told the detective she would have to call him back when it was less busy. She cut the call short and was about to get up from her desk when Lorelei returned from her dinner break.

"I got this, sugar," she said.

Agnes pointed at the attorney's office.

Lorelei nodded.

"Thanks," Agnes said.

"You'll need a steno pad," the attorney said.

Lorelei turned around, grabbed one from her desk, winked at Agnes, and then stepped inside his office.

Agnes reached for the telephone to call the detective back. Her cell phone rang.

"Jesus Christ," she said in frustration.

She answered her cell phone.

"Agnes, it's Jack."

"Oh, thank God," Agnes said. "How's your son?"

"He's resting now, but he's gonna be in a lot of pain. He's got pins and rods and two plates in his leg. It's a mess."

"I'm so sorry, Jack."

"Thanks," he said. "What about you? How're you doing?"

"I had a break-in at the apartment," Agnes said. "I didn't want to tell you before because of your son."

"What do you mean break-in? Where you live? Were you home?"

"No, thank God. I had just left for work but forgot something and went back. I saw them kick the door open, two men. I took off and came straight to work."

"What two men? Did you call the police?"

"Yes, but they wanted me to go to the precinct. I was too scared at the time. I also had some phone calls, Jack. Somebody with a Russian accent called my cell phone. He wanted to know where I was. He kept saying—"

"Back up a second. Who called you?"

"I don't know. He called before I left for work and then again when I was going back to the apartment for my CD player. I saw the calls were from my friend's cell number. I'm afraid it has something to do with her."

"With who?"

"Rachel. She's missing, Jack."

"The hooker?"

"Rachel," said Agnes with a slight edge to her voice. "She's been missing two days now. Her ex-husband left a message on my phone. When I called him back, he said she hasn't even called her kids. It's not like her."

"Did they report her missing? Did you?"

"No, not yet, but then I got that call, and when I saw it was Rachel's cell number, I asked for her. He wouldn't put her on. He kept saying she was busy. I'm sure he was Russian, Jack. That was right before I saw the two men kick my door in."

"Jesus," Jack said. "You have any idea where she is, your friend?"

"She had mentioned something about working for Russians. Then when I called Nelson, he said she had been traded to them."

"Who's Nelson, and what the hell does 'traded' mean?"

"Nelson is her pimp, the guy she used to work through sometimes."

There was a pause on the line.

"Jack?" she said.

"Give me a moment," he said. "I'm trying to sort this out."

Agnes waited.

"You mention any of this to the police, about your friend, I mean?" Jack asked.

"I started to tell the detective dealing with the break-in, but I got busy here. I figured I'd tell him when he came to get the report."

"What report?"

"The detective said he'd come here to the job to get a report about the break-in."

"What's his name?"

"White. George White."

"They wouldn't send a detective to your job, Agnes."

"What?"

"They wouldn't send a detective to your job. Not for a simple break-in. Something isn't right. Which precinct was he calling from?"

"He didn't say. He gave me his cell number. His direct line, I guess."

"And you called it?"

"Not yet, no," Agnes said. "That kind of freaked me, too. After I told him I had a friend missing, he knew it was a woman. I didn't tell him it was Rachel."

"He knew her name?"

"No, but I never told him it was a woman."

"Look, don't call him back. I'll come pick you up as soon as I'm finished here."

"You sure, Jack?"

"Positive. I don't like this, what you're telling me. That bit about your friend being traded to the Russians and all. If it has to do with prostitution, you're talking about the Russian mob, Agnes. I would think your friend would know better."

"Oh, God," Agnes said. She felt a pang of guilt. She remembered trying to talk Rachel out of the job, but then backing down for the sake of their friendship.

"Look, I'm just waiting on one of the doctors," Jack said. "Nicholas had surgery today. He's gonna be on morphine the next few days."

"God," Agnes said, "the poor thing."

"He'll be okay, but I want to be here tomorrow afternoon to see him. In the meantime, I'll come get you soon as I talk to one last doctor."

"What are you thinking about all this, Jack?"

"I don't know," he said. "But I don't like that the Russian mob might be involved. I don't like that some detective claims he'll come to you to fill out a break-in report. I don't like what you said, that he knew your friend was a woman without you mentioning it, and I definitely don't like the break-in, the fact you saw two guys a few minutes after some Russian was on the phone asking where you were."

Agnes could feel the color draining from her face. "Poor Rachel," she said.

"Just stay calm," Jack told her. "I'll pick you up, and maybe we'll start with the pimp after that. You know where we can find him?"

"He's on Second Avenue in East Harlem. One sixteen on Second." Another line rang. "Hold a second," she said. She took the call, transferred it to the attorney, and was back on the line with Jack. "One sixteen twenty-six, apartment three-B."

"We'll go see him after I pick you up. Can you leave early?"

"Of course, sure."

"What about the detective? Did you tell him where you're working?"

"Shit, I think so, yeah. But I can give him another address if he calls back."

"Good," Jack said. "Just don't call him back. I'll call you when I'm downstairs. Get me a building pass or something, and I'll come up to meet you."

"You sure about this?"

"Soon's I'm done with the doctor, I'm on my way."

•◆•

Lorelei stepped out of the attorney's office and went to Agnes's desk.

"You okay, sugar?" she asked. "You looked a bit harried before."

"I'm fine," Agnes told her. "I had a little scare before I left for work. Someone broke into my place."

"Oh, lord," Lorelei said. "You sure you need to be here?"

"Actually, she does," the attorney said. He had just poked his head out of his office doorway.

Agnes ignored him. "I already called the agency," she said. "I told them I might have to leave."

"Excuse me?" the attorney said.

Agnes turned to him. "You don't want to push this," she said. "If I have to, I'm going."

He looked at both women, muttered something under his breath, and withdrew back into his office. Then he closed his door.

Lorelei winked at Agnes. "You go, girl," she whispered.

One of the lines rang. Agnes put the caller on hold until she cleared it with the attorney.

"Put it through," he said.

Agnes put the call through at the same time her cell phone rang. She apologized to Lorelei before answering the call.

"Don't mind me," Lorelei said. "I'm gonna get a cup of tea. You want?"

"No, thanks," Agnes said before answering her cell phone. She didn't check the number and was surprised when she heard the detective's voice again.

"Ms. Lynn? Detective John White."

Agnes was positive he had said his name was George White earlier. She didn't respond.

"Hello?" he said.

"Ah . . . yes, hello. This is Agnes."

"Oh, okay. How are you making out? Working a late one?"

Agnes remembered what she had told Jack about giving a phony address if the detective called back.

"Ah . . . actually, if it's not too much trouble, I was wondering if you could come meet me," she said.

"Okay, sure. Where at?"

"Ah, Midtown," Agnes lied. "Near the Garden. I'll be leaving around midnight."

"Excuse me?"

"I'm at our Midtown office. It's near Madison Square Garden."

The detective didn't say anything.

"Detective White?"

"That's fine, ma'am," he said, but Agnes could detect a change in his tone. "What's the building address?"

Agnes was caught off guard. "Ah, three-forty-one," she said.

Another moment of silence unnerved Agnes.

"Detective?"

"What street, ma'am?"

"Ah, Thirty-fourth, I'm sorry," Agnes said.

"Okay," he said. "I'll see you there."

"Thanks, detective," Agnes said. "I was just handed some more work. I'll see you later."

She hung up just as Lorelei returned with her cup of tea.

"This is crazy," Agnes said.

"You should go home, sugar."

Agnes saw the attorney's line had stopped blinking on her desk phone. She looked up when his door opened. He stepped out of his office with a big smile.

"You know you two look almost identical," he said.

"Thank you," Lorelei said. "I know in my case that's a compliment."

Agnes noticed he was avoiding direct eye contact with her. She forced a smile to be polite.

"Well, you're both very pretty," he added, "but we still have some work to do. Lorelei, can you stay another hour?"

"I guess," she said, "but that's it. One hour and I'm out of here."

The attorney crossed his heart. "Swear to God," he said.

"Oh, shhh," Lorelei said. "And don't blaspheme."

Agnes was wondering about the change of tone in the detective's voice. It was as if he knew she was lying.

Lorelei saw something was wrong.

"Sugar?" she said. "You sure you're okay?"

Chapter 11

"WHAT SHE SAYS?" Pasha Chenkov asked Detective Michael Lyons.

Lyons was a dirty cop connected to Viktor Timkin's crew since the day he had assassinated a rival Russian mob leader for fifty thousand dollars two years ago. He had picked up Chenkov on his way into the city and, using a phony name, had spoken with Agnes Lynn a few minutes earlier.

"She lied is what she said," Lyons said. "Before she gave me a downtown address, and now she told me she's near the Garden. That's Midtown. Your guys found her car in some garage downtown, right?"

"Maybe she takes train from garage."

Lyons was a thin man with pale skin and a drinking problem. He took a sip from a pint of Jameson he kept in a flask.

"Yeah, right," he said, "that makes sense."

Chenkov's cell phone rang. Lyons took the picture of the blond woman the Russian had left on the console. He looked at her face and wondered what the hell they wanted with her. He asked when Chenkov was off his cell phone.

"She is to help friend," the Russian said. "Now woman is downtown near ferry, One New York Plaza."

"The first address she gave me."

"Is busy there, no?"

"Not at this time, but there are plenty of cameras down there since the Trade Center."

"You come, eh?"

"I come, no," Lyons said. "Whatever you're up to isn't my problem, Hojo."

"What time she says she leaves work?"

"She didn't say."

"She goes with you?"

"Even if I did go down there, why would she do that? She has her own car, right?"

The Russian mobster thought about it. He bit at a fingernail.

"You go with her," he said. "You bring her to Brooklyn."

Lyons didn't like Chenkov and knew the feeling was mutual. He especially didn't like having to help the Russian enforcer out of a crisis he knew nothing about.

"What's so important about this broad?" he asked. "She

didn't like it when I asked her friend's name earlier. She rushed me off the phone after that. What's it about?"

The Russian ignored the question. "Viktor wants her," he said.

"Yeah, so why's he need me to get her?"

"Business."

"What business? He didn't say anything to me."

"He calls you later, eh? For now we get woman."

"I don't think so," Lyons said. "You figure out what you're gonna do, because I'm not involved with the broad beyond this. Besides, I have to get uptown for your other adventure, right?"

"Pimp, yes, but that is later."

"I don't care when it is. I'm not sticking around downtown with two thousand cameras all over the place."

"I get you her car and you can take her?" the Russian asked.

Lyons turned to him and stared.

"Yes?" the Russian said.

"*Nyet*," Lyons said. "Or you want me to write it out for you? I'm not going near this broad. I tried to set it up for you and that's it. You're on your own now."

The Russian cursed under his breath.

Lyons took another hit from his pint.

•◆•

When she called the agency to tell them she'd be leaving at midnight, Agnes was surprised to learn a man with an accent had also called and claimed to be her boyfriend.

"What boyfriend?" she asked. "Who?"

"Oh, God, I'm sorry," the dispatcher said. "He said he was your boyfriend and that he'd just missed you at the apartment. He knew where you lived and all. I'm sorry, Agnes."

"Did you tell him where I am?"

"No, they'd fire me for giving that information out. I just told him you were working on assignment. He said he was a boyfriend the second time, because I wouldn't tell him anything the first time. I wasn't sure if he knew you or not, but he had your address."

"Did he ask where I am?"

"Yes, actually, he did. I didn't tell, though. I swear it."

You told him enough, Agnes was thinking.

"Are you okay?" the dispatcher asked. "Is he some kind of a nut? A stalker or something?"

"I don't know who he is," Agnes said, "except he's not my boyfriend. I don't have one."

"Oh, shit."

"When did he call?"

"Half an hour ago? I meant to tell you when the phones got busy here."

"Do you have the number he called from? You have that kind of thing on your phone?"

"It was a private line. Sorry."

"Shit," Agnes said. She turned on her chair for privacy.

"Agnes?"

"Huh?"

It was the attorney. He was standing behind her. He had forgot himself and tapped her shoulder to get her attention. Agnes jerked away from him.

"I'm sorry," he gasped.

"Don't put your hands on me," Agnes said.

"I'm sorry," he repeated. He took a step back. "Jesus, I didn't mean anything. I was just . . . ."

He turned to Lorelei, swallowed hard, then pointed to the prospectus he had set on Agnes's desk. "I need that back as soon as possible," he whispered. "ASAP, please."

"I'll take care of it," Lorelei said.

"Agnes?"

It was the dispatcher.

"Hold on," Agnes said.

"Please," the attorney repeated.

Agnes was still shaken from being surprised by the attorney. She didn't see him step back inside his office.

"Agnes?" Lorelei said. "You're looking pale, honey."

• ◆ •

Half an hour later, after she had completed a round of edits to a real estate document, and while Lorelei was taking dictation in the attorney's office, Agnes was using the Internet to find out what she could about the Russian mob in New York.

She used Google to find information about the different factions of Russian organized crime in the United States and was surprised at how most of the articles referred to the Russian mob as the Red Mafiya.

Agnes narrowed her search to New York City and was further surprised at how many neighborhoods the Russian mob had infiltrated on a map of the five boroughs. One of the maps presented a legend showing various degrees of shading to highlight Russian Mafiya influence. The darker the shade of red, the more influential the Russian Mafiya were.

She read about a pair of stepbrothers believed to be running the Russian criminal enterprise out of Brooklyn. The darkest shade of red was centered in Brighton Beach on the map. Although the article was nearly a year old, when she searched for more recent stories, the same names appeared: Yuri and Viktor Timkin.

Viktor had emigrated first from Russia and then from Israel. At fifty-two years of age, he was believed to be the smarter of the two stepbrothers and the official head of the New York Red Mafiya. Physically, Viktor Timkin was described as a little fireplug of a man with a calm disposition and patience for seeking vengeance.

Yuri Timkin was the younger of the stepbrothers and was described as vicious, ruthless, and stupid. He had served time for assaulting a Red Sox fan at a Yankees baseball game.

Agnes searched for Russian mobsters linked to prostitution and found a few who were involved in both the porn industry and prostitution. Igor Mahalov and Aaron Tevya Bartnev were the two names most often noted. Agnes wondered if Mahalov knew something about Rachel.

Mahalov was known as the Red Mafiya's pimp; evidently he often smoked Cuban Churchill cigars while holding court on Surf Avenue in front of the New York Aquarium. Bartnev was called the porn king in Brighton Beach and was known to hang out in a video store on Brighton Beach Avenue.

According to Internet articles, there seemed to be two types of Russian mobsters: street thugs who handled the day-to-day businesses long associated with organized crime—the extortion, loan-sharking, gambling, prostitution, and porn—and then there were the more sophisticated white-collar criminals who were involved in Wall Street high finance. Allegedly, the Russian Mafiya had managed to move billions of dollars from Russia through accounts at the Bank of New York in an elaborate money-laundering scheme that proved to be the downfall of the bank.

Agnes was sure the Russians her friend was involved with were the more dangerous street thugs. She printed two of the articles that provided the names and locations of Russian mob hangouts and stuffed them inside her purse.

A few minutes later, Lorelei stepped out of the attorney's office. She held a hand up to her mouth as she yawned.

"Excuse me," she said.

"How'd that go?" Agnes asked.

"I'm not sure, but it seemed like forever, and I am dog tired, girl. I can use a hot bath and a massage. Maybe an orgasm or two if I can find the strength."

Agnes motioned toward the attorney's office. "What time's he leaving?"

"Soon, let's hope. You rocked his world twice tonight, but he was back to giddy a few minutes ago. Hopefully, he'll ask to have the last set of edits sent to his house by car. That shouldn't take long."

"Well, I'm here until Jack picks me up," Agnes said.

"I can use a pick-me-up myself," Lorelei said. "I'm going to splash some water on my face. Then, when I come back, if he is finally through, I'm calling for a car. It's been a long day and one I'm supposed to be off."

"I can have Jack wait a few minutes if you want to go now."

Lorelei waved the offer off. "I'll wait him out. If your man comes to get you first, consider yourself lucky."

"I owe you, Lorelei. Pick a night next week for dinner."

"I'd rather drink."

"Okay, drinks, then. Say when."

"When."

Lorelei's cell phone rang. Agnes jumped at the sound.

"Hey, I think you're the one needs that drink, sugar," Lorelei said.

Agnes swallowed heard. "I'm fine," she said. "Sorry. Take your call."

•◆•

Nelson Freeman spent his afternoon drinking before packing two suitcases. He intended to leave New York to visit with his sister in Alabama the next morning and wasn't sure if he was coming back to New York. When the apartment buzzer sounded, Nelson let it ring a few more times before stumbling out of bed to answer it. Sometimes people looking to gain access into the building rang as many buzzers as it took for someone to let them inside.

The buzzer sounded again a moment before he responded. The noise hurt his ears.

"Who is it?" he asked.

He waited a few seconds, but there was no answer.

"God damn it," he muttered.

Freeman stopped in the bathroom on his way back to bed. He had just flushed the toilet when there was a loud knock at the front door.

"Jesus fuckin' Christ," he said. He grabbed his straight razor from the medicine cabinet and looked through the peephole in the apartment door.

"Yeah?" he asked.

"Police," a deep voice said.

"Police who?" Freeman asked.

"Open door," the voice said.

This time Freeman heard an accent. "Police who?" he repeated. "Show some ID. Hold it up to the door."

"Okay," the voice said. "See?"

Freeman was staring at a middle finger when a series of shots filled the hallway outside his door. He felt two jolts in his stomach before flying backward into the wall directly behind him. He was sitting propped up against the wall with his hands clutching his bloody stomach when the apartment door was kicked open.

He was starting to lose consciousness. A man kneeled in front of him and pointed a gun at his head. He barely saw the flash from the muzzle before the bullet entered his forehead.

•◆•

Five teenagers wearing high school football jerseys were roughhousing on the sands of Plum Beach off the Belt Parkway in Brooklyn. It was a frigid cold night with a full moon and a clear sky. The headlights from two cars the boys had driven onto the beach provided just enough light for a game of two-hand touch. The boys had been drinking most of the night and were sloppy drunk.

They stopped to line up for a new play. A tall kid with the

name Miles stitched on the back of his jersey was quarter-backing. Both of his receivers lined up to his right, a few yards from the surf's edge. The defenders lined up directly across from them.

Miles yelled, "Go," and his receiver broke from the line. One slanted across the middle until he tripped and fell. Miles faked a quick throw, then stepped up to throw a long pass to his other receiver, a tall kid wearing a white doo-rag.

The ball was overthrown. The receiver barely tipped it with one hand. The ball bounced to his right and was headed for the water.

The receiver turned quickly to retrieve the ball. He was about to make a dive for it when he suddenly stopped and covered his mouth.

Both defenders teased him about drinking too much wine before switching to beer. The quarterback joined in when he heard his receiver gagging.

"Get the ball!" the other receiver yelled.

The tall kid began to retch.

"Yo, Sims, I'm gonna kick your ass you leave that ball in the water like that," the quarterback yelled.

The tall kid had started to spew. All four of his friends ran to his side, but Miles spotted it first, the body floating close to the water's edge. He walked closer to the surf and stopped when it appeared to be a woman.

"Yo, that's some lady in there," he said.

The others, except for the tall kid, joined him. They took half steps at a time.

"She bald," one of the boys said.

"Oh, man, she all cut up or somethin'," another said.

A wave flipped the body over. They could see open wounds running across her entire torso. Her head was bald. Her face was bloated from being in the water. Both of her eyes were opened wide and colorless.

Two more of the boys lost what was in their stomachs before they could turn away.

Chapter 12

LORELEI WAS CONCERNED about Agnes and insisted she work on the last document the attorney dropped off. Agnes tried to take the work from her, but Lorelei wouldn't hear of it. Agnes used the downtime to search the Internet for more information on the Russian Mafiya.

A few minutes after the attorney finally left, Lorelei was finished with the document. She prepared it for a package delivery, called the car service for a pickup, then organized her desk and was ready to leave. She went to the closet alongside the printers and took out her jacket. She pulled something red from one of the pockets and proceeded to unfold a red kerchief. She wrapped it around her head, tied a knot under her chin, and then posed for Agnes.

"Voila," she said.

Agnes pointed to the kerchief. "I love it," she said.

Lorelei touched the kerchief. "This thing?"

Agnes nodded. "I love the look, too. I hate wearing hats, because they're so overdone. I love the practicality of a kerchief."

Lorelei glanced over her shoulder a moment. "Tell you a secret?"

"Sure," Agnes said.

"My boyfriend likes me to wear them in bed."

"Really?"

"Seriously. He says he likes the peasant look."

"Oh, God."

"What do I care if it keeps him at it?"

"Sure," Agnes said.

"Anyway, you really like it?"

"I love it."

Lorelei undid the knot and pulled the kerchief from her head. She walked it to where Agnes was sitting and set it on her desk.

"There," she said. "It's yours now."

"No, I can't take that."

"Please, it's just a piece of silk."

"No, it's expensive, I'm sure."

"It was a gift."

"So? What will your boyfriend do?"

"I have a closetful, honey, trust me."

Agnes stood up at her desk. The two women hugged.

"Thanks for handling that last document," Agnes said.

"You sure you're okay?" Lorelei asked. "We can talk if you need to."

Agnes shook her head. "Thanks for this," she said. She held up the kerchief. "I mean it."

Lorelei waved it off. "It's my pleasure."

"You working tomorrow?"

"I'll be in around ten. You?"

"I wasn't booked, but I think I'm going to take the day. I don't even know if there's any damage to the apartment. I can use a day to relax anyway. Maybe I'll see a movie with my friend."

Lorelei smiled. "You keep calling him that you're like to believe it, honey. What's his name? His real name?"

"Jack," Agnes said.

"He's the one on his way to get you?"

"Uh-huh," said Agnes, smiling now.

"Okay, then. You take care of yourself and your friend."

"Okay," Agnes said.

"'Night, sugar."

"Good night."

Agnes felt nervous as soon as she was alone. She watched the clock as she waited for Jack's call from downstairs. She remembered her car and called the garage to let them know she'd be late picking it up.

"You won't date me because I'm married, but here you are seeing another guy wearing a wedding ring," the garage attendant said.

It was Louis, an older Hispanic man from the parking garage. He liked to play a flirting game with her but was always courteous. Now she was terrified about what he had just said.

"What guy?"

"The guy waiting outside with his friend," Louis said. "You want me to go get him? He said he'd wait for you up the ramp."

"He have an accent?"

"Russian, I think. Maybe Polish. Hey, you know this guy or what?"

"No, Louis, I don't, but he's been asking about me. He called my agency before, too."

"He a cop?"

"No. I don't know who he is."

"You want me to go see he's still outside? It's just up the ramp."

"No, don't get involved," Agnes warned him. "He might be dangerous. I don't know him. You said there were two?"

"Two guys, yeah. Black leather jackets, sunglasses. They looked like they had money."

"Jesus," Agnes said. "Look, if he comes back, I didn't call for my car yet, okay?"

"You sure, kiddo? I can call the cops from here, you want? He'll never know."

"No, don't do anything. Just say I didn't call for my car yet if he comes back down and asks."

"Okay. But you call me later and let me know you're okay, understand?"

"I will, Louis."

"Promise."

"I promise."

"Okay, kiddo. You take care of yourself."

Agnes spotted Lorelei's glasses on the desk when she

hung up. She grabbed them and her purse and headed for the elevators.

•◆•

Pasha Chenkov stood inside a bus stop shelter on Water Street in front of the building where Agnes Lynn was working. He had one of his men waiting in a car parked off the corner of Whitehall Street and two more of his men stationed outside the garage where she had parked her car.

Chenkov had already screwed the silencer onto the barrel of the Beretta nine-millimeter tucked inside the waist of his pants. If the woman headed straight for her car when she came out the front entrance of One New York Plaza, he would leave her to his men waiting for her at the garage. If she headed for Water Street, he would kill her himself.

It was a quiet night. The little traffic there was came and went with each changing light. The few corporate cars parked at the curb in front of the building were heeding the taxi signs more than fifty yards from the bus stop where Chenkov waited.

At exactly eleven forty-eight, Chenkov noticed a blond woman leaving the building. He checked the picture one of his men had taken from Agnes Lynn's apartment, then stashed it inside his jacket pocket while he watched to see which way she was heading. When she veered right, toward the corporate cars parked at the taxi stand, Chenkov turned to his driver off the corner of Whitehall Street and waved him on.

Chenkov then approached the woman from behind, about twenty feet from the last car at the cab stand. He waited until he was sure he could catch her before he pushed down the wool face mask he was wearing up on his forehead. He kept the pistol hidden in a deep jacket pocket as he looked up to grab her attention.

"Agnes?" he said.

The woman seemed startled at first, then turned and smiled. "Oh, you must be—"

Chenkov pulled the gun from his jacket pocket and shot her two times in the chest. He took a quick glance around the area before leaning over her body and firing another two shots into her forehead. Then he got inside the car that had pulled up to the curb and it raced away.

• ◆ •

Agnes was running through the lobby when she spotted Lorelei heading for the corporate cars parked at the curb on Water Street. One of the security guards yelled to her to slow down as she went through the revolving doors.

She was about to call out Lorelei's name when she saw a man pointing something at her friend. There were two flashes. Lorelei went down. Agnes gasped as the man leaned over and seemed to shoot her friend in the head.

Agnes screamed for help. The man got inside a car that then raced through the red light at the far corner. She ran down the stairs to her friend and kneeled alongside the body. She saw the two holes in Lorelei's forehead and knew she was dead.

Agnes screamed again, louder this time. Two of the security guards were outside the lobby doors calling to her. She waved them over.

The drivers of the cabs and corporate cars at the stand were out of their cars now. They gathered around Agnes and Lorelei. Agnes stood up and shrank back toward the building. One of the security guards told her to stay put until the police arrived. She told him she was cold and needed her jacket. She headed for the subway instead.

•◆•

Jack had been driving across the Brooklyn Bridge when a radio report suggested that an apparent purge within the Russian mob had taken place in Brooklyn. Three minutes later he turned up the volume at "the possibly related story of a woman's body found washed up on a Brooklyn beach."

He wondered if the woman could be Agnes's friend. The shitty feeling in the pit of his stomach suggested it probably was. He tried calling Agnes to meet him downstairs but she didn't answer. He left a message for her to call him back.

Then he saw the commotion outside the building as soon as he turned onto Water Street. He pulled up at the curb behind the taxi stand and could see two uniformed security guards talking to a few men around a body that lay on the sidewalk. Jack saw it was a blond woman and panicked.

He found his way to the body just before the first of several police cars arrived at the scene. He kneeled down, saw it wasn't Agnes, and felt a wave of relief.

"You know her?" someone asked.

Jack looked up and saw it was one of the security guards. "No," he said. "I don't."

"There was another woman, another blonde came out

looking for this one, but she took off. She said she needed to get her coat, but then she headed down the subway."

"You know her name?"

The security guard read from a log-in sheet. "Woman named Agnes Lynn," he said. "She was temping for Burrows and Lang upstairs. She had one of their building passes."

"She's okay?"

The guard pointed toward Whitehall Street and said, "She was when she took off for that subway."

Thank God, Jack thought. Thank God.

Chapter 13

THE TWO DETECTIVES stood on the Starrett City side of Spring Creek in Brooklyn and surveyed the waters where the bodies had been found floating more than two hours ago. Two police boats idled in the middle of the creek.

Detective Robert Moss nudged his partner, Anita Nance, with an elbow and said, "I'll lay three to one they were all face down."

Nance scoffed at her partner's attempt at humor.

They had been working homicide together three years

now. Moss, at forty-six, was an eighteen-year veteran of the force, the last ten with homicide. Nance was twelve years on the job, her last three with homicide. It was a windy night. The cold chill whistled in off the water.

"Been two hours already," Moss said. "The time this Russki gets here, they'll all be at the morgue, the bodies."

"You know anything about him?"

"He's the head of the redfella squad. Supposed to have a reputation for pushing the envelope. He was some kind of warrior back in Russia, in the army there. That's about it."

Nance was a tall, athletic African American woman with a big chest and broad shoulders. She motioned toward the water. "You think OC will take this off our hands?"

"If they're mobsters, yeah, I guess so," Moss said. "I hope so." He pointed to several local news vans parked along Vandalia Avenue. "They're sure hoping so. Nothing like a little gang war to jumpstart media ratings."

"What about the woman called in on the beach? You think she's part of this?"

Moss picked at one fingernail with another. It was a habit he couldn't control. "She could be," he said. "Plum Beach isn't very far from here. The kids found her said it looked like she was cut to pieces. I'll guarantee these guys are part of some war. Maybe it's all connected."

A banged-up Chevy Impala pulled up on along the curb. Both detectives turned to see who it was.

"This him?" Nance asked.

Moss didn't respond.

A tall, broad man with white hair and blue eyes got out of the Impala, spotted the two detectives on the embankment, then climbed it quickly and introduced himself.

Detective Ivann Koloff was with the Brooklyn organized crime task force investigating the Russian Mafia in Brighton Beach. He went by his nickname, Vanya.

Nance said, "They were probably dumped off by boat and floated down here. They're sending divers in to see if there are any on the bottom."

"The ones they already pulled were Russian mob," Moss added. "Had the tattoos on their shoulders and knees. One had a star. Why they called you, I guess."

"Any names?" Vanya asked. Although he'd been in the United States more than ten years, his Russian accent was still pronounced.

Nance read the names from her notes. "Oleg Kephik, Sergei Zennan, and Konstantin Gregorovich. At least that's what their driver's licenses read."

"This a war?" Moss asked.

"Not that I know," Vanya said. "Is too obvious, they dump bodies together like this. Not war, something else, I think. Names you mention are Yuri Timkin crew."

"They from Canarsie?" Moss asked.

"Maybe," Vanya said. "Most are Brighton Beach. Sergei, is same one, is Canarsie."

"I live in Canarsie. I know they're there, near the projects, across the water there." Moss pointed to the opposite bank of Spring Creek. "They still picking the Italians' scraps?"

Vanya saw Nance was paying attention. He smiled at her. "These guys not interested in scraps anymore," he said. "The people who did this are looking to take over."

.◆.

Thirty minutes after the last body had been pulled from the water Vanya showed the two homicide detectives a book he kept of the Russian Mafia crews he was investigating. He explained the makeup of the crew from Brighton Beach and how all of the bodies in the water were from Yuri Timkin's crew.

"So what you're saying is this was some kind of a purge," Moss said.

They were having coffee in the Seaview Diner in Canarsie. Vanya sipped at a black coffee. Moss carefully buttered a piece of rye toast. Nance, both elbows on the table, leaned in close to pay attention to what the Russian detective had to say.

"Yes, purge," Vanya said. "Viktor Timkin is leader, stepbrother to Yuri. This one—" he pointed to a picture of a bald man— "is dope, eh? Wild animal, no brains. This one is different." He pointed to Viktor Timkin's picture. "This one is smart." He looked from Moss to Nance. "How you say, cunning."

Nance moved up on her chair. Moss saw his partner's interest in Vanya and interrupted her admiration. "So Viktor whacked Yuri's crew. What about Yuri?"

"Probably he's dead, too. We know crew is, eh? Except for reason we don't know. Has to be reason. They don't like each other, but is big move to make. One of the names you have, Konstantin, is genius. He is know computer engineering, software, coding. Viktor doesn't want to lose him, I'm sure. Viktor is low-profile, not make drama. Why he does this? Why now?"

"We know that, we're wasting our time here," said Moss, before picking at his fingernails again.

"You think this can have anything to do with the Italian mob?" Nance asked. "The Corellis had a small war going on for a while. That crap going on within their family has been in the papers the last couple of weeks, something about the guy just out of prison wanting to take over. He had something to do with Coney Island. That borders on Brighton Beach."

Vanya shook his head. "Is too deliberate, what happened tonight," he said. "If this is somebody else, Italians, they don't leave bodies to find. Not to put on display like this. Not anymore. This is deliberate. This is Timkin."

Nance was impressed again. Moss saw it and said, "You pretty sure of yourself on this."

"Positive," Vanya said, eyeballing Moss this time.

Nance said, "Why the tattoos? Why on the knees?"

"Is history of criminal from Russia," said Vanya, turning away from Moss. "Long story short, knees mean he doesn't bow to anyone. Stars, pointed stars, are big shot. Leadership. Goes back to *Vors* in Russia, criminal-in-law. Long story. Criminals form union, crews, in prison. Tattoos are in prison. Distinguish what is do, who is what." He turned to Moss. "If John Gotti is wear special tattoo on chest, say he is boss."

"Gotti wore expensive suits to show that," Moss said. "Painted a target on himself because of it."

"Gotti was tough guy," Vanya said. "Would've been boss in Russia, too."

"What about the woman who was found at Plum Beach?" Nance asked. "Could she be part of what we found in Spring Creek?"

"I hear this on radio in car driving here," Vanya said. "Is possible. Do you know about woman?"

"Not yet," Moss said. "We headed to the medical examiner from here."

"Preliminary report was that she was mutilated," Nance said.

"A Russian bachelor party gone bad," Moss joked.

Nance shot her partner a hard look.

"I don't think so," Vanya said to Nance. "Anyway, we know from Viktor Timkin soon enough. Time is tell. Timkin is ruthless, eh? Is careful, not make move without reason. Is reason we need."

"Back to that again," Moss said. He peeked at his watch. "Well, we'll have plenty of paperwork to follow up on after the medical examiner. I'm glad you guys are handling this, tell you the truth. We're already overworked. You coming?" he asked his partner.

Nance extended her hand to Vanya. "I'd like to talk to you about this again if I can," she said.

Vanya took Nance's hand. "Anytime," he said. "You have number."

"Yeah, and isn't she the lucky one for it," Moss whispered to himself.

•◆•

Agnes was fortunate to have taken her purse, but her jacket was back at the office. She was shaking from the frigid temperature when she finally stepped on the R train.

She would have to wait until she was out of the subway before she could use her cell phone. In the meantime, as she rode the train three stops to Canal Street, she struggled with what had happened to Lorelei.

Agnes was sure Lorelei had been killed by mistake. She couldn't forget what the attorney had said about her and Lorelei looking so alike earlier.

She switched trains at Canal Street and took the Lexington Avenue number six train. She stood near a heat vent but was still shaking when a homeless woman pushing a shopping cart got on at Spring Street.

"You okay, honey?" the woman asked.

Agnes pursed her lips. "I'm okay," she said.

"Need something to wear?"

Agnes looked at the clothes the woman had inside a paper shopping bag. She saw a roach crawling across a blue sweatshirt and said, "No, thanks."

"You'll catch your death of pneumonia, you don't put something on," the homeless woman said.

"I'm almost home," Agnes told her. "Few more stops."

The homeless woman yawned. Two minutes later, her chin rested on her chest as she lightly snored on a corner seat.

At Thirty-third Street Agnes got off the train and hustled up the stairs to Park Avenue. It was freezing outside. She looked both ways on Park Avenue but didn't see anything open. She knew there were twenty-four-hour delis and Indian restaurants in the twenties on Lexington Avenue where yellow-cab drivers congregated during their breaks. It was also one of the few areas where streetwalkers continued to operate in Manhattan. It gave her an idea.

Agnes crossed Park Avenue and headed south before turning east.

It was a few minutes before midnight when she spotted a black woman hiding inside a recessed doorway as a police car passed. It was a hooker working the streets. Agnes approached her once the police cruiser was gone.

"Where you working from?" she asked.

"Excuse me?" said the black woman, her voice filled with suspicion. "I'm waiting on someone."

Agnes noticed the fake-fur jacket the woman was wearing. "You have another coat nearby?"

"Excuse me?"

"I need a jacket. A coat or something. I'll pay you if you have one."

"You must be trippin'."

"I'm not, but I am freezing."

The tall woman looked Agnes up and down. "You a cop?"

"I'm no cop. I need a jacket, though. Really, can you help me or not? I'll pay you."

The black woman pointed east on the street. "Try the deli up the block," she said. "Man there is okay. He don't have something, come back and I'll see what I can do."

"The guy in the deli?"

"Big man there, yeah, he's all right."

"Thanks."

Agnes ran to the corner and stepped inside the delicatessen. She ordered a cup of hot chocolate and a toasted bagel. She waited until after she paid before asking the Arab man behind the counter if he had a jacket he wanted to sell.

"You lost your coat?" he asked.

"I left it in a cab."

"Oh, boy. It's too cold to be walking around like that."

"Can you help me? I'll pay for it."

He pointed toward the back of the store. "Let me see what I can do."

He walked down the narrow aisle behind the deli counters and disappeared behind a door. A few seconds later he came back holding a dark green down jacket.

"I tell you what," he said. "You give me some money to hold on to the jacket until tomorrow, okay? You bring back the jacket, and I give you back the money."

"Thank you," Agnes said. "Thank you so much."

"How much you can give me?" the Arab asked.

Agnes went through her purse. "You have a cash machine?"

"In back."

"Is a hundred good enough."

The Arab handed her the jacket. "Hundred is fine," he said.

Agnes put the jacket on and zipped it up to her neck. She shivered one more time before sipping the hot chocolate and heading to the cash machine.

"Thank you so much," she said again.

A few minutes later she handed the Arab five twenty dollar bills. She thanked him one more time and then motioned for him to come closer.

"I need something else," she whispered.

"What?"

"A gun."

This time the Arab pulled away. "Sorry, I can't do that."

"Do you know where I could get one?"

"No. Please don't ask this."

"Sorry," Agnes said.

"Is okay, but you bring jacket back tomorrow, yes?"

"I will," she said, "I promise."

She left the deli and turned the corner onto Lexington Avenue. She saw another hooker palming off something, probably money, to one of two men sitting in a BMW parked near the corner of Twenty-seventh Street. Agnes ducked into a doorway to stay warm. A few minutes later the hooker she had seen with the men in the BMW was standing outside the doorway.

Agnes tapped on the glass. The hooker turned to her. Agnes opened the door.

"How come there are two of them?" Agnes asked.

"Excuse me?" the hooker said. "Who the fuck are you?"

"Agnes. And you are?"

The hooker started to walk away.

"Please, I need help," Agnes said. "Please."

The hooker stopped and did a slow turn. She was a thick black woman wearing white tights under a short yellow skirt with white leather boots. The wig she was wearing was red and long. She looked both ways on the street, then pointed to the doorway and stepped inside the vestibule with Agnes.

"What's it about?" she asked.

"I'm in trouble," Agnes said. "I need a gun."

"The fuck I look like, Kmart?"

Agnes motioned toward the door. "Those your guys out there?"

"Excuse me?"

"I'll pay for the connection. I'll pay good, but I need your help if you can do it."

The hooker squinted. "That your real name, Agnes?"

"Yes, but don't tell them that."

"Right, and I'm J-Lo."

Agnes smiled. She put out a hand. "I like some of your music."

The hooker smiled back, then took Agnes's hand. "One's the friend of the other," she said. "He's a cheap motherfucker, too, the friend. Jimmy tells me to give his friend a blow job at the end of the night, and the man doesn't even tip."

"Then you should lose Jimmy," Agnes said.

"I would if I could. You on the street?"

"No. Not anymore."

"I know you're not a cop, right?"

"I'm not a cop."

"You sure?"

"I'm not a cop."

"You want me to go to Jimmy for a gun, it'll cost you."

"I understand. That's not a problem."

"What the hell you need a gun for anyway?"

"Protection."

"Yeah, right, what else. Okay, I'll go talk to him, but there's no guarantee on this. He gets in my face, I'm not gonna push him."

"I appreciate it, but I'd rather do this through you. Pay you, I mean. I don't want to meet Jimmy if I don't have to."

"He probably don't wanna meet you either, but he might to make sure you're not the law."

"I'd rather not."

"That's up to Jimmy, if he goes for it."

Agnes handed the hooker five twenties. "That's for you," she said.

The hooker lifted her skirt and stashed the cash inside the top of her stockings. "Okay," she said. "I'll go talk to him, see what he says."

"Thank you," Agnes said.

Chapter 14

VIKTOR TIMKIN SAT with Fat Tony Gangi, the underboss of the Vignieri crime family, in an Italian restaurant on Houston Street in Greenwich Village. It was a few minutes past eleven o'clock. The restaurant was empty except for two women stragglers sitting at the bar.

The two men sat alone. Gangi picked at the provolone cheese on a plate of cold antipasto. Timkin buttered one end of a bread stick before biting the tip off.

"In your father's language, I would tell you that I need a

stone removed from my shoe," Timkin said. "*Ho bisogno di una pietra rimossa dal pattino.*"

"That's pretty good," Gangi said. "You speak any other languages I should know about?"

Timkin held both his hands over the table like a typist fingering a keyboard. He said, "I get that from the Internet, what I just said, translation program, but you understand what it is."

"Your guy the feds are holding at the Metropolitan Correctional Center," Gangi said, "I understand he's trying to hang himself."

"Taras Sadova," Timkin said. "This is good, he hangs himself. Sadova is rat. He looks to make deal and decides, no, he can't do it. He would rather die. I like he does this, hangs himself."

Gangi sipped from a glass of water.

"And I am told that your problem is solved in the morning," Timkin continued. "Something about Albanians taking revenge, if I'm not mistaken."

"Richie Marino is a problem we can all do without," said Gangi after setting down a glass of water.

"So that Coney Island would be open to us," Timkin said. "The boardwalk and the Astroland."

"As we already discussed," Gangi said, "everything except the baseball stadium."

"Is done, then," Timkin said.

"Good. Now there's another issue to discuss. I was told a little while before you got here that a pimp up in Harlem was killed."

Timkin waved a hand. "Was stepbrother," he said. "Yuri."

"I have a captain of mine is very upset. That pimp was worth a good deal of money to my guy."

"What to make for compensation?"

"Right now he wants blood."

"I already take care of that."

"What do you mean?"

"You will see in papers tomorrow," Timkin said. "Crew that makes mistake is taken care of."

Gangi was impressed. "Your stepbrother?"

"Was another stone in my shoe. Since he comes here, he was problem. Finally, was removed tonight."

"Okay, good. That will take care of his anger. What about his wallet?"

"Name price."

"Say, fifty grand, but I'll tell him it's only forty."

"Is done," Timkin said. "I send you in morning."

Gangi set a one-hundred-dollar bill on the table, waited until Timkin saw it, and then pushed it at the Russian mob boss.

"As a symbol of prosperity," Gangi said. "And friendship."

Timkin pocketed the bill and raised his glass of water. "To friendship," he said. "*Tovarich.*"

•◆•

The pimp and his friend had left with the deposit money Agnes had passed them through the hooker, and now they were parked back on Lexington Avenue where they had been earlier. Agnes checked the side-view mirror on the driver's side as she approached their car. She could see the guy sitting behind the steering wheel was short and bald.

"Got a light?" she asked him.

The bald man looked Agnes up and down before smiling. "You want a light or a gun?"

"Both," she said without hesitation.

He leaned to one side and fished a lighter from a pants pocket. Agnes winked at the man sitting in the passenger seat. He was tall and thin and a cheap motherfucker, J-Lo had said.

The bald man flicked the lighter. Agnes took a long drag on the cigarette. "You just coming home or on your way out?" he asked.

"I'm heading home as soon as I get what I need," she said.

"I got that here, but I need to see some more green," the bald man said. "You can reach in and lay it on my lap."

"I like to see what I'm paying for first," Agnes said. She noticed the keys were still in the ignition.

The bald man reached under the seat and pulled out a .38 revolver.

"Bullets?" Agnes asked.

He opened the cylinder and showed her it was loaded before he spilled the bullets into his free hand. He handed her the bullets.

"Put those in your pocket now so I know you're not looking to rob us after you get the piece," he said.

Agnes did as she was told.

"The money?" he said.

She pulled out three hundred in cash she had stashed inside one of the jacket pockets. "It's a pretty expensive antique you're selling me," she said. "Does it come with a holster?"

"You a funny girl," the bald man said. "It's what I could get in a hurry, but don't worry, you shoot somebody with it, it'll work."

The tall man said, "We give you a discount you wanna take it in trade."

Agnes leaned down closer to the window. "Not with that antique to my head," she said. "No offense."

The tall man lost his smile.

Agnes handed the bald man the money through the window. He didn't let go of the gun.

"Don't be a prick," she said.

"First you insult my friend and now me," he said.

"Then I apologize," she said coolly, looking into the eyes of the bald man. She leaned inside the window. "I apologize," she told the tall man.

He grabbed his crotch and said, "Apologize to this, bitch."

Agnes knew she'd be robbed unless she did something fast. She looked at the bald man one last time to see if he'd do the right thing. She knew he wouldn't when he avoided her eyes.

"Look, I'm not fucking you two guys out here in a car, okay?"

"You can suck my dick, though," the tall man said.

"Not out here. No way."

"Then I guess you beat," the bald man said.

"How about a hand job?" she offered.

"Say what?" the tall man said. "I look like a schoolboy to you?"

"Look, I really need to get going, and it's all I have time for right now. I have my own issues, okay?" She pointed inside her mouth. "A canker sore if you know what I mean."

"The fuck she talkin' about?" the tall man said.

"Take the hand job," the bald man said. "She poisoned."

"Oh, shit," the tall man said.

"Open them up," Agnes told the tall man.

"What?"

"Your pants?"

The tall man did so, then arched his back enough to pull his pants down over his hips.

"You gonna reach me from there?" he said when he was exposed. "You Gumby or some shit?"

"No, but I'm not doing anything until I can put my hand on the gun I just paid for," Agnes said. "If that's okay with you?" she asked the bald man.

He removed his hand from the gun. Agnes put her left hand on the weapon and checked the traffic behind her on Lexington Avenue. She was timing the lights so there would be yellow cabs passing when she took the gun.

"You reach in further and I might grab those titties you hiding under that coat," the bald man said. "Give you a little thrill while you working my friend's pole."

"What a treat," Agnes said.

"Well?" the tall man said. "It's fuckin' cold, bitch. My balls are turning to ice."

"Okay," Agnes said. She started to lean in the window, but stopped to throw a hard right elbow into the bald man's face. The crack was loud. She flattened his nose on contact. He winced from the force of the blow and was stunned from the pain.

Agnes grabbed the car keys from the ignition next. The tall man grabbed her by the hair with both hands. He tried to pull her inside the car when she stabbed him in the balls with the lit cigarette. He screamed before letting her go.

She ran back two blocks to Twenty-fifth Street and caught one of the yellow cabs heading south. She had him turn west on Twenty-seventh and pushed an extra twenty-dollar bill through the Plexiglas window for him to run the light at Park Avenue.

Agnes waited until they were downtown before tossing the BMW's keys out the taxi window.

•◆•

Jack had called Agnes as soon as he learned she had run down to the subway. He left a message when she didn't respond.

"It's Jack. The security guards said you were heading for the subway. The police are here now, and they're going to question me about this. I don't know what happened. I'm going to say I came here to pick you up, but that's all I'll say until I hear from you. Call me back as soon as you can."

It took half an hour before two detectives spoke with Jack. He told them he was there to pick up his friend from work and that he hadn't seen the shooting. One of the detectives had told him the dead woman had been working with Agnes Lynn.

"Upstairs?" he asked.

"According to the security guards," the detective said. "They both signed in for the twenty-eighth floor."

Jack shook his head. "I didn't know the woman who was killed."

"Did your friend Agnes mention anything to you about Ms. Beauregard?"

"Nothing, no."

There were a few more questions before Jack was permitted to leave. One of the detectives had taken his name and address and said they might be calling him again. Jack told them it wasn't a problem and got out of there. As soon as he pulled away from the curb, he tried calling Agnes again. He left a second message when she didn't answer.

"It's me. Call me, please. I'll stay in the city until I hear from you."

It was one o'clock in the morning when he stopped at a diner on the West Side of Manhattan. He continued to wonder where the hell Agnes had gone without a jacket. He ordered a sandwich and a cup of coffee while he waited for her return call. His cell phone didn't ring.

Jack watched the television above the counter and saw the report of the shooting on the local cable channel. A few minutes later the story switched to the one Jack had heard on the radio in his car earlier about the Russian mobsters found in Spring Creek in Brooklyn. Jack asked the guy working the counter if he could turn up the volume.

He caught the last of the report, something about a suspected gang war within the Russian mob. The news report flashed the mug shot of one of the gangsters believed to be the head of the crew found in the water.

The reporter said, "Yuri Timkin, a stepbrother to the alleged leader of the Russian mob in New York, Viktor Timkin, is believed to be missing. Police would not speculate as to whether or not the younger stepbrother was also killed in the apparent gang war."

"In an unrelated story, the mutilated body of a woman found washed up on Brooklyn's Plum Beach, some four miles from Spring Creek, has been identified and the family notified. Rachel Wilson . . . ."

The night manager of the diner turned down the volume.

"Hey," Jack said. "I was listening to that."

"Sorry, boss, but it's too loud," the manager said.

Jack paid his bill and ran out to his car to catch the story on the radio. On 1010 WINS they retold the story but didn't mention Rachel's name. He switched news stations three times before giving up.

Jack was tired and needed sleep. He tried Agnes again several times in a row. Finally, after twenty minutes of dialing, Agnes picked up on the third ring.

"I'm sorry I didn't call you back," she said, "but I don't want you involved."

"Where the hell are you?"

"Hiding for now," Agnes said. "They're after me. I don't know why, but they are. They killed the wrong person tonight. They must have thought Lorelei was me and killed her by mistake."

"You have to let me help you, Agnes."

"No, I don't want you involved. I don't know what's going on, except Lorelei is dead and maybe Rachel is too. And that cop who called me was a fake, Jack. He called me back and couldn't even keep his name straight."

"I told you not to talk to him."

"I picked up by accident. It was busy at work and I didn't notice the number. He wanted to pick me up from work, but I told him I worked near the Garden. I called the Staten Island precinct a little while ago, and they said there was no such detective. Not a George or a John White, the two names he gave me."

Jack was thinking the situation was a lot worse than he had thought earlier.

"Then maybe they have a cop on the payroll and you're in more danger than you know," he said. "You need my help."

"No, Jack. I don't want anyone else getting hurt. They killed Lorelei because she looks like me. She went downstairs without her kerchief on, and somebody must've thought it was me and killed her instead."

"Do you have a jacket? You must be freezing."

"It's back at the office, but I have another one."

"Are you home?"

"No. I bought it from someone."

"You have to let me help you. Where the hell are you?"

"No, Jack. They found me at work, and they were waiting for me to leave, I know it. They also knew where I had parked my car and had two guys waiting there for me. I don't know why they're after me, but they are. I'm sure it has something to do with Rachel."

Jack closed his eyes at the mention of the dead woman's name.

"Look, I don't like not knowing where you are," he said. "I can't help you like this."

"I don't want you to help, Jack."

"You have to go to the police. Let me bring you in."

"I have to go now."

"Wait, damn it. What about the pimp?"

Agnes didn't respond.

"Agnes?" he said.

The connection was broken.

Chapter 15

NANCE WAS HORRIFIED at what she saw lying on the stainless steel slab in the examination room at the medical examiner's office. Moss guided her out of the room into a hallway. She spent the next several minutes trying to keep her stomach in check.

When she was finally calm again, Nance pointed back into the examination room. "Who would do something like that?"

"I don't know," Moss said.

She felt dizzy. She held her forehead with one hand and reached out for Moss with the other. He helped her to a bench in the hallway.

"You gonna be sick?" he asked. "You wanna use the bathroom?"

"No."

Moss waited until she seemed okay. He offered her a stick of gum. Nance waved it off.

"She might've been involved in rough trade," Moss said. "I know how upset you are, but sometimes those things happen."

"Don't marginalize this one," Nance said. "That woman in there was fucking slaughtered."

"I'm not marginalizing anything," Moss said, "but the woman was a hooker. Hookers sometimes get involved with sickos."

Nance looked up at her partner. "Jesus Christ," she said. "Could you be any more insensitive? She was slaughtered, damn it."

Moss, frustrated now, said, "Look, I don't mean to sound insensitive, okay? I'm just saying this might not be what it looks like. It might be something random."

"A serial killer?"

"Maybe. It could be."

"We have anything like it on file?"

"Not that I know of, maybe not recently, but we'll have to run it through Virginia."

"The feds?"

"It could be a guy getting his kicks up and down the coast. It could be a local whack job just got started. It could be anything."

"None of the fucking wounds would have killed her instantly," Nance said. "That's what they think in there."

"At first examination, yes. That might be."

"She was cut up and down the backs of her legs. She was cut across her stomach. On her arms and face."

"Granted, the guy who did it was a maniac. Maybe he knew her. We have to look into it."

"She was fucking tortured, Bob. And raped, at least abused vaginally and anally."

"Maybe."

Nance grabbed onto Moss's right arm. "We have to get whoever did this."

"We will."

Nance tugged on his arm and said it again. "We have to."

•◆•

Detective Vanya Koloff's men had learned from one of the informants that Leonid Fetisov was forcibly taken out of a bar by two of Yuri Timkin's crew the day before the bodies were discovered in Spring Creek. The informant had also mentioned that Leonid was carrying his haircutting bag when he was last seen.

Vanya's men brought Pavel Chenkov's brother-in-law to the roof of an apartment building under construction on Bay Parkway. Leonid Fetisov was blindfolded, tied, and gagged. Vanya brought him to the edge of the twelve-story building and removed the blindfold. He gripped the thin man by the back of his neck and pushed him forward just enough so Fetisov could see the street below.

The hairdresser felt dizzy, lost his balance, and collapsed. He lay on the roof without moving.

Vanya tossed his cup of hot coffee on Fetisov's legs. The

hairdresser screamed from the burn before rolling away from the edge of the roof.

"Get up!" Vanya yelled.

"Please," Fetisov begged in Russian. "Please don't kill me."

Vanya spoke English. "Tell me about woman," he said.

"What woman?"

"Woman is found on beach in Brooklyn."

Fetisov covered his face with both hands.

Vanya kicked him. "Tell me about woman!"

The hairdresser gasped from the kick. He rolled onto his back and held both hands up.

"Tell me," Vanya said in Russian.

"I am dead man," Fetisov cried. "Please."

Vanya asked for another cup of coffee one of his men was drinking. Fetisov wet his pants.

"I am cut hair," he cried. "Shave hair."

"Why?"

"They tell me to shave."

"Who tells you?"

Fetisov bit his lower lip. Vanya held the cup of coffee over the hairdresser's head.

"Yuri!" Fetisov yelled.

"Who else is there?"

"His men. Some of them, not all."

"Who else?"

"I don't know."

Vanya stepped on the hairdresser's left ankle.

Fetisov winced from the pain. "Actors," he cried. "Actors are there. Two men."

"Actors?"

"Pornography actors."

"They make film?"

"I don't know."

Vanya kicked again. "Don't fock with me. Why Chenkov kills Yuri Timkin crew?"

Fetisov was weeping now. "I don't know, I don't know. I'm not there. I am gone."

Vanya finished his cigarette. "You can fly?" he asked. He pointed to the street. "From here. You think you can fly?"

Fetisov refused to look.

Vanya said, "What happened to woman?"

Fetisov shook his head.

"What happened? Why she is cut?"

"I don't know," Fetisov cried. "I swear, I don't know."

"Where is Yuri? Is dead? Why his crew is dead?"

"I swear, I don't know," Fetisov pleaded. "I swear."

Vanya lit a fresh cigarette. He checked the time on his watch and told his men he had another appointment.

"Can I go now?" Fetisov asked. "Please, can I go?"

Vanya spoke to two of his men in whispers. He told one of them to look into local porn dealers and to try and find the actors Fetisov had mentioned. He told the other to keep the hairdresser hidden.

"Please?" begged Fetisov when Vanya was finished talking to his men. "Can I go now?"

Vanya blew smoke in the hairdresser's face. "What do you think?" he said.

Chapter 16

JACK KNEW AGNES would head uptown to Harlem as soon as she broke the phone connection. He drove across town on Fifty-seventh Street until Second Avenue, where he turned north. There was hardly any traffic up into the one-hundreds, but then he spotted flashing lights farther up on the east side of the avenue. Jack spotted a street sign and realized he was close to the address Agnes had given him. Two blocks from the flashing lights, he grew nervous. The police activity was where the pimp lived.

The crime scene tape extended out onto the stoop of a

building facing Second Avenue. Jack pulled over to the curb one block south of the action. He approached what was left of the police barricade in front of the building with the taped-off stoop. He was surprised to see somebody he recognized from his time on the force.

"What's inside, hot shot?" he asked detective Michael Lyons. Jack wasn't a fan of the cop, but they had once worked a homicide together.

Lyons's eyebrows furrowed when he recognized Jack. "Holy shit," he said. "The late, great Jack Russo. How the hell are you?"

"Good," Jack said. "Retired a few years, but doing good. How you doing?"

"Good as a guy can, I guess," Lyons said. "I'm out and about."

The men exchanged a handshake. Jack motioned toward the crime scene tape with his head. "What's up in there?"

"Some pimp bought it," Lyons said. "Looks like somebody shot through his apartment door, then kicked it open to finish the job."

"Sounds exciting," Jack said.

"Happened a few hours back, I guess. Of course nobody heard anything, saw anything, or knows anything."

"Some things never change."

"At least this one is fresh meat," Lyons said. "I had one the other night cost me lunch and dinner. Guy found in a closet must've been there two weeks."

"Thanks for the graphic," Jack said. "I'm retired, remember?"

"I hear ya. What are you doing up here?"

"I was thinking of giving acting a shot," Jack said. "I hear the big shots hang out at Rao's up here."

Lyons said, "Rao's, huh? You switch sides or something?"

"I'm pulling your chain," Jack said. "I was visiting a friend nearby. I saw this and thought I saw you. Figured I'd say hello."

"Lady friend, I hope. From up here?"

"Close," Jack said. "Walking distance."

"Good for you," Lyons said. "I've tasted the dark side myself. It isn't all that bad, they trim the Brillo pad."

One of the forensic team called to the detective from the doorway at the top of the stoop. Lyons put out a hand for Jack. "Well, it's good seeing you again."

"You, too," Jack said.

He waited until Lyons was inside the building before leaving. Jack didn't like it that Michael Lyons was involved in the investigation of the pimp's murder. He wasn't sure if it was too coincidental or just a gut feeling he used to rely on as a detective, but Jack sensed something wasn't right with all that was going on around Agnes Lynn. He got in his car, started the engine, and was about to pull away from the curb when he spotted her sitting in a yellow taxi across the street.

•◆•

Agnes had taken a room in a Howard Johnson's downtown on the border of Little Italy and Chinatown. She tried to pay cash to avoid an electronic record but was required to provide a credit card for incidental charges.

She had started to watch the local news when Jack called. She did her best to keep him informed without involving him, but then he had mentioned the pimp and Agnes had to hang up.

Confronting Nelson Freeman was next in her plan of action. She took a taxi uptown to Harlem and was surprised when she saw the police activity outside the address where Nelson Freeman lived. Afraid to get out of the cab, she offered the taxi driver a twenty-dollar bill to find out what had happened.

The driver took the twenty and crossed Second Avenue. He spoke to one of the uniformed policeman on the scene and was back a few minutes later.

"A man was killed inside," the driver said.

"Did you get a name?"

"Sorry, no. Policeman doesn't tell me. Should I try again? I can go ask, no charge."

"No," Agnes said. She thought she had a better idea and was about to call Nelson Freeman's home phone again when the car door on her right opened. She reached for the gun inside her jacket pocket, saw it was Jack, then let go of the gun.

"Jesus Christ," she gasped. "Jesus Christ, Jack."

"Is everything okay, miss?" the taxi driver asked.

"Yes," she said. "I think so."

Jack sat in the back of the cab with her. "Don't go anywhere," he told the driver. "You have any idea what you're doing?" he asked Agnes.

She pulled out her cell phone. "I was about to call Freeman. If it was him who was killed, the police would answer, right?"

"No, they wouldn't," Jack said. "They'd let you talk and then trace your number if they could."

"Is it him? Is it Freeman?"

"Yeah, it is," Jack said. He thumbed toward the east side of the street. "That's what the sideshow out there is for."

Agnes leaned over to look out the window. "What the hell is going on?"

"I'm not sure, but I think you're right about Rachel," Jack said. "It has something to do with her."

"How did you know to come here?"

"You hung up on me soon as I mentioned the pimp. I was lucky you gave me his address earlier. I saw some cop I know from back in the day, and I chatted with him. I was about to leave when I saw you. I'm parked back there."

"How was he killed?"

"Shot through the door, but it was a hit, an execution."

"Jesus Christ."

"There's something else."

Agnes felt a pain in her stomach. "Rachel?"

"I'm sorry," he said.

Agnes closed her eyes.

"Are you okay, miss?" the driver asked. "I can get the police."

"She's fine," Jack said.

Agnes crumpled against the door.

"She knows the man who died?" the driver asked.

"It was a friend of hers," Jack said.

"I'm sorry," he said.

"What's she owe you?" Jack asked.

The driver pointed to the meter. "Eighteen fifty."

Jack pulled his wallet out. He pulled a twenty and a ten from inside and stuffed them through the Plexiglas opening. "Thanks," he told the driver.

"Thank you, sir," the driver said. "I hope she feels better soon."

Jack helped Agnes out of the cab, but made sure Michael Lyons wasn't on the street when he walked her across Second Avenue. He helped her inside his car and offered a cigarette. Agnes waved it off.

"How'd she die?" she asked once Jack started the engine.

He pulled away from the curb and headed north on the avenue. "It was bad," he said.

"Tell me."

Jack told her what he'd seen on the news and had heard over the radio as he drove. Agnes's eyes were red, but she hadn't cried yet. Her anger had taken over.

"Mutilated, why?" she asked. "Why the hell would someone mutilate her?"

"I don't know, Agnes, but these Russian guys obviously think you know something or they wouldn't be looking for you."

"I can't believe this is happening. Rachel and then Lorelei and now Nelson. God damn it."

"We have to decide what to do."

"I do. This isn't about you, Jack."

"I'm not gonna watch you get yourself killed."

"It's the Russian mob, right?"

"It looks that way."

"Well?"

"I can bring you in to the police," Jack said, "except I just saw somebody back at the pimp's place I don't trust. A detective I know used to be dirty."

"You think he's involved?"

"I don't know, but I don't like it that he's the responding

detective to this particular homicide. It might be nothing, but I don't like it."

"Could he have been the guy who called me earlier, Detective White?"

"That could've been anybody."

"I don't understand. How could they know so much about me so fast?"

"They have your address from your telephone number," Jack said, "probably when you called Rachel."

"And what about my car? How did they trace that to a garage in Manhattan? How did they know to call the agency I work for?"

"Probably when they broke into your apartment," Jack said. He reached for her hand. She pulled away. "Sorry," he said.

"Me, too," Agnes said. She had curled both her hands in her lap. She looked out the window.

Jack saw a sign for the Harlem River Drive and turned east. "There was a bunch of Russian mobsters found in the water in Brooklyn," he said. "It might be a mob war, something internal, but then there's this, what's going on with you. The beach where they found your friend is a few miles from where the mobsters were found. Those guys were found in a creek in Starrett City."

She closed her eyes upon learning that Rachel's body had been dumped in the water like so much trash. Her jaw clenched.

"What the hell is going on?" she yelled.

"We should call the detectives investigating Rachel's murder," Jack said. "They should know what's going on. I'll make the call."

Agnes shook her head. "What about your son?"

"He's in recovery until tomorrow afternoon. I'll be there. In the meantime I need to know you'll be safe."

Agnes was determined to keep Jack out of danger. When he turned onto the entrance for the Harlem River Drive at 139th Street, she screamed for him to stop to the car.

Jack hit the brakes. A taxi rear-ended them.

"Shit," Jack said.

Agnes got out of the car and ran.

●◆●

When Michael Lyons learned about the shooting downtown he began to panic. He assumed it was the same woman the Russian had tried to get him to drive to Brooklyn. If it was, then his relationship with the Russian mob had run its course. It was dangerous enough, knowing what he was doing. Now, if they were willing to trick him, it meant he was expendable.

His sense of panic was further heightened later on, when Jack Russo showed up at the Harlem crime scene. Lyons had thought nothing of it until he returned to the apartment with the forensic team and spotted Russo crossing Second Avenue with a blond woman who looked like the woman in the picture Chenkov had on him earlier.

"Jesus Christ," he said aloud.

"Excuse me?" one of the forensic investigators said.

"Nothing," Lyons said.

"It looks like the answering machine tape is missing."

Lyons's mind was still focused on Jack Russo and the blond woman. "Huh?" he said.

"The answering machine. Somebody took the tape out."

"Oh," Lyons said. "Well, dust it for prints."

The next few minutes were impossible. He had to wait until he was alone before he could call Pasha Chenkov from a pay phone on the street. Lyons was crazed by the time he spoke with the Russian thug.

"Who this is?"

"You made a big fucking mistake," Lyons said.

"What?"

"The woman."

"Who this is?"

"Tell your boss we need to talk—and fast. You guys are fuckups. I just saw the woman with an ex-cop uptown."

"What woman?"

"Asshole, pay attention."

"Who is asshole?"

"I just saw the woman you were looking for," Lyons said. "Figure it out."

"You can talk, Michael. What you are saying?"

Lyons cursed under his breath at the mention of his name. "Who's Michael?" he said before he killed the connection.

Chapter 17

DETECTIVES MOSS AND Nance found Roger Wilson at his third-shift job at a soda distributorship in Valley Stream on Long Island. Wilson was working a skid loader, moving Diet Rite soda from one side of the warehouse to another. It was cold inside. Wilson appeared puffy from layers of sweatshirts he wore under an army field jacket. His skull cap was pulled down to cover his ears.

Moss and Nance flashed their badges.

"I don't know what happened," Wilson said, "except she left me with two kids. I'm gonna have to raise them with my mother."

"You seem more angry than upset," Moss said.

"I'm both. I had my own share of troubles. I'm sure the two of you know about that."

"Ossining," Nance said. "We know."

"I'm out just a few months and working here mostly. I also pump gas closer to where I live. For Indians, you can believe it."

"It's a job," Moss said.

"Yeah, so I shouldn't complain."

"Did you know the man Rachel was working for?" Nance asked.

"Freeman?"

"That his name?" Moss asked.

Nance wrote it down.

"That's what I know him by. Rachel also worked for an escort service. At least they sent a guy with her when she went out."

"You know the name?"

"I can find the number. I don't know the name. Look, I didn't like what Rachel was doing, so let's not get confused here. In fact, I hated it."

"That's noble of you," Nance said. "I guess you don't feel the need to grieve."

"I can't afford to grieve," Wilson said. "Especially now, it's all on me."

"Bitter, too, huh?"

Wilson dead-eyed her. "It's the way I feel."

"You ever get into it with her?" Moss asked. "Get violent, I mean."

"No. I'm not about that, hitting women."

"Two points," Nance said.

"You know what?" Wilson said. "I need to get back to work."

"Before you do," Moss said: "Where were you the day Rachel went missing?"

"Here," Wilson said. "We spoke to each other while I was here. I was here when she didn't pick up the kids, and I dropped them off at my mom's. I been back and forth since, work and home. The only other person I talked to was her friend called after her."

"What friend?" Nance asked.

Wilson smirked. "Now we pals, huh?"

Nance waited.

"I forget," Wilson said. "I guess you out of luck on that one, but I will call you with the number of the escort service once I'm home. I'll do that much for you."

•◆•

"You see, that's what pisses me off about these people," Moss said.

They were back in the car after speaking with Roger Wilson. Nance was checking her notes. Moss started the engine.

"One's a hooker and the other is an ex-con, and here we are begging one to help us solve the other's murder," he said. "Makes no fucking sense. Who cares what happened, that's how I feel about it now."

"I should've kept my mouth shut," Nance said.

"Huh?"

"I shouldn't have pushed him. That crack about being noble. It was dumb."

"You couldn't help yourself. You said what I was thinking. I was the good cop for a change."

"And I shouldn't have said anything. Somebody called looking for Rachel, and he isn't telling us."

Moss pulled away from the curb. He said, "Some other john pro'bly, but we can find out easy enough. Pull her phone records and this guy."

"Whoever Rachel's friend is, she might know something can steer us toward whoever butchered the woman."

Moss made a U-turn and headed back toward the Belt Parkway.

"You're not saying anything," Nance noted.

"I'm too insensitive, remember?"

"No argument here."

"Yeah, well, wait'll you learn about the Russki, you think I'm insensitive."

"Vanya?"

"Vanya, is it? You really are smitten."

"I'm not smitten, Bob. I'm just not as jaded as you yet, thank God. You've had a bug up your ass since we met with Vanya, and now you're taking it out on the victim of a murder."

"Your powers of observation are wanting," Moss said. "I could give a fuck about the comrade. The fact he's organized crime and has a reputation as a loose cannon and that he probably won't share dick with us is for you to learn. You'll probably learn how the Russkies feel about blacks, too, you give him the chance, but again, that's for your edification. As for the dead hooker, well, I'm not as moved by that one as you. It doesn't mean I won't do my job."

"Except you're blowing off following up on potential evidence."

"We can check phone calls through records in the morning

or have it done overnight. I'm not blowing it off. I'm just not as enthusiastic as you."

Moss turned left at a light and hit the gas hard. The car bucked and caught Nance by surprise.

"Hey, fuck you today," she said.

Moss remained silent as he drove onto the Belt Parkway heading east.

·•·

When she left Jack on the entrance ramp to the Harlem River Drive, Agnes ran along Madison Avenue until she saw a yellow taxi she could flag. She got in at 138th Street and told the driver to use Fifth Avenue to head back downtown.

Agnes felt guilty for running from Jack Russo, but she was sure it was for his own good. The Russian mob had killed her friend and the pimp she worked for. They had also killed an innocent woman by mistake. Agnes couldn't risk having Jack become another victim.

It was after three o'clock in the morning. She was exhausted and needed to sleep a few hours. If the Russian mob could locate her through phone records, they probably had the same access to credit cards. Tomorrow she would take more cash from her bank account and find a short-stay hotel where she could avoid leaving an electronic paper trail.

When she was back at the hotel, Agnes went up to her room and ran hot water in the shower until it was steaming. Images of Rachel and Lorelei filled her head as she stepped under the hot water. At first the shower relaxed her. The intense spray on the back of her shoulders and neck was calming.

After a while, Agnes was haunted by the last conversation she had had with her best friend.

I have a job requires I shave my head, Rachel had told her.

That doesn't sound good, Agnes remembered telling her.

It pays more than I can afford to ignore, except the guy's an Arab.

Agnes remembered Rachel had mentioned the Arab had a boat somewhere on the East River and that she had been with him before.

He has a big-ass boat parked on the East River not too far from the yacht club there. Liked me to wear boots while I handled him.

Agnes turned off the shower, dried herself, and then went through the Manhattan yellow pages until she found a marina located on the East River. She circled the number before writing it down on a piece of hotel stationery.

She would call the marina in the morning and learn what she could about the rich Arab Rachel had shaved her head for. She closed her eyes and thought of her best friend and Lorelei. A surge of rage ran through her body. She grabbed the bedspread with both hands and clenched her fists until they hurt.

Chapter 18

"YOU CATCH DEAD body in there before fish," Viktor Timkin said. "Maybe car or television, but no fish."

Aalam al Fahd handed his fishing pole to one of the deckhands. He pushed himself out of the portable fishing chair along the railing of his yacht, *Jamal*, and crossed the deck to shake hands with Timkin.

"What a pleasant surprise, Viktor," he said with a thick British accent. "What takes you out of Brooklyn so early in the morning? Or should I say late at night?"

"Both," Timkin said. "Business brings me." He held up two fingers. "Two things."

Fahd was born in Saudi Arabia and raised in Great Britain. He was a huge man of four hundred pounds. He wore his long black hair in a thick ponytail wrapped with a silk scarf.

He motioned for his guests to step inside the cabin. "Come," he said. "Let's go where it's warm at least."

Timkin and his bodyguard stepped inside the cabin. They both sat on a couch off to their left. Fahd took a chair facing them. He stroked his beard with one hand while petting his pit bull, Kasib, with the other. His bodyguards stood on either side of him. Both were holding shotguns.

"I'll assume weapons are one of the reasons you've come," Fahd said. "I'm not sure I know the other reason."

Timkin had showed up unexpectedly. Fahd was suspicious as to why.

"Most important reason, yes, is guns," Timkin said. "I need six tonight. Hungarian model, nine millimeter."

"I believe I have some nearby I can get to you."

"Can you deliver them to Brooklyn?"

"Now?"

"Is great help if you can do this as soon as possible."

"Then it is done," Fahd said. "And the other business?"

"I think you know, eh? Woman from Yuri to make film . . . is big trouble now."

Fahd tilted his head to one side. "Is that why all those fellows were found in the water last evening, because of the woman?"

"Yuri was told not to do this, eh? He does anyway. He is idiot. My mother's son, so I have to live with him. But this is dangerous business he does with you with woman. I can't have this come to me."

"It was just one film, Viktor," Fahd said. "And I paid Yuri for it. I paid him well and in cash."

"Aalam, listen to me, eh? He is idiot, my stepbrother. He doesn't supposed to do this with you. I tell him never to do this. He does anyway and for what, fifty thousand dollar? Is lunatic, Yuri is. Why I send him to Canada, eh?"

"If it's a matter of money, I'm sure I can appease you, my friend. Besides, I paid Yuri seventy thousand dollars cash, not fifty."

Timkin opened his hands. "Is Yuri. He tells me fifty."

Fahd said, "I have cash on the yacht, Viktor. If Yuri cheated you and that's an issue, I'm more than anxious to make up the difference for the sake of friendship."

"No," said Timkin, waving the offer off. "No need. Was business with you and Yuri. Is over, eh? Is done."

"Had I known how much it would upset you, I would've taken the business elsewhere, I promise."

"South America?" Timkin said. "They do this shit there?"

"In some third world countries, sure," Fahd said. "It is a form of commerce to some."

"Maybe I am dinosaur, eh? What my daughter calls me."

"Nonsense," Fahd said. "It's just not for you, Viktor. I understand."

The two men sat smiling at each other until Fahd offered his uninvited guests coffee.

"No, thanks," Timkin said, "or I don't sleep rest of the week."

"Well, I shall have the weapons delivered to whatever

address you say within the next few hours. And because of the mishap with the woman, there'll be no charge."

"No, this isn't necessary," Timkin said. "I pay."

"I insist," Fahd said.

"Please, I am embarrassed for my stepbrother."

"No, no, the guns are on me. And may there never be another issue between us. I consider you a true friend, Viktor."

The two men exchanged hugs. A few minutes later Timkin and his bodyguard were ushered off the yacht. Fahd watched from the railing while the Russian crime boss and his chubby bodyguard left the marina in a black Mercedes.

It was close to five o'clock in the morning. The sun would be up in another hour. Fahd yawned before nodding his approval at his two bodyguards for a job well done.

Both men bowed their heads.

"He comes to kill me," Fahd said. "He is cunning, that one. He comes to do it himself. The other one was his backup, but Viktor was going to kill me himself."

"What with?" one of Fahd's bodyguards asked.

"Why, his hands, of course," Fahd said. "I believe he would've strangled me."

He dismissed his bodyguards before heading up to the master cabin and crawling into bed. He tried to sleep, but it wasn't easy. As cordial as he had spoken to the head of the New York Russian mob, Fahd couldn't ignore why Viktor Timkin had showed up at the yacht so early in the morning.

He wasn't sure if Yuri Timkin was in Canada or dead or what, but he was sure why Viktor had paid a sudden visit. Fahd tried calling Yuri three times before giving up and taking a sleeping pill.

•◆•

The taxi had slammed into the rear bumper a moment before Agnes left the car. Jack was caught off guard. By the time he realized she'd fled, it was too late to follow. He couldn't leave the car.

"God damn it," he said.

He got out of the car, but not to argue with the taxi driver. He was watching to see where Agnes had run. He cursed again as he watched her heading south.

She had timed her escape perfectly. He hadn't seen it coming, and now he felt foolish.

The taxi driver leaned on his horn. Jack turned and saw the man was waving his hands. Jack flipped him the bird before getting back inside his car. He couldn't leave it on the ramp and had to drive to the next exit before circling back to look for Agnes on the streets.

After twenty minutes of driving around an eight-block radius, he gave up and started for home. He tried calling her again and wasn't surprised when she didn't answer.

He didn't understand what was going on, but Jack was sure Agnes was in danger and that she would need help to survive. He had an ex-partner from his undercover days who was still on the force. Jack hadn't spoken to Jerry Klein in months, but the two had remained friends. He tried Klein's cell phone. His former partner had left a message saying he was on vacation in Israel and would be back at the end of the month.

The mention of Israel gave Jack pause. The tiny country was a dark memory for him. His only brother had been killed there five years ago.

There were a few other guys still on the force he could call, but Jack decided to call the detectives investigating the murder of Rachel Wilson instead.

He was at the end of the Brooklyn-Queens Expressway heading onto the Verrazano Narrows Bridge when he called the police hotline. He gave the operator his name and address and was transferred to a female homicide detective.

"Detective Nance speaking," she said.

"It's about the woman found on the beach," Jack said.

"And your name?"

"Jack Russo. Actually, I'm calling about a friend of the woman you found on the beach. She's in danger."

"What do you know about the woman on the beach, sir?"

"Not much, except what her friend told me. She was a single mother hooking to support her kids. Apparently she was working for Russians."

"Can you tell me anything else about her?"

"Look, detective, I'm familiar with the procedure, so let's skip it and get to the issue. The woman you found on the beach is Rachel Wilson. She had a friend named Agnes Lynn. Agnes is the woman I'm trying to help. Her apartment was broken into yesterday on Staten Island, and she's had Russians stalking her ever since. You can check with the Staten Island police about the break-in."

"What do you mean, Russians stalking her?"

"What I said, as in the mob. They had something to do with killing her friend Rachel, and they probably killed another woman downtown by mistake. They're looking for Agnes. She doesn't know why, but they are."

"Where's your friend now?"

"Hiding. She just took off on me. I don't know where she went."

"We can't help her if we don't know where she is."

"Yeah, I know that. Neither can I. I'm calling to let you know she's out there without protection. I'm also calling because Rachel's pimp was killed in Harlem last night, which is something else that's more than a coincidence. I was at the crime scene earlier, and I saw a guy from the force I don't trust as far as I can throw. He was investigating the pimp's murder."

"I'm not sure I understand. What were you doing at a crime scene?"

"Looking for my friend," Jack said, "but I saw Michael Lyons. He was a dirty cop back when I was working, and I doubt he's changed. It's more than suspect he's at the scene of a murder that probably involves the Russian mob."

"You were on the job?"

"A few years back, yeah. Look, I'm on my way home right now. My kid was hit by a car yesterday. He's in a Brooklyn hospital and I need to be with him tomorrow, but I also need to know you guys are aware of what's going on with Agnes. She's afraid to talk to you because some guy claimed he was a detective called her about a break-in at her apartment last night. She thought he was trying to find out where she worked. She thinks that's how they killed the woman she was working with. She thinks the Russians thought the woman was her."

"Where are you now?"

"Heading home to Perth Amboy," Jack said. "I've tried

calling Agnes, but she isn't answering. I have no idea where she is. She was afraid of getting me involved, why she ran off."

"Can we have Agnes's number?"

"Sure, but she probably won't answer a number she doesn't recognize. She also might hang up if she does answer and she hears you say you're a cop. She won't come in unless I'm there."

"Can we meet with you?"

"You feel like making the drive, sure."

"Can't you come here?"

"I just left from there. I'm closer to home now. Just went over the Verrazano."

"Give me your address?"

Jack gave the detective his address and phone number, then Agnes Lynn's cell phone number.

"Tell me more about Michael Lyons," she asked. "Is there anything specific you know about him being dirty?"

"He was up on charges a few times, I know that much. I'm sure IA has a file on him. He was with narcotics for a while before moving over to homicide. I worked a case with him myself before retiring. No problems there, except I was uncomfortable because of his reputation."

"I see."

"Look, this all has something to do with the Russians found in the water last night. I don't know what, but there has to be a connection. The fact Lyons shows up is another red flag."

"Will you wait up for us?" the detective asked.

"If you move your asses, yeah, sure," Jack said.

"We're on our way."

"I'll wait downstairs in front of my building. It's the last one on your left before the water, directly across from the park."

Jack hung up and noticed the sun had started to rise. He looked at himself in the rearview mirror and saw his eyes were bloodshot. He yawned long and loud before stretching his neck from side to side.

"I'm supposed to be retired from this bullshit," he said.

The highway curved east. The glare of the rising sun blinded him. He turned down the visor, then looked at his cell phone on the console.

"Call me back, Agnes," he said. "Call me before it's too damn late."

Chapter 19

VANYA FOUND VIKTOR Timkin outside a pastry shop on Brighton Avenue. The Russian mob boss was eating a cream puff pastry. He waved off his bodyguard as the detective approached.

"I wondered all day and night when you would come to break my balls," Timkin told Vanya in Russian. His voice was pleasant but loaded with sarcasm.

The detective took the cream puff from Timkin's hand, pulled it apart, and ate the end the gangster had yet to bite into. He handed what was left back to Timkin.

"If you're hungry, I can get you another one," Timkin said.

"Why'd you kill Yuri's crew?" Vanya said.

"Excuse me?"

"Why did you kill your idiot stepbrother's crew? Why? Did you kill Yuri, too?"

Timkin looked to his bodyguard. He was also eating a pastry. "I don't know what you're talking about," Timkin said. "I didn't kill anyone, and Yuri is on vacation in Canada. Montreal, I think."

Vanya turned to the bodyguard. "You're too fat, Misha, put down the cake."

"Fuck you," the bodyguard said.

Vanya turned back to Timkin. "Montreal? Why'd you kill him?"

Timkin smiled. "I told you, he's in Canada."

"Bullshit."

"Now you are being rude, eh?"

"What happened? Why did you kill his crew?"

"I don't have time for this nonsense, Vanya. You break balls for nothing. You're always breaking balls. You don't belong, eh? You're not one of us."

"Why didn't Pasha kill the faggot hairdresser?" Vanya asked.

"What hairdresser?"

"He wasn't there with the woman?"

Timkin turned to his bodyguard. "What woman?" he asked Misha.

Now Vanya smiled. "You didn't know he was there, the hairdresser? Ah, why he's still alive. I understand now. You didn't know he was there."

Timkin waved the comment off. "This is bullshit, Vanya. Is

too early in day, eh? I didn't even sleep yet. Don't fuck with me now."

"He's missing, no?" Vanya asked. "The hairdresser is missing. You know that, right?"

Timkin thought about it a moment. "Did you kidnap him, Vanya? Is that what this is? You want money? How much?"

Vanya said, "Tell me, why you killed Yuri?"

Timkin motioned at his driver to get in the car. "I don't know what you are talking about," he said as he walked away. "And I am busy, eh? I have to leave. Go back in the store and tell them I buy you a dozen cream puffs. On me, no charge."

"I'll find out from the hairdresser now," Vanya said. "I'll make him tell me."

Timkin sat in the Mercedes parked at the curb. His bodyguard stood staring at Vanya. Timkin yelled at him to get in the car.

This time Vanya spoke in English. He said, "Go with Daddy, fat Misha, before you get beating, he can't help you."

The bodyguard grabbed his crotch. Vanya blew him a kiss.

• ◆ •

The triple assassination Viktor Timkin had arranged to secure Coney Island for the Russian Mafiya began when six Albanians picked up their weapons at the bakery on Brighton Avenue at eight o'clock in the morning. They left in pairs of two with three cars of the same model and color. Each car had Pennsylvania dealer plates.

The Albanians drove the half mile from Brighton Beach to Sheepshead Bay and parked side by side in the parking lot of a twenty-four-hour convenience store on Emmons Avenue. All six men used black face paint to disguise themselves with phony mustaches and beards. One had painted black circles around his eyes.

A white van with block lettering that read BRIGHTON ROOFING was parked at the curb a few doors down from the convenience store. Three of the Albanians stepped inside the van through the side door. The other three stepped inside the convenience store and acted drunk. Each carried a ski mask attached to a clip on his belt.

At eight fifteen a black Cadillac Seville pulled into the convenience store lot. Three men got out of the Cadillac; they all looked tired. Two appeared disheveled and drunk. They walked to the back of the parking lot and used a garbage bin to shield themselves from view as they urinated.

The third man, Richard Marino, was heavyset and well dressed. He wore Ray-Ban aviator sunglasses. He lit a cigarette alongside the Cadillac, then stared at the three cars parked side by side. He pointed to them when his friends rejoined him.

"Too bad we don't have one of the kids with us," he said. "Dealer plates. We could've taken them from here back to Canarsie and chopped them up before the idiots parked them here knew what happened."

The three men shared a laugh before turning toward the store.

Inside the store, the three Albanians covered their heads with the ski masks. One held a gun on the man behind the counter and told him to get on the floor. The other two stood on either side of the doorway.

Richard Marino and the two men he intended to make his

underboss and consigliere once he took control of the Corelli crime family stepped inside the convenience store without a care in the world. As was their routine a few times a week since Marino's release from prison three months earlier, they had stopped there on their way home to pick up daily racing forms, some instant lottery tickets, cigarettes, and coffee.

Two of the three Albanians in the van stepped out and hustled to the convenience store a moment before the shooting started. Two of the men they were there to execute fell backward onto the sidewalk in front of the store. The Albanians from the van fired two shots each into the dead men's heads.

Inside the store, Richard Marino was already dead from the barrage he had walked into. The man working the counter was spared. The three Albanians inside the store joined the ones outside as the white van pulled up out front. The van took off and headed east.

Thirty seconds after the van left, a local taxi stopped at the curb and let three men out. They ignored the two bodies on the sidewalk and headed into the parking lot. Each drove one of the three identical cars out of the lot and headed west on Emmons Avenue. The taxi driver got out of the cab and stared at the two bodies on the sidewalk. He turned and watched the three cars as they drove away. He looked back at the bodies again, then got inside the taxi and sped away.

•◆•

He'd had a pasty complexion and was at least sixty pounds overweight. She had met him at the bar alongside the

Cleopatra Barge in Caesar's Palace. He was there on business, he had told her. She noticed his wedding ring, a good sign, before she spotted the loose-fitting, diamond-studded Rolex. She had preferred married men, because they were less likely to make trouble.

He had bought her a drink before fumbling through awkward conversation. She helped him along, but only because she was tired and anxious to get home to take a hot bath.

"You looking for a date, hon?" Agnes had asked him.

"Uh, yeah, sure," he'd said.

Agnes waved him closer. "You have a room here?" she asked.

"Ah . . . yes, as a matter of fact. Yes, right upstairs."

The fact he was nervous was another good sign. If she was lucky, she'd be his first and he'd overtip her when they were through.

"You're not a cop, right?" she asked. It was standard procedure to ask, even though she was sure he wasn't the law.

"No, I'm not a cop," he half giggled. "I'm in real estate."

"Good for you," Agnes said. "Five hundred an hour."

The big man cringed.

"Good luck," Agnes said.

"Wait," he said. "I'm sure we can work something out."

He put a hand out to stop her from getting off the bar stool. She froze a few inches from his hand and stared into his eyes until the big man removed his hand from her path.

"Sorry," he said.

"What's to work out?" she said. "Five hundred an hour. A grand for two hours. Five grand for the night."

The big man nodded. "Okay," he said.

"I need to hear you say it," she told him.

"Five hundred for the hour."

The time it took between the walk from the lounge to his hotel room was less than seven minutes, but it had felt like an eternity. It was a routine Agnes had come to hate, a symbolic reminder of the dull recurrence her life had become.

Agnes hated this man. She hated him and all the others she had been with before him. Most of all she hated herself for the emotional suicide she knew she was committing with each new john.

Agnes glared at the pasty man a few minutes later when she had to help him explain what it was he wanted. He had already paid her the five hundred dollars, and she had just removed her top. The trick couldn't keep his eyes off her cleavage accentuated by a black lace push-up bra.

"Just ah, ah . . . oral," he had managed to say.

"A blow job," she said, embarrassing him on purpose.

"Well, ah . . . you know, sixty . . . ah, ah . . . sixty-nine."

Agnes was suddenly horrified. "You wanna do me, too?"

"Well, ah . . . yeah. Is that extra?"

She could've taken him for a few hundred more right there and then. Most girls would have. Men were tricks and tricks were business; whatever you could get from them was what you charged. Agnes didn't let men perform oral on her, though. She took care of them and was done with it.

Something about this request stopped her from explaining it to him. She had reached the end. She could no longer numb herself through the performance. What she did was quit the business instead.

"What I do wrong?" he had said when she grabbed her

blouse from the back of the chair she had laid it across. She ignored his question as she put her blouse back on.

"You want more? I'll pay it. Five-fifty?"

Agnes continued dressing.

"More?" he asked.

She gathered her purse and sweater and started for the door. The big man was so dumbstruck, he had forgotten to ask for his money back. Agnes remembered for him. She pulled the five hundred from her purse and tossed it over her shoulder on her way out.

"Bitch!" she heard him yell when the door closed.

It had come back to her in a series of dreams. She was aware of her dreams but wouldn't let herself wake up until the dream turned to a nightmare, and the same man with the pasty skin was kneeling alongside her trying to lay his hands flat against her naked body. She was trying to slap his hands away and kept missing. She felt one hand touch her stomach. She jerked onto her side in the bed. She felt more hands touching her and Agnes forced her eyes open.

She was in a cold sweat. She turned to the windows and saw the sun was up. She turned to the clock and saw it was only eight fifteen. She was still tired. She pulled the sheets down until she was cold. She pulled the sheets back up, curled up, and closed her eyes again, but knew in her heart that sleep would not come.

Chapter 20

VIKTOR TIMKIN SPOTTED the wall of darkness in the distance off Coney Island Beach. He could see the shadow beneath the great mass of cloud and knew it was rain. Whitecaps spotted the water from the beach to the ocean.

Timkin was tired and cranky and anxious to sleep before news of the mob rubout in Sheepshead Bay brought extra attention to Brighton Beach. At some point later in the day Joseph LaRocca would be crowned as the new boss of the Corelli crime family, and the small peninsula located in southernmost Brooklyn, except for a minor league baseball stadium and its parking lot, would become a territory under the control of Timkin and his organization. The famous beach lying on the Atlantic Ocean, with Seagate to its west, Brighton Beach and Manhattan Beach to its east, and Gravesend to the north, would be his to do with as he pleased.

He pointed at the dark mass of cloud that seemed to glide east across the ocean.

"This is us, Pasha, the sky like that, the dark cloud," he said. He waved his arm east to west. "Soon we cover everything, eh?"

Chenkov was holding onto bad news. A few hours earlier what the cop had told him was confirmed—he had killed the wrong woman. Fearing his boss would learn about it from the local media, Chenkov had come to tell Timkin firsthand his version of what had happened.

"For now, though, I'm exhausted," Timkin said. "I come to smell the sea every chance I get, but the chances are less and less."

"We have a problem," Chenkov said. He waited for Timkin's full attention. "The woman, Agnes Lynn."

"What?" Timkin said. "What about the woman?"

"The Irish cop fucked up," Chenkov said. "He tells me the wrong woman."

Timkin was confused. "What do you mean, the wrong woman?"

"Lyons, he didn't want to stay to help with the woman, and he tells me the wrong one and I kill her."

Timkin was about to yawn. He froze instead.

"What are you talking about, Pasha?"

Chenkov played fast and loose with the facts.

"What else?" Timkin asked.

"Lyons says there's an ex-cop with the woman now,"

Chenkov said. "Lyons said the same guy asked him about the pimp. He said he saw Agnes Lynn with him after he went up to the pimp's apartment. The woman went with the ex-cop in his car."

Timkin closed his eyes before shaking his head. He opened his eyes again and asked if Lyons had taken the license plate of the car the ex-cop was driving.

"We don't need it," Chenkov said. "Lyons knew the guy. He gave us his name. One of my guys found it on the woman's telephone bill. We have what we need. I sent two of my men. We don't need that asshole cop anymore. And now he knows too much. Too much about me, eh?"

"Lyons called Misha's cell all night," Timkin said. "He's nervous. He left a message at the bakery for me. He wants papers to leave the country."

"We should get rid of him."

Timkin yawned again. "Maybe," he said.

"No maybe, Viktor. That drunken cop has a big mouth, and then he gets brave because of his badge. He thinks he's untouchable. He talks shit."

"Now we may need him," Timkin said. "If he knows the ex-cop the woman is with. We might need him to draw the other one out."

"He's afraid to go near the woman. He was afraid last night and he's more afraid now. Why he wants his paperwork. He wants to run away, the bitch that he is."

Timkin took his time thinking it over.

"Cops are the first ones to flip and make a deal," Chenkov said.

"If he goes, he has to disappear," Timkin said. "All the way disappear." He clapped his hands. "Poof, eh?"

Chenkov grinned. "I do that Irish pig for the pleasure."

Timkin saw the clouds were coming closer. He said, "Your brother-in-law is missing."

"Two days," Chenkov said. "How did you know? I just found out myself."

"Vanya Koloff."

"The cop?"

"He came to break my balls at the bakery. He has the faggot."

"Vanya kidnapped him?"

"The faggot told him about the woman. He shaved her head."

"You didn't mention Leonid to me."

"Fucking Yuri didn't mention him to me."

"Shit."

"Vanya says he is going to make him talk."

"He will. Leonid is faggot. He'll talk."

"Fuck."

"He's a faggot."

Timkin said, "You have to get the woman." He turned to the west and pointed toward the Astroland Playland. "We have this place to ourselves, Coney Island, except for the baseball. The mess Yuri made is the only thing that can fuck this up. Fahd knows I went there to kill him this morning. He had bodyguards with shotguns for me and Misha. He's nervous because of what happened to Yuri's crew. He called Yuri's phone all morning already."

Chenkov shrugged. "Fahd can't talk to the FBI, Viktor. He's a gun dealer."

"Exactly why he can, because he is a gun dealer," Timkin said. "Pay attention, Pasha. Fahd is an international trader, eh?

How many names can he take to the FBI if he wants to deal? A dozen, maybe a hundred. The FBI made a deal with Sammy Gravano, that piece of shit, after he admitted killing nineteen people. Now they learning he killed more than nineteen. Now they learn? They give deal to whoever they want for whatever they want. If that fucking film gets to CNN, trust me, Fahd isn't going to jail."

Timkin stopped to point to himself and Chenkov, back and forth. "You and me will go to jail, Pasha," he said. "You and me."

Chenkov bit his lower lip. "We get woman, Viktor. I get her."

Timkin patted Chenkov on the back. "You should probably call your wife," he said.

"Later."

"Tell her the faggot ran away."

"Later."

"Tell her he went on vacation."

"Okay, I tell her later."

"And then get rid of Leonid as soon as Vanya lets him go."

•◆•

Detectives Nance and Moss had stopped at the Friends of 24-7 escort service in Springfield Gardens after Roger Wilson called with the number. Neither had gotten any sleep. Nance was cranky. Moss was getting there.

The service was located above an all-night bodega and was nothing more than a three-room apartment. Nance had called from outside the bodega and asked for the dispatcher to come down to talk. When the dispatcher hung up, Moss called back from his cell phone.

"If you want, I'll come back with a warrant, but then you'll be hounded twenty-four seven, just like your service provides. We have questions we need answered. We're not here to bust you. You have two minutes to get down the stairs."

Less than a minute later an obese Hispanic woman wearing a red kerchief poked her head out of the door alongside the doorway to the bodega.

"We're not here to arrest you," Moss said.

The obese woman lumbered out of the doorway. Nance stepped back and looked up at the windows on the second floor. She could see the blinds move.

"We're here about Rachel Wilson," Moss said.

The obese woman remained silent.

"We need to know if she was working for you the last few days. Was she?"

The obese woman shook her head no.

"Say it," Nance said.

"She no work for us three weeks now."

"You sure?" Moss said. "We check your records, her records, we find she's been out for you, we're coming back."

The obese woman continued shaking her head. "She don' work here three weeks."

"Who was her last trick?" Nance asked.

"Last customer is same one she always have from here."

"Who is he?" Nance said.

"Old man lives in Port Washington."

"His name," Nance said.

"I give you, he doesn't call again. Please?"

Moss interrupted Nance. "It's okay," he said. "But you're sure Rachel Wilson hasn't worked for you in three weeks, that's it?"

The obese woman crossed her chest.

Nance rolled her eyes.

Half an hour later the detectives were driving across the Verrazano Narrows Bridge into Staten Island on their way to Perth Amboy. Nance was still upset with Moss for not pushing the Hispanic woman a little harder back at the escort service. She asked about Michael Lyons before covering her face as she yawned.

"Michael Lyons is a cracker prick scumbag used to be hooked up with the Irish over in Sunnyside," Moss said. "The guy got so hot about five years ago, even his dirty friends walked away. Word is, he's not welcome at the watering holes in Sunnyside anymore."

"*Hot* meaning 'dirty'?"

"Filthy dirty. He's had Internal Affairs on his ass more than once, but some undercover cop everybody knows was set up took the fall for Lyons and some of his cronies a few years back. Since then, most of them counted their blessings and retired. Lyons was too young for retirement. Brass moved him from drugs to homicide."

"You know this and he's still operating?"

Moss veered to the extreme left tollbooth once they were off the bridge. "Everybody knows it and he's still operating," he said. "But for all anybody knows, he's got people watching him twenty-four seven. Or there's nobody watching him. You know how it goes. NYPD can be accused of a lot of things, but being on top of its own isn't one of them."

"Well, if what Russo claims is true, that he saw Lyons at the pimp's murder scene and that the woman killed downtown was supposed to be Agnes Lynn, Lyons is probably hooked up with the Russian mob."

Moss was through the toll and using all three lanes on the Staten Island Expressway to weave through traffic.

"Tell me that again," he said. "Agnes Lynn looked like the woman was killed?"

"What Russo claims she said. Apparently this Agnes Lynn was working with the woman who was killed. The woman Agnes Lynn was working with was also blond. First responders claim it was an execution-style murder."

"Which wouldn't make sense if it was random," Moss said.

"Unless it wasn't and the killer thought it was Agnes Lynn."

Moss said, "Which now makes me a lot more enthusiastic this morning than I was last night."

"Except you let that substitute pimp off the hook back in Queens," Nance said. "That routine of hers, the phony broken language and then the sign of the cross."

"She was telling us what she could," Moss said. "The guy Rachel Wilson serviced for them was some old dude on Long Island."

"And you believe her. She worked for an agency for one customer."

"Maybe she's what the customer requested. It happens."

"And she worked, what, once a month for the guy."

"You're looking for a fight now," Moss said. "Let it go."

Nance rubbed her temples. She felt a headache coming on. "You're right," she said, "I am looking for one. I'm sorry. Exhausted, too. And I'm getting a headache."

"Caffeine headache probably," Moss said.

"Technically, it's still last night, by the way, but thanks for being enthusiastic about it."

Moss ignored the shot. "The pimp was killed where Russo saw Lyons, Rachel worked for him?"

"I also learned that from Russo."

"And not from Lyons," Moss said.

"Lyons probably has a few dozen names to look into," Nance said. "If the guy was a pimp, I mean, to be fair to Lyons."

"You're being too fair," Moss said. "He's the one on the scene, there's probably a reason. And with all the bodies in Brooklyn yesterday, the mob guys in the water near Starrett City and then Rachel on Plum Beach, it's no coincidence she was working for the pimp killed in Harlem."

"That's what Russo said, it's no coincidence. He also said there are Russians stalking Agnes Lynn. I'll put in a call to Vanya once we hear what else Russo has to say. This Agnes is probably the friend the ex-husband was talking about last night."

"And Russo mentioned Lyons for a reason," Moss said. "He gonna wait for us? This is getting a lot bigger than a simple homicide investigation should be."

"I told him we're on our way half an hour ago," Nance said. "He said he'd wait in front of his address. He gave me directions. It's just over the Outerbridge in Perth Amboy. He's not far from the bridge."

Moss said, "Yeah, so let's hope we get to him before the Russians do."

•◆•

Vanya had his men bring Leonid Fetisov to the Kings County morgue to view the body of Rachel Wilson. The hairdresser was panicked when they brought him into the examination room. Vanya stood behind Fetisov and motioned at the attendant to remove the sheet from Rachel Wilson's face.

Fetisov gasped. He jerked away from Vanya and turned his back to the body.

"She was butchered like a piece of meat," Vanya told him in Russian. He grabbed the hairdresser by the shoulders and turned him to face the body again. "Look," he said.

Fetisov slowly opened his eyes. The sheet had been completely pulled off. He saw an open stomach wound, gagged, and was sick into a plastic bucket.

Vanya waited until Fetisov was finished vomiting before taking him outside the examination room. He sat the hairdresser on a bench in a hallway and squatted down to look into his eyes.

"You cut her hair?" he asked.

Fetisov nodded.

"For Yuri?"

Fetisov nodded again.

"Who else?"

This time the hairdresser looked down.

"Leonid, don't fuck with me, okay? Viktor Timkin doesn't know you were there, or you'd already be dead with Yuri and his crew. Understand? Now he knows because you didn't tell me last night. You didn't tell me, and now he knows you were there. You're a dead man when I let you go."

Fetisov grabbed his hair with both hands.

"We'll protect you, but you tell us everything you know," Vanya said. "What was the haircut for? What did Yuri do with the woman? Who was there? Who was it for?"

Fetisov's body heaved.

"Tell us or I'll let you go home," Vanya said. "I'll let you go home right now. I'll call your brother-in-law if you want. Maybe he'll pick you up. Pasha Chenkov and Viktor Timkin will come to pick you up."

Fetisov choked.

"Why did you cut the woman's hair? For who?"

Fetisov held his hands together in prayer.

Vanya pointed a finger back toward the examination room. He said, "Motherfucker, I'll put you in the same drawer with the woman. You'll spend the day in there with her."

Fetisov bawled.

"Okay, you want to pray?" Vanya said. He made the sign of the cross with a tight fist. "I swear on my father's grave, Leonid. You'll stay in the drawer with that woman all day."

Fetisov dropped to the floor and curled into a fetal ball.

Vanya grabbed him by the back of his collar and pulled him up. He'd dragged him two feet toward the examination room when Fetisov began to talk.

Chapter 21

JACK STOPPED AT a diner on Fayette Street in Perth Amboy to pick up an egg on a roll and a container of milk. He was hoping to get a few hours' sleep after meeting with the New York detectives. He ate the makeshift breakfast in his car before pulling out of the diner parking lot.

When he was finished, Jack called the hospital to check on his son. He was told Nicholas was resting well and that the doctor would be making morning rounds in a few minutes. Jack thanked the nurse and said he'd call back.

He called his ex-wife next and grimaced when her boyfriend answered the phone. Paul passed the phone to Lisa, and Jack told her what he'd just been told by a nurse at the hospital.

"He'll be out of it until the afternoon," Lisa said. "You're gonna have to take them for their word."

"Yeah, I know. I'm just anxious to see him."

"Me, too, but he's okay. Just try and relax about this. Nicholas will be fine. He's gonna be hurting for a while, but he'll be fine when it's all over."

"Right," Jack said. "I'll see you later."

He put his phone in his pocket as he approached New Brunswick Avenue. He saw the time and remembered to take it slow. The Perth Amboy police were notorious for making their ticket quota early after the start of a new month.

Jack was careful not to drive along the street where he lived. He circled around the area using Sadowsky Parkway and Linden Street. If the Russian mob had gone through Agnes Lynn's telephone bills in trying to find her, his phone calls had probably flagged him as somebody she might have been with two days ago.

The other thing in the back of Jack's mind was Michael Lyons. If the detective was on the Russian payroll, then Jack's sudden appearance at the Harlem crime scene had probably put him in jeopardy.

He drove around the area a few times before parking on Linden Street, opposite Roessler Park. High Street and the apartment building where Jack lived were across the park. Raritan Bay bordered the west side of the building.

Jack was sitting low behind the steering wheel when he

spotted a blue van pulling up to the front of the building. He kept his car running in case he had to get out of there fast.

Two Hispanic men got out of the van and unloaded a bed from the back. Jack figured they were tenants moving in. Most of the occupants in the building were Hispanic.

He was planning on giving it another ten minutes before heading up to his apartment. Five minutes passed before his cell phone rang. Jack saw it was a 917 area code and took the call. He was surprised when the detective identified herself.

"This is Detective Nance. Anita Nance."

Jack hesitated.

"Mr. Russo?"

"Speaking," he said. "What you find out?"

"About Lyons?"

"Yeah."

"He wasn't assigned to the Freeman murder. He was on the scene and wound up with it."

"Convenient, huh?"

"It could be coincidence."

"Could also be too late."

"Meaning?"

"What about the Russians?"

"I spoke with the head of the red squad myself."

"And his name?"

"Vanya Koloff."

"Oh, great. He on their payroll, too, or the thought didn't cross your mind?"

"He's not the type. Trust me."

"I can't afford to trust you or anybody else, not so long as Michael Lyons is involved."

"He's not involved with the Rachel Wilson case. You still at your place?"

"I'm outside, but not for much longer. I need to see my kid later, and I need to be awake for that."

"We're just over the Outerbridge now."

"Then you're close. I'll be here." He closed his phone.

Jack got out of the car and walked to a nearby park bench that faced the apartment building where he lived. He glanced at his watch and saw it was close to 9:00 a.m. He finished a cigarette, crushed it under his right foot, and took in the saltwater smell of Raritan Bay.

At 9:03 a strong breeze rattled the branches of the tree Jack was sitting under. At 9:04 Jack was about to get up and cross the park when he flinched from the cold metal of a gun barrel pressed against the back of his neck.

•◆•

"What flag is that, Jeffrey?" Agnes asked the black man wearing a blue maintenance uniform. She had read his name off the tag above his left breast pocket.

"Huh?" he said. He looked up at where Agnes was pointing. "Somewhere Middle East," he said. "Saudi Arabia, I think. They're Arabs, I know that much."

They were standing under the FDR Drive near Twenty-third Street. Agnes couldn't sleep after dreaming about the last man who had solicited her for sex. She had gotten up, showered, and then called the Harbor Marina for directions before checking out of the downtown hotel.

Jeffrey had just tossed a bucket with rope inside the trunk

of a car. Agnes asked him if he had worked on the big yacht
with the Arabic writing along its hull.

"Not on it, no, but I work in the marina there," Jeffrey said.
He slammed the trunk shut. "I'm just getting off."

"Who owns something that big?" Agnes asked.

"Somebody with a ton of money. People like me wash the
docks down."

Agnes smiled. "You working here long?"

"Six months."

"How's the job?"

"You a reporter or something?"

"Just curious."

Jeffrey's eyebrows raised. "About washing boats?"

"I'm a private investigator."

"Uh-oh."

"Not to worry; it has to do with somebody visiting the
yacht there. I'm working for his wife."

"Just don't ask me anything that'll get me fired."

"No problem."

Jeffrey had folded his arms across his chest. He was a big
man, broad across the chest and thick with muscle. "Wanna do
this in the car, where I won't freeze to death?" he asked.

"Good idea," Agnes said.

He unlocked the doors and they sat in the front. Jeffrey
started the engine and turned up the heater. "It'll blow cold air
a couple minutes before it gets warm," he said.

"I'm fine," Agnes said. "So are there many visitors to the
yacht?"

"The Arab one? A few. Guy works nights says they have
women come in limousines all the time. Sometimes guys go up

there, too, before the women arrive. Usually well dressed, which means they have money, too. Some mornings when I start, they just getting off the yacht and heading home."

"You know if a Russian guy named Viktor Timkin goes up there?"

Jeffrey shrugged. "I don't know names. What's he look like?"

Agnes remembered his being described as the older step-brother at fifty-two and that he was built like a little fireplug.

"A little fireplug," she said. "Somewhere in his late forties, early fifties."

"There's been a few guys look like that," he said. "Was a Russian dude here before talking to one of the bodyguards I see around the big guy when he comes down to the cars to go someplace."

"How you know he was Russian?"

"I don't, but he sounded like it. The regular guard was taking his break, and I sit there when he's out, sometimes for overtime, too. Man said his name was Tevya, had me call up to the yacht for clearance. I asked for his last name, but he told me to tell them who he was. His name wasn't on the list, but they let him up. Came down 'bout an hour ago."

Agnes remembered the name from her research. Aaron Tevya Bartnev was in charge of porn for the Brighton Beach Mafiya.

"He was here? He went up to the boat?"

"Once I called it in, yeah."

"You don't remember a Timkin, though, huh? He'd have a Russian accent, too."

"I don't really get to talk to the people getting on and off the yacht. That was an accident tonight, with the guy Tevya.

Like I said, the regular guard took his break. I know the guy owns the yacht has a British accent, if that helps."

"British? I thought he was an Arab."

"He is. Guess they grow them there, too."

"You ever speak to anybody else going up to the yacht?"

"A couple of the women on nights I filled in; the regular guard was out, they couldn't get anybody to replace him."

"Uh-huh," Agnes said. "And?"

"I assume they were escorts or something. I know two were from high-profile strip clubs. The limos had the names on them."

"Any black women?"

"Sure, a few. One I talked to not long ago. Couple weeks now, I guess. She was fine-looking. Wore those boots go all the way up the legs? I told her 'good evening,' you know."

"Taking a shot?"

"Something like that. She was decent about it, though. She smiled."

"What you talk about?"

"Nothing important. The weather, how cold it's been. The time, because it was pretty late, after midnight, when she got here. She said her name would be on the visitors' list and it was. I figured she was a hooker, but I didn't ask. I told her to watch out for the dog, though. Man has a nasty one he keeps on board, a pit bull."

"When was that?"

"Couple weeks ago, I guess. Hey, I thought you were investigating some dude?"

Agnes winked at Jeffrey. "My client thinks the black woman was for her husband. Know her name by any chance?"

"See, now this the kind of thing can get me fired."

"No way," Agnes told him. "This goes nowhere. She's just looking for grounds, my client. She doesn't care much more than that."

Jeffrey thought about it a moment. Agnes opened her purse. He took offense and reached out to stop her. She lurched back and pinned herself against the door.

Jeffrey was confused. "You don't need to pay me," he said. "I was trying to stop you from insulting me."

Agnes put her hands up. "I'm sorry," she said. "You surprised me."

Jeffrey remained silent.

"I am sorry," she repeated.

Jeffrey looked straight ahead. "Something with an *R*," he said.

"Roberta?"

"No, not that."

"Ronnie?"

Jeffrey shook his head.

Agnes said, "Rachel?"

"That's it," Jeffrey said. "She was nice. Friendly."

Agnes saw Jeffrey was still uncomfortable. She reached across the console to touch his hand. He pulled away.

"I'm sorry," she said again.

"You think I was gonna rob or rape you?"

Agnes turned on her seat to face him. "Neither," she said.

Jeffrey watched a city bus navigate around a construction crew filling potholes along Marginal Street.

"I do want to thank you," she said.

"No need," he said, "but I got to get home now."

They had been pulled over for speeding on Amboy Avenue alongside a cemetery. Both detectives had flashed their badges before the patrolman got out of his car, but it still took a few minutes before they were on their way again. At the corner of Amboy and New Brunswick Avenue they were nearly hit by a black van speeding through a red light. Nance had offered Moss a two-to-one bet that the cruiser sitting at the speed trap along the cemetery was no longer there.

When they made it to High Street near the water, Jack Russo wasn't waiting outside the apartment building address he had given them. Instead, there was a crowd of people and two Perth Amboy police cruisers on the opposite side of the park.

Moss let Nance out to try Jack Russo's doorbell while he headed around the park. He pulled up alongside one of the two police cars. A group of people stood at the curb. A woman in a pink robe and fuzzy slippers pointed to a nearby bench.

"What's going on?" Moss asked one of the patrolmen. He held his badge out the window.

"A woman thinks she witnessed an abduction," the patrolman said. "Less than fifteen minutes ago, she says."

"Uh-oh," Moss said. "Was it a guy, the person she saw abducted?"

"What she says," the patrolman said. "Three white guys grabbed another white guy from the bench there and tossed him into a black van. She said the van turned the corner and took off up High Street. I already called it in."

"A black van?" Moss asked.

"What she said, yeah. We've got cars heading for the Outerbridge in case they're still around."

"Was the guy hurt?"

"I don't know for sure," the patrolman said. "The woman said he seemed to be unconscious. She saw it from her kitchen window. She lives across the street here."

Moss thanked the patrolman and took off around the park to pick up Nance. He used his cell phone to alert the Staten Island police about the van maybe heading their way.

"He's not there," Nance said when she was in the car again.

"He was abducted," Moss said.

"What?"

He filled her in. Nance called Vanya Koloff.

• ◆ •

Once Vanya learned about the movie and the mysterious Arab Yuri Timkin had serviced in the Brooklyn basement the day he had Leonid Fetisov shave Rachel Wilson's hair off, the Russian detective stopped at a Sheepshead Bay fish market and purchased six fresh blue-claw crabs for two dollars each. He brought the pot of live crabs to the basement of a bar his men frequented after work.

Waiting for Vanya were two of his men and a local porn dealer with connections to the Timkin crime family. The porn dealer went by the name of Tevya. His real name was Aaron Bartnev. He was a Russian-American immigrant in the United States for more than forty years. He spoke fluent Yiddish and fairly good English.

Vanya saw his men were letting Bartnev drink water. He knocked the plastic bottle out of the porn dealer's right hand.

"What do you want from me?" Bartnev asked in English.

Vanya spoke in Russian. "Yuri Timkin went to you for actors," he said. "Who were they? Who was it for?"

Bartnev made a face at Vanya. "What are you talking about?" he said, also in Russian. "I don't know what you're talking about."

Vanya set the pot with the live crabs on the table. He motioned at Bartnev to look inside, then said, "Don't fuck with me, okay?"

Bartnev balled his hands into fists on his lap.

"Who were the actors? You got them. Who were they? What did he want with them? Who were they for?"

"I don't know anything about actors," Bartnev said.

Vanya smacked the porn dealer hard across the face.

Bartnev closed his eyes tight. "Leave me alone!" he yelled.

"I'll let the crabs bite your fucking nose off," Vanya said.

Bartnev opened his eyes to glance at the pot.

"What was it about?" Vanya said.

Bartnev shook his head.

Vanya pointed to the porn dealer's hands. One of his men held Bartnev around the neck while the other pulled one of his hands away from his lap.

"Okay," Vanya said. "Now the crabs eat your fingers."

Bartnev's hand slipped free. He balled it into a fist in his lap again. Vanya grabbed one of the crabs and set it on the porn dealer's face. The crab latched onto Bartnev's chin and neck. The porn dealer screamed. He tried to shake the crab free, but it was already drawing blood from his chin.

Vanya gave a head nod to his men, and they let go of Bartnev's hands. He slapped the crab off his face. One of the claws clung to the fleshy part of his neck, even though the body of the crab had been knocked across the room.

Vanya had another crab now. He dropped it on Bartnev's lap. The porn dealer jumped up from the chair. He smacked the crab off his lap, then pulled off the claw still hanging from his neck and flung it.

Vanya removed his belt and had his men strap the porn dealer into the chair this time. When he was secured tightly, Vanya told one of his men to go find the two crabs on the floor before he used the other four in the pot.

"You are focking crazy bastard!" Bartnev yelled.

Vanya's cell phone rang. He saw it was Anita Nance.

"Let me go!" Bartnev screamed.

Vanya motioned at his men to take over. He left the basement to answer the call.

Chapter 22

MICHAEL LYONS HAD already put in twenty-two years with the
NYPD. He'd been a detective the last fourteen. He owned a
two-family home in Woodhaven, Queens, where his ex-wife
lived with their two sons. He had lived in an apartment since
his divorce ten years earlier.

Lyons had managed to hide most of the dirty money he'd
taken over the years. Three safe-deposit boxes in three different
banks contained fifty thousand dollars each. There was thirty
thousand in another.

Lyons had mostly worked shakedown scams with vice and

narcotics detectives. When Internal Affairs starting looking into dirty cops, a group of older detectives decided that a younger detective should be the sacrificial lamb. Lyons was part of the crew that killed the young cop and planted evidence that would end the investigation into police foul play.

"One gets sacrificed so that the rest can survive" was how it had been put at a dinner meeting when the six detectives decided the fate of another.

Lyons could never accept the math and had turned to alcohol to numb his guilt.

Now he was one day from the sixth anniversary of the cop murder. Each year it was a little more difficult to deal with. The past two years Lyons had fought bouts of paranoia that sent him on weeklong drinking binges.

This year it was worse than usual. He wondered if it was because he had seen Jack Russo at the Harlem crime scene with the woman he was sure the Russian mob was trying to kill, or if it was because one of the detectives investigating the murder of a prostitute in Brooklyn was leaving voice messages for him about the pimp. Whatever it was, the coincidences unnerved Lyons.

He had planned to leave the United States with phony paperwork he had been promised by Viktor Timkin. Lyons needed the phony passport and airline tickets to flee the country in the event things went from bad to worse. He had called the Russian mobster a few times to request a meeting, but so far Timkin hadn't returned any of his calls.

He would need a day to get his money from the banks. Then he would have to hide somewhere safe until the paperwork was ready. The phone calls the investigating detectives had left on his voice mail had already alerted the homicide department to his sudden disappearance. It would only be a matter of time before his colleagues came looking for him.

If it was all coming apart, Lyons knew he wouldn't be able to do the time and would have to flip on his Russian employers if he were caught before he left the country. He had witnessed the breakdown of crime organizations from two-man stickup teams to wiseguy crime families since he first joined the force. The one thing he had learned that the law could count on sooner or later was a snitch. He might be vilified as a dirty cop, but what he could give the feds on Viktor Timkin just might save him from the abuse he would receive in jail.

Usually it was the guys who killed the most and cursed the loudest about rats who snitched. He tried to guess which Russian would be the one to destroy him if he didn't talk first. Lyons guessed it would be the stocky prick he had been with the night before. He knew it wouldn't be Timkin, but Pasha Chenkov was exactly the kind of killer the feds usually turned.

Now he had a drink to settle his nerves. He tried to convince himself there was nothing to worry about. He was on his way from the bedroom to the kitchen when he was stopped by the sight of the bank calendar hanging from the back of his apartment door. Lyons saw the date of the anniversary of his participation in the cop killing. He tried to look away but couldn't. He was paralyzed by fear.

•◆•

When he was able to think clearly, Jack realized his hands had been cuffed behind his back. He remembered being in a van and bouncing whenever it hit a bump in the road. He remembered trying to look up and feeling a knee in the middle of his back pushing him down. Then the van had stopped, and he heard the doors open a moment before another electric shock put him out a second time.

He had just started to regain consciousness when they pulled him up off the floor of a car. He could see they were in a garage with a small loading dock. He saw a freight elevator at one end of the platform a moment before the blindfold was tied around his head.

He was shoved up a ramp into an elevator and pulled out again when it stopped on about the fourth or fifth floor. Jack was led down a carpeted hallway into a room where he remained standing a few minutes before he heard men speaking Russian.

Then Jack was pushed into a chair and the handcuffs and blindfold were removed. He counted four men, two of them armed, in what appeared to be a hotel room. A couple of hours passed before a fifth man entered the room. He was short and stocky. Jack could tell he was the one in charge because of his body language and the way the others looked to him.

The leader smoked a cigarette. He set one foot on a chair and motioned at one of his men with his head.

A small bottle of water was held up to Jack's mouth. He sipped when the bottle was tilted up.

"Where is woman?" the stocky man asked.

"She doesn't know anything," Jack said. "You made a mistake with her."

"Where she is?"

"I don't know."

The stocky man pointed at one of his men, and Jack was punched across the right side of his mouth. The blow stunned him. He tasted blood when he licked his lips.

"Where woman is?" the stocky man repeated.

"Fuck you," Jack said.

This time the punch came from his left and without warning. Jack saw tiny lights inside his head. His vision was blurred when he opened his eyes.

When Jack could focus again, the stocky man said, "Where woman is?"

•—•

"God damn it, I know something is wrong!" Lisa Russo told her boyfriend. "He can be an asshole sometimes, but Jack isn't neglectful. Not ever."

Paul Werner stroked Lisa's arms to try to calm her down.

"I have his friend's number back at the house," she said. "He's still on the force. Maybe I should call him."

"You left messages, right?"

"Yes, I did. Six now. I know something is wrong."

They were in the lobby of the hospital waiting for Jack to show. The last time she had heard from him was earlier in the morning. The doctor had let her see their son a little after noon. When she tried calling again, Jack's voice mail picked up.

"Do you want to call the police?" Paul asked.

"I might have to."

"I can do it if you want."

Lisa had just come down from seeing her son. Nicholas was barely able to speak with the morphine being pumped through his system. He had been in pain, though, and it had upset her more than she thought it would.

Now she was frustrated. "If I send you back to the apartment, would you know where to look for my telephone book? It's in the junk drawer near the phone."

"Yeah, I'll find it, don't worry."

"Just bring the book here. I'm not sure where I filed his name."

"What is it?"

"Jerry Klein, but just bring the book back here."

"You sure?"

"Please, Paul."

"No problem." He reached out with both hands. "I'll get it."

Lisa pulled away. "I'm going back upstairs."

"You okay?" Paul asked.

"No."

"You need something? Valium maybe?"

"No. Just go and get the telephone book, please."

"Okay, I'll be back soon as I can."

Lisa stopped herself from turning her back on Paul. She reached up to kiss him instead. "Thanks," she said. "I'm sorry for being such an asshole."

Paul hugged her. "No problem. I'll be right back."

"Thank you."

Lisa watched her boyfriend leave the hospital before heading back toward the elevators. She was about to step inside when her cell phone rang. Assuming it was Jack, she answered.

"Where the hell are you?" she asked.

"Who this is?" a man with an accent asked.

"Who's this?"

"Who you are?" the man said.

Lisa checked the number to make sure it was Jack's. It was.

"Where's Jack?" she asked.

The caller hung up.

"Shit," Lisa said. Then she called 911.

Chapter 23

"I KEEP GETTING her voice mail," Nance said.

She had been trying Agnes Lynn's cell phone ever since Jack Russo gave it to them. Nance left voice messages requesting an emergency callback.

"She's probably afraid to answer calls from numbers she doesn't recognize," Moss said. "You try punching in nine-one-one?"

"She's got nothing to lose answering the call," Nance said. "She doesn't have to speak."

"She might be scared because of Lyons."

"How the hell are we supposed to help her if she doesn't answer?"

They were driving east on the Belt Parkway. Moss saw the exit for Bay Parkway up ahead and switched lanes. "We keep trying," he said. "In the meantime, I need coffee."

"Me, too."

"The other thing is Russo," Moss said. "We can let Perth Amboy handle the abduction end, but since our guys on Staten Island found the van, we'll have to report it over here."

They had returned to New York without telling the Perth Amboy police about Russo. The Staten Island police had located a stolen black van abandoned off an exit of the Korean War Veterans Highway. Neither detective was sure how they should handle the Jack Russo dilemma.

"Then again," Nance said, "they found *a* van, not necessarily *the* van."

"We're betting the coffee on this one," Moss said. "I say it's the van."

"I'll call Vanya back and see what he says," Nance said.

"What's this guy, the answer man all of a sudden? A couple hours ago he was too busy to give us spit. He tells us not to report Russo yet, but it's not his ass if we don't."

"He's the head of the Russian mob squad, Bob. With what's happened the last couple of days, maybe he was busy."

Moss pulled off the parkway into a Burger King parking lot. He went inside while Nance dialed Vanya Koloff on her cell phone. It took him ten minutes to get two coffees and two Danish. When he came back out, Nance had just turned off her phone.

"He still says we shouldn't report it," she said. "Especially not to the feds, not if we expect to find Russo alive."

Moss handed her a coffee. "That his confidence in redfellas or his distrust of all things federal?"

"A little of both probably, but you know what'll happen if we don't report it and Russo winds up dead."

"It would be our careers."

Both detectives sipped their coffees.

Nance said, "At the least."

"Then we report it."

"But not to the feds."

"Not our call. Once we report it to our people, we're off the hook."

"Okay," Nance said. "In the meantime we need to find Agnes Lynn. If she's not dead, she's hiding from the wrong people."

Moss checked his watch. "And still no word from Michael Lyons."

"How the hell does he explain that?"

"He doesn't. He won't. We can forget about him helping us until we make a stink, which I'll definitely do if he doesn't return my calls in the next hour."

"Vanya is probably right about Russo. If this gets out to the media, he's a dead man."

"Like I said, we can defer to Perth Amboy PD," Moss said. "We can say we thought they had it and hold onto the information a little longer. We might need to for Russo's sake."

"If you say so," Nance said. "I was supposed to meet with Jerry Pirella today. We could wait until after I talk to him."

"Your ex-boyfriend the fed? I thought we're not going that route?"

"It's personal, Bob, me and Jerry."

"I thought you were finished with him."

"I am. He keeps calling. I was going to cancel until all this happened. Then I wondered if he might know something we don't."

"I don't like it. I don't trust the feds, especially a jilted one."

Nance gave him a look. "That your idea of chivalry?"

"Something like that," Moss said. "What else was the Russian answer man up to?"

"He mentioned something about porn actors. He's got his men questioning someone about them."

"Porn actors?"

"It's what he said. A pair of Russians."

"It have anything to do with us?"

Nance bit her lip. "He didn't say."

"Uh-oh."

"It could be he doesn't know yet."

"Yeah, right."

"You think he's holding back?"

Moss motioned at Nance's coffee. "Finish it," he said. "It'll help wake you up."

•◆•

Agnes realized her cell phone battery was dead when she tried to call a Hertz car rental after leaving the Harbor Marina. She found her way to an electronics store on Park Avenue South and bought a new charger and battery. She was sitting in a yellow taxi on her way to the Hertz place when she noticed she had phone messages.

She listened to a few messages from Jack and then a few more from one of the detectives claiming to be investigating

Rachel's murder. It was a woman detective and she sounded anxious. Detective Anita Nance's message mentioned Jack's name and said that he had contacted them the night before. Then Nance said something Agnes didn't understand.

"We were on our way to meet with him, but he wasn't there. We need to talk to you about that."

Agnes felt her stomach drop.

The taxi stopped at the curb in front of Hertz. Agnes paid the driver and got out. She dialed Jack's cell phone number and stopped in her tracks when a man with an accent answered.

"Who this is?" he said.

Agnes killed the connection.

•◆•

Vanya received the call from his men and rushed to the Gowanus Expressway under the BQE. Two bodies had been fished out of the canal. Both were male, naked, and missing their penises. They both had been shot in the back of the head. Vanya had the forensic unit search for tattoos that might confirm their identities. Both men had small hearts on their right ass cheeks.

He called Detective Nance.

"Hey," she answered.

"Bad news," he said.

"What?"

"Porn actors are dead."

"What's it about?"

"I'm thinking snuff film," Vanya told her.

"Jesus Christ," Nance said. "You mean Rachel?"

"I think so. Actors are dead. Yuri's crew is dead. Yuri is probably dead, too, eh? Viktor cleans mess."

"And now they have an ex-cop and maybe the woman we're looking for. We can't find her."

"Ex-cop is woman's boyfriend?"

"We don't know. He's definitely a friend. He told us he was trying to protect her."

"You think they have her, too?"

"They might. We can't get her to call back."

"Maybe she's afraid."

"Maybe, but we can't do anything unless she talks to us. We have to get her off the street."

Vanya was thinking something else.

"You there?" Nance said.

"I'm here," he said. "If woman is hiding, they'll use boyfriend."

"What do you mean?"

"Why they kidnap him, to get her. If she's hiding, they'll contact her."

"We're going to have to report it," Nance said. "Moss is going to after I talk to a friend with the FBI."

"You go to feds and they kill ex-cop," Vanya said. "Timkin doesn't take chances with FBI."

"I'm talking to a friend with the FBI," Nance told him. "I'm not reporting anything to them."

"Be careful, eh?"

"I understand."

"Let me know what your friend says."

"Where are you?"

"Gowanus Canal."

"That where the bodies are? In the water again?"

"Yes. Executed like Yuri's crew. Also they cut off penises."

"Part of the snuff thing?"

"No, I don't think so. More diversion. Is bullshit."

"You sure?"

"I think so."

"Okay, I'll call you back."

"Bye-bye."

Vanya closed his phone as the morgue van pulled away. He lit a cigarette and stood facing the cold wind blowing across the canal. The situation had changed. Viktor Timkin was involved in something a lot bigger than covering up a snuff film. Vanya wasn't sure what it was, except the body count suggested it was a lot more important than it appeared.

As much as he tried to avoid department bureaucracy, it was time to talk with the man running the organized crime task force.

Vanya gave him a call.

Chapter 24

DETECTIVE MICHAEL LYONS met Pavel Chenkov in the lounge of the Brooklyn Inn. It was close to two o'clock. The bar was empty except for two of Chenkov's men sitting with a worn-looking woman at one end. Lyons had a bad headache and was anxious to speak with Viktor Timkin about the phony passport and airline tickets he would need to leave the country. He asked Chenkov for aspirin and a glass of water.

Chenkov served Lyons the aspirin and water before pouring two shots of vodka. He set the drink in front of Lyons and raised his own in a toast.

"Yeah, yeah," said Lyons, barely raising his glass off the bar before leaning forward to sip the drink. "Where's your boss?" he asked after setting the glass down.

"We have friend upstairs."

"What friend?"

"Jack Russo."

Lyons did a double take. "You fucking serious?"

Chenkov topped off Lyons's drink. He said, "Jack Russo, upstairs he is."

"That's why I'm here, the guy you have upstairs. Where's Timkin?"

"He's be here later."

Lyons took a look around the lounge. "I hope you intend to get rid of Russo," he said. "The guy probably knows enough to bury you by now. I know he knows enough to bury me."

"What he knows?" Chenkov said. "Girl he knows?"

"He knows about the woman you're looking for, that's more than enough."

"Girl is come to save him, eh? Why we keep him."

Lyons downed the shot this time. "Unless she brings the militia, yeah, sure," he said. "You do that, keep him. Very smart. Now I know why the Soviet Union fell apart."

Chenkov turned to his men and spoke Russian. He told them what Lyons had said. The two men glared at the cop.

"When's he getting here, your boss?" Lyons asked. "I don't have time to waste."

"Little while. Don't worry, he's come."

"When? I don't like being here with Russo upstairs."

"Have 'nother drink," Chenkov said. He poured another shot.

Lyons ignored it. "Look, I appreciate the clever conversation and all, but I have better things to do."

"First you come upstairs, see Jack Russo, eh?" Chenkov said.

"What the hell for?"

"Maybe you kill him for us."

"Fuck you," Lyons said. He slid off the bar stool.

Chenkov waved at Lyons. "Come upstairs to see this guy," he said.

Lyons pointed a threatening finger. "You go and get your boss on the phone right now."

"Come upstairs," Chenkov said. He came out from behind the bar. "Viktor wants this."

"Yeah, well, let Viktor tell me. Whacking Jack Russo isn't part of my deal."

Chenkov pulled a nine-millimeter from the waist of his pants. His men grabbed Lyons by his arms.

Chenkov said, "Come upstairs anyway, big mouth, cocksucker-motherfucker. First we talk to you, and then you talk to Jack Russo."

• ◆ •

Agnes took the chance and used her credit card to rent a car. She chose a navy blue Chevy Cabriolet and used the road atlas to find the New York Aquarium located in Coney Island. According to the map, she could take the BQE to the Prospect Expressway, which would turn into Ocean Parkway. At the end of Ocean Parkway the street name changed to Surf Avenue.

She wasn't sure what she might learn from Igor Mahalov, but according to the articles she had researched, he was the man in charge of prostitution for the Russian mob. She already knew the one involved in porn, Tevya, had been to the yacht to meet with the Arab.

Agnes was sure the Russians had Jack and was terrified for him. She called the detective back once she was through the Battery Tunnel. She recognized the voice of the woman who had left the message.

"Nance," the detective answered.

"This is Agnes Lynn."

"Agnes? Thank God. Where are you?"

"What happened to Jack?"

"We think he was kidnapped. Are you okay?"

"I'm fine. What happened?"

"He was waiting for us outside his building in Perth Amboy. He had called earlier, and we were on our way to meet him. He was gone when we got there. The Perth Amboy PD had a witness said she saw a man being abducted. We just missed him. Where are you?"

"I called his phone and one of them answered."

"A Russian?"

"Yes."

"What he say?"

"He wanted to know who was calling."

"They call back?"

"Not yet. Jack has a son in the hospital he was supposed to visit today."

"We know. We're going to do whatever we can for him. Where are you? You need to come in."

"Not yet."

"Why not?"

"I'm busy."

"Agnes, you can't fight these people alone. They're too powerful."

"What happened to the cop Jack said was dirty?"

"Nothing yet," the detective said. "We're trying to contact him, but he isn't returning calls. Nobody knows where he is. Nobody has seen him since the crime scene last night."

"What's his name?"

"Lyons. Michael Lyons."

"How do I know you're not dirty? How do I know you didn't set up Jack this morning?"

"You can call any precinct you want and walk in," the detective said. "You can call City Hall if you want. However you want to handle this is fine with us, but we need to get you off the streets before they find you. We're not dirty, Agnes. We're looking into Rachel's murder. We know you were friends. We need to protect you. We can't get the people who killed Rachel without you."

"We need to get Jack first."

"We can't do that with you out there. You can't fight the Russian mob by yourself."

"I'll call you back," Agnes said.

"When?" the detective asked.

"After I help Jack."

"How are you going to—"

Agnes hung up when she saw the street sign up ahead for Ocean Parkway.

•◆•

Detective John DeNafria had been promoted to gold shield status one week before he was put in charge of overseeing the investigations of all five New York crime families. Prior to his promotion, DeNafria had been assigned to the Vignieri crime family. Vanya had worked with him twice before when the Russian and Italian mob organizations had crossed swords in disputes over territory. Vanya was hoping DeNafria could tell him something about what might be going on besides the obvious and was surprised at how anxious the head of the task force was to see him.

"I was about to call you," DeNafria said.

Vanya pointed at his right temple. "I sense this, eh?"

"One of Timkin's guys hung himself this afternoon."

"Sadova?" Vanya said.

"At the MCC."

"In the Metropolitan Correction Center? He's not hanged himself. He's killed."

"What we figure, yeah, but who?"

"Italians have people inside," Vanya said. "Probably was somebody with Vignieri. You're checking guards, no?"

"Yeah, of course, like it'll do anything," he said. "Take a seat. I wanna show you something."

They watched a videotaped surveillance of three Corelli family members talking with Igor Mahalov, the mobster responsible for Russian prostitution in New York. The four mobsters stood at the curb on Surf Avenue outside the aquarium. Mahalov was puffing on his trademark Churchill cigar and was animated on the tape. He waved his hands when he spoke. The Italian mobsters seemed friendly and were laughing at whatever the Russian gangster was telling them.

Vanya turned to DeNafria. "When this was?"

"A couple days before Richie Marino and his two best friends were whacked in Sheepshead Bay," DeNafria said. He used the remote to stop the tape. "An hour before the aquarium opened. They were back again one day after the hits, the two on the left, about the same time of the morning. Those two are both with Joe LaRocca, directly under him. The other one—you can't tell there, but he's young—is LaRocca's nephew, his sister's kid. Probably just a gopher."

DeNafria handed Vanya a folded *New York Post* and pointed to the headline. Vanya read it aloud. "Meet the new boss."

Vanya looked down from the headline at a picture of Joseph LaRocca hugging another mobster outside his home in Howard Beach.

"We also have a sit-down between Viktor Timkin and the underboss of the Vignieri family," DeNafria explained. He switched VCR tapes and hit PLAY.

Vanya watched Viktor Timkin and his bodyguard crossing Houston Street. DeNafria stopped the tape when the Russian mobsters stepped inside an Italian restaurant.

"This was around midnight the night before the hits," he said. "From the looks of it, Timkin was summoned to this meeting."

"Who is connection?" Vanya asked.

"The pimp somebody whacked up in Harlem might be," DeNafria said. "He was operating under a Vignieri skipper there. It could be they're inquiring about that. We know Timkin's stepbrother played cards with the guy. We have that from a few sources. They did business in the past."

"Woman found on beach worked for same pimp," Vanya

said. "Yuri Timkin kills woman, Viktor kills Yuri and pimp to cover it up."

"You found Yuri Timkin's body?"

"No, but is dead, no doubt."

"So, what, they went into the contract business?"

"Worse."

"Worse like what?"

"I think they make movie."

DeNafria was puzzled. "Movie? What movie?"

"Snuff film," Vanya said. "Yuri, not Viktor. Yuri was stupid, not Viktor. We find two actors we think they used in Gowanus Canal today. Both executed."

"That explains the fax up from Florida this morning," DeNafria said. He went to his desk and pulled the fax from a folder.

"Vladimir Gregor was another guy in the porn business," he read from the fax. "They found him in some South Beach hotel. Also executed."

"You get fax from where, FBI?"

"FDLE. Florida Department of Law Enforcement. Probably their OC task squad. How come you didn't get it?"

"Who knows," Vanya said. "Somebody with FDLE is on payroll maybe?"

"For Timkin?"

"Who else?"

"We figured it's something to do with porn, but we didn't tie it into Timkin. Not directly."

"Is Mahalov's business, porn. This is what you were going to call me about?"

"That, the meeting between Timkin and Gangi, and the

guy hung himself. We figure it all has something to do with what happened in Sheepshead Bay. That went down as professional as they get. Now you're telling me two more Russians are dead."

"Porn actors."

"Whatever. What do you make of it?"

"I think you know something you don't want to share, eh? I think you know more than you make believe."

"Come on, Vanya, that's not my style."

Vanya chuckled. DeNafria did, too.

"Not usually," DeNafria added, "not with you. We're sharing here. I showed you the surveillance tapes."

He fast-forwarded the tape in the VCR a few seconds before stopping to hit PLAY again. This time Viktor Timkin and his bodyguard were recrossing Houston Street back to their car. DeNafria stopped the tape.

"I need something concrete," DeNafria said. "Something like what the fuck is going on would be a good starting point."

Vanya pointed to the screen. "I think he kills Yuri to clean mess," he said. "I think Yuri does film with woman, snuff film maybe, or something goes wrong and they kill woman by mistake, and Viktor kills Yuri and his crew to clean mess."

"What about contract killers Timkin might've supplied Joe LaRocca to kill Marino? That hit, the three guys killed in Sheepshead Bay, that could've been Timkin, no? Maybe LaRocca repaid the favor and killed Yuri's crew for Viktor Timkin."

Vanya lit a cigarette. "Timkin doesn't trust Italians to do this," he said. "Maybe Timkin helps LaRocca, but not without okay from Vignieri. Maybe what meeting was about, not pimp. No way Timkin lets Italians kill Yuri's people."

"You're sure? What about the guy hung himself at the Metropolitan Correctional Center today?"

Vanya shook his head. "Not same thing," he said. "Sadova was rat, eh? Timkin kills Yuri's crew."

"So what are LaRocca's guys doing with Timkin's pimp in Coney Island?"

"I don't know this," Vanya said. "You don't have anybody with LaRocca's crew?"

"A rat? Not us, not yet. The feds probably do, but they're not sharing."

"No one you can turn to make flip?"

"Not anybody the feds aren't on."

"Nobody you can squeeze?"

"Not like you, no."

Vanya looked up and frowned. "So this is bullshit, your questions."

"We can use your help."

"Yes, you can use help, and . . . ," Vanya said.

"I have a name."

Vanya chuckled again. "You want me to squeeze somebody," he said. "Next time just say so, eh? Saves time."

Chapter 25

SHE SAW THE Russian mobster exactly where the news articles said he would be. He stood on the edge of the curb and was smoking a long cigar. Two younger men in leather jackets stood facing him.

Agnes pulled into a spot alongside a parking meter a few hundred yards from the aquarium. She watched and waited while the three men talked near the curb. She wasn't sure if the Russian would take her message to his boss, the man named Viktor Timkin, but she had run out of options. If they were holding Jack, she had to do something besides trying to save herself.

Twenty minutes passed before the two younger men got

into a black BMW and took off. The man with the cigar started walking her way when her cell phone rang. Agnes peeked at the number but didn't recognize it. She answered anyway.

"Hello?"

"Agnes?"

It was the Russian accent again. "Who is this?" she asked.

"We have boyfriend."

Agnes swallowed hard. "What are you talking about?"

"Jack Russo is boyfriend, no?"

"Put him on."

"Maybe later. Where you are?"

"Put him on."

"Where you are?"

Agnes saw Mahalov was almost directly across the avenue from her. She disconnected the call and made a sharp U-turn. She pulled up alongside the Russian mobster.

"Excuse me," she called out the passenger window.

The Russian stopped to look at her. She waved him over.

"What I can do for you?" he asked with a big smile.

"Are you Mahalov?" she asked.

The Russian lost his smile. "Who you are?" he asked.

"I'm not a cop," she said. "I need to get some information to your boss. Viktor Timkin, right?"

The Russian was squinting now. "What you are talking about, lady?"

"Are you Mahalov? Igor Mahalov?"

This time the Russian waved her off. "I don't have time to jerk off, eh?"

Agnes pulled the gun from her jacket pocket and held it between her legs. "Hey!" she yelled.

The Russian ignored her and started walking. She leaned on the horn. When she saw he wasn't going to stop, she continued leaning on the horn as she drove alongside him. He covered his ears and finally stopped. He looked at her a moment before approaching the car again.

"What the fock you want?" he said.

Agnes raised the gun so he could see it.

"You want to shoot me?" he said.

"No, but I need to get a message to your boss," she said. "I'm Agnes Lynn. He's looking for me. I need him to set Jack Russo free, and then I'll do whatever he wants."

"I don't know what you are talking about," he said. "You want to give me a ride maybe?"

He reached for the door and Agnes pointed the gun at his head. "Don't," she said.

The Russian stopped. "What you want from me, lady? I'm busy, eh?"

"Call him for me," Agnes said. "Call your boss right now."

The Russian shrugged. "I don't have phone."

"Yeah, you do. I saw you using one before."

He smiled again. "What happens I don't make call?"

"I'll shoot you," Agnes said.

"So shoot me," he said.

Agnes shot him.

•◆•

"You got an ex-cop was abducted by the Russian mob, you're nuts to even consider not reporting it, you and your partner," special agent Tommy Pirella told his former girlfriend.

"The guy winds up dead, you'll both be persecuted and rightfully so."

Pirella had showed up with a bag of Chinese food a few minutes after Nance stopped home. He had just ended a long day's surveillance of wiseguys playing cards on the back patio of a home on Long Island.

"We are going to report it," Nance said. "We're just trying to stall for the guy's sake. From the looks of this, the sooner his name is public, the sooner they'll kill him. They already killed a lot of people."

"This about the bodies in Spring Creek the other day?"

"That seems to be part of it. We're working with the head of the red mob squad, Vanya Koloff. You know him?"

"I do indeed," Pirella said. "Very privileged gentleman from what I hear."

"What's that supposed to mean?"

"Let's just say he has special dispensation."

"How so?"

Pirella took a bite from his egg roll. He spoke as he chewed. "He's known to go a little overboard with the redfellas. To be fair, from what I understand, it's the only way to deal with those guys. The Russian mob got a big head start when they came over here in the seventies. We were busy infiltrating the Italian mob. Now we're all playing catch-up. Vanya Koloff does his thing, and people above him look the other way."

"Like what?" Nance asked. "Stop dancing around it. Does his thing like what?"

Pirella lit a fresh cigarette. "I stopped boozing six months now, and I still can't stop myself with these things," he said, then pointed at her. "Your fault, I might add."

They had been involved for a year before Pirella was reassigned to Miami. When Nance refused to make the move south, he ended their relationship. Two years passed before he was brought back to New York. When he returned six months ago, Nance was no longer interested.

"It was my fault you gave me an ultimatum?" she asked. "Come on, what's this guy Koloff do? He looks rough, physically, but he didn't seem to be the type that acted without thinking things through. I think he annoyed Moss because of it, the way he kept focusing on one thing. 'The reason,' he called it, why this one stepbrother might've whacked the other one."

Pirella waited for more. Nance used a fork to cut a piece of shrimp toast in half.

"What?" she said. "Come on, Tommy, what's he do, his thing?"

"He likes to work with crabs, the big blue claws. He likes to use them during interrogations. That's one I heard about. Good source, too."

"And nobody talks because . . . ."

"Who're they gonna talk to?"

Nance dipped a piece of shrimp toast in a small tub of mustard.

"Another one?" Pirella said. "He went up to Saratoga to grab some Russki on the run, caught him and brought the guy to a bee farm. Supposedly exposed the guy's legs from the knees to his feet to a disturbed hive. The guy wouldn't talk. Koloff exposed his privates. The guy eventually talked, but he had to get stung a few hundred times first."

Nance was suspicious. "And you're saying Internal Affairs doesn't touch him?"

"From what I hear, they don't go near the Russian mob

squad," Pirella said. "It's a choice job you want that extra excitement in your life. Of course the risks are real. Worse that can happen to me watching wiseguys I get a gravy stain on my shirt. The redfellas will kill you to test a new gun they bought off the street."

"They all Russian, Koloff's squad?"

"I don't know. But they all speak the language. My guess is we're keeping an eye on them, sort of." He turned his face to one side and held a hand up to cover his eyes. "Like this, know what I mean?"

"What about you guys? You have a red squad. What do they say?"

"Ours is involved in the higher-profile stuff," Pirella said. "Money laundering, weapons dealing, and some drug stuff the Russians do with the cartels. For the most part, we're ignoring the street stuff, leaving it to NYPD and the OC task forces. Don't forget we're also looking for Islamic fundamentalists and other crazies. We're stretched pretty thin since nine-eleven."

Nance was forking lo mein into her mouth.

"This was about the floaters in Brooklyn, right?" Pirella asked.

"I said yes. It's where I met him. Moss and I showed up before Koloff. He gave us a quick rundown of what he thought had happened."

"You interested in this guy or what?"

Nance ignored the innuendo. "There's something else we need to look into," she said. "A homicide detective named Lyons. Michael Lyons. Ever hear of him?"

Pirella shook his head.

"He's got a dirty rep," Nance said. "Last night, early this

morning, he investigated some pimp who was killed in Harlem. The woman that was found on the beach, she's our homicide. She worked for the murdered pimp. Rachel Wilson was her name. She was cut up bad. Tortured, it looks like. This morning we got the call from the ex-cop we're positive now was abducted. Then there's a woman we're trying to save, apparently the one the Russians are after. She was Rachel's friend, a woman named Agnes Lynn, and now she's looking to do something on her own and doesn't want our help."

"International intrigue," Pirella said.

"Yeah, well, Moss wasn't into this case when we first got it, but now he's fixated because of Lyons. I have to get back from here and try to find this woman before she turns up dead, too."

"You talking with your Russian friend about this?"

"He knows a lot more than us right now. Why?"

"Be careful of stepping into unchartered waters, my dear. The Russians aren't known for their love of African Americans."

Nance feigned interest. "Really?"

"How many sisters you know living with comrades?"

Nance called Pirella a jerk.

"Well, what the comrade have to say?"

"He gave us some ideas."

Pirella sighed. "Well, if you want I could ask around, see if we're looking into any of this. I got a friend with OC mentioned something about the Corelli thing. The dissension was between the guy was clipped in Sheepshead Bay and the guy was acting boss, Joe LaRocca. Now that that's settled and LaRocca's the new boss, my friend might be able to tell you something."

"No, thanks," said Nance as she wiped her hands with a

paper towel. "Your special agent friends are too self-important. The one time I had to deal with you people, it was nothing but bullshit and bureaucracy."

"Whereas your Russian friend is suave and smooth?"

"Not to mention handsome."

"Uh-oh," Pirella said. "And here I was ready to offer you a real meal of Peking duck at a real-to-life Chinese restaurant next time."

"To get down my pants again?"

"At this stage a hand job'd do just fine."

Nance bagged the leftover containers, set them on his lap, and opened the apartment door. When he stood up to leave, Nance held the door for him.

Pirella extended his free hand to shake. He said, "I'll assume you won't tongue-kiss me good-bye."

Nance rubbed his free hand in both of hers.

"Consider this your hand job, Tommy," she said. "Thanks for the meal."

•◆•

After several years of discontent with police work, Jack had resigned from the New York City police department at age thirty-five. The long hours of detective work, coupled with a failing marriage and a lacking sense of purposefulness, had brought on an early midlife crisis. Jack yearned for freedom from conformity. He'd spent a total of twelve years and six months on the job. His life had been mapped out by police procedure through what he had believed were the best years of his life.

After killing an armed robber during a stickup his last year of service, Jack was frightened by the lack of guilt he felt after the incident. It wasn't until after he was promoted for his performance in the face of danger that he realized he needed to quit police work.

He divorced the same year, a full six years ago, but his relationship with his ex-wife was mostly good. His parents were both dead. His only brother, two years his junior, had been killed in a terrorist bombing while on assignment in Israel. John Russo had been a freelance journalist.

He had often wondered if his brother was killed instantly or if he had lingered after the bomb exploded. He did know that John was pronounced dead at the scene of the carnage when medical help arrived. Jack knew that his brother had never made it off the bus alive.

It was a thought that bothered him now, so close to his own death, he was sure. He saw his brother's eyes over and over and imagined their look at the moment of the explosion.

Then he thought about Nicholas and how he had already disappointed his son by not making it to the hospital today. The thought of never seeing him again hurt deep. He closed his eyes and envisioned his son lying helpless in a hospital bed.

After a few minutes, anger replaced emotion, and Jack could focus again.

His ribs and back were sore. He could taste his own blood. He knew his lips were swollen and that he was missing at least one tooth. It didn't matter. He had to do something to try to save himself.

He opened his eyes again and saw Michael Lyons standing

across the room between two Russians. The cop had been beaten. His face was bruised and bloody.

The stocky one in charge was also there. One of the Russians was holding a small handgun, Lyons's throwaway piece, Jack guessed. The Russian tossed the gun on the bed. It landed on the near corner. Lyons looked at it. The one in charge slapped Lyons across the face.

"What you thinking, Michael?" the Russian said. "You going to shoot us? All of us?"

The other Russians laughed.

Jack wet his bruised lips with his tongue and swallowed what little saliva he had. A bottle of water was handed to him. He sipped from it slowly. When he looked up again, he noticed Michael Lyons was wearing handcuffs.

Lyons turned to the one in charge. "I'm a fuckin' cop," he said. "You really think you'll get away with this?"

The one in charge didn't answer.

Lyons said, "You think I don't have you guys on tape? This is the first place they'll come looking for you, you dumb shit."

Jack realized what was going on. He smirked at Lyons. The dirty cop saw it.

"The fuck you looking at, Russo?"

Jack managed to whisper, "You piece of shit."

"What he say?" Lyons asked. He tried to step forward. One of the Russians pulled the cop back by his hair.

"He says you are piece of shit," the one in charge told Lyons.

Lyons was punched in the crotch. The cop winced before dropping to his knees. His handcuffs were removed and his leather jacket was pulled off and tossed on the bed. Jack noticed the jacket had partially covered the gun.

"I'm a fuckin' cop," Lyons gasped. He rubbed his left wrist with his right hand.

"Shhh," the one in charge said. "You talk too much. All the focking time you talk."

Lyons looked up from the floor. "You can't do this," he said. "Where's Timkin?"

The one in charge motioned to one of his men. Lyons was kicked in the face. Blood spilled from his broken nose. Both his hands were cuffed again, behind his back this time.

Jack managed another smirk.

Chapter 26

JOSEPH LAROCCA LOST his FBI tail without much trouble once he crossed the street to where two of his men were buying frankfurters at a stand across from Battery Park. He had timed the move to coincide with a four-thirty ferry departure. Another two of his men were already waiting at the ferry gate in case they needed to stall the trip.

LaRocca had waited until he was sure the agents following him had remained in their car before he hustled to the ferry. His men were at the frankfurter stand to obstruct the agents if they followed.

By the time the agents reacted and got out of the car, the ferry had already left.

LaRocca was there to meet with Fat Tony Gangi. The big man was waiting for LaRocca across from the concession stand. He offered LaRocca a piece of hot pretzel covered with mustard. The new boss of the Corelli crime family respectfully declined.

"What's it about?" Gangi asked.

LaRocca leaned in close to Gangi's ear to whisper. "These crazy Russians," he said. "You're not gonna believe what two of my guys come to me with."

Gangi glanced around the area before motioning at LaRocca to get up. The two men left their seats and headed toward the front of the ferry. They stepped outside and were hit full in the face with an icy wind.

"Jesus Christ," LaRocca said. "Fuckin' hurts, this wind."

"Turn your back," Gangi said.

The two men huddled together with their backs to the wind.

LaRocca said, "One of Timkin's people told my guys they might have a snuff film for sale."

Gangi was confused. "The fuck is that?"

"When they film a porno and kill the broad," LaRocca said. "Sick shit."

Gangi was mortified. "Are you kidding me?"

"It's what the guy down the aquarium there, the one handles the Russian hookers, Mahalov, what he told my guys. He said he heard it from the other guy handles their porn, the one at the video store on Brighton Avenue."

"Jesus Christ."

"Yeah, what I was thinking. Just what we need now, a fuckin' scandal to bring some more attention."

A gust of wind whistled in Gangi's right ear. He turned to his left and bumped into LaRocca.

"We know this as fact?" Gangi asked.

"It's what my guys came to me with," LaRocca said. "Whether it's real or not, what Mahalov told them, who the fuck knows? If it is, though, it's not good."

"If it is, they can forget taking Marino's old turf, I'll tell you that much," Gangi said.

"What do we do in the meantime?"

"Disassociate, completely. Nobody goes near those guys. Keep your people out of Coney Island."

"What if Mahalov gives them a call?"

"They don't answer it. They're involved in that shit, they're stupid enough to talk about it, we can't be connected."

Another gust of wind forced LaRocca to cover his face with both hands.

"Now I know why the stepbrother isn't around anymore," Gangi said.

"Yurell?"

"Yuri."

"He involved in this snuff thing?"

"What's the difference? I'll find out what I can from Timkin, but I guarantee you when I mention this Mallov, whatever the fuck his name is, he won't be around much longer afterward."

"I wouldn't mind splitting Marino's turf with you," LaRocca said. "Be a shame it goes to waste."

"Yeah, well, I hope you don't mind going to war, because that's what we might have to do if Timkin is behind this shit. There are certain things you can't do. Videotaping a murder is up there near the top of the list. They made it a fuckin' porn movie, and we'll do ourselves a big favor taking them out for it. Even the feds'll appreciate it."

The ferry began a turn toward Staten Island. LaRocca shivered from a sudden blast of wind. "Sounds good to me," he said, "but can we go back inside now? My fucking face is burning out here from this wind."

Gangi motioned toward the door. The two mob leaders stepped back inside the ferry and out of the cold.

•◆•

Agnes didn't realize how calm she was after shooting the Russian mobster until a woman in a van that was stopped at a red light alongside her beeped to get her attention.

"Do you know how to get to the BQE?" the woman asked.

Agnes pointed straight ahead. "This turns into the Prospect Expressway, and then you'll see the BQE on your left," she told the woman. "Just stay straight on this."

The woman thanked Agnes. They both proceeded ahead when the light changed.

She was using the same route in reverse on her way back to Manhattan. It was sunny but cold outside. She turned the heat up, because she had kept the rear windows opened a crack to get rid of the cordite smell.

She couldn't stop thinking about Jack and wondered if she had made it worse for him by shooting the Russian. She was anxious for the Russians to call her back and grew nervous when she had to take the Battery Tunnel for fear she wouldn't receive their call.

She checked messages when she was out of the tunnel. There was one from the detective. She didn't bother listening.

Twenty minutes later she parked in an open lot on the Lower East Side. She found a room at a cheap hotel on Avenue C that accepted cash in advance for a two-night stay and didn't require credit cards for incidentals.

She ran back out to a deli for something to eat and drink. Then she stopped at a Gap to buy herself a few changes of clothes and a new winter jacket. She stopped at a pharmacy for lipstick, eyeliner, blush, and perfume, then at a shoe store for a pair of heels. She was anxious when she headed back to her hotel room, but needed to bring back the jacket she had borrowed the night before. She took a cab north on Park Avenue and had the driver loop around the street where the deli was. She gave him half the fare and asked him to wait while she dropped off the jacket. The man from the night before wasn't in yet. She left the jacket without asking for her money back.

When she came back out of the deli, she suddenly felt vulnerable on the street. She had the driver use the FDR to take her downtown. She was dropped off in front of the dump where she had taken the room on Avenue C. She had just gotten settled in her room when her cell phone rang at exactly six o'clock.

"Agnes Lynn," she answered.

"What you are doing shooting people?" the man with the accent said.

"Let me speak to Jack," she said.

"You don't kill Mahalov," the man said. "Just wound."

"Let me speak to Jack. I'll do whatever you want if you let him go."

"Where you are?"

"Arkansas."

"You make joke, eh? I call you back in two minute. Don't go away."

"Wait!" Agnes yelled, but the connection had been broken.

• ◆ •

"What turn around is turn around again," Boris Chenkov had told his son before the two were separated more than fifteen years ago.

It was the night Pavel left Russia for America. His father, the captain of a crime crew in St. Petersburg, had purposely given his son the advice in broken English.

"Sometimes you are fight, sometimes you are turn around," Boris had told him. "Sometimes you turn around, is turn around again, eh?"

It was a lesson Chenkov had learned many times since his father first explained it to him, how patience on the street was sometimes more important than showing balls. It was a lesson about to bear the sweet fruit of revenge.

Since Yuri Timkin was gone, Chenkov expected to move up in the organization, maybe even run the new territory in Coney Island with his crew. He might also become second in command under Viktor Timkin. It was the next position in line and one step closer to what Chenkov had craved since first becoming the head of his own crew, being boss someday.

Although Timkin had always favored the more cerebral earners who worked the money-laundering end of their business, it was Chenkov and his crew who held the bread-and-butter street businesses of the organization together. It was Chenkov and his men who were the enforcers.

Today it was up to him to handle the cop. He enjoyed watching the big mouth squirm. Michael Lyons had irritated Chenkov since they first met. When Chenkov thought about the verbal abuse he had taken from Lyons the day before and again earlier downstairs in the lounge, a rush of adrenaline fueled his blood lust.

He thought about his father's advice, how what "turned around is turn around again," and he called the woman back, Agnes Lynn.

"Go ahead," she answered.

"Agnes?" Chenkov asked.

"Go ahead," she repeated.

"Listen careful, okay? Don't get nervous. Just listen."

There was a pause. The woman remained silent.

Chenkov walked up close behind Michael Lyons and held the phone alongside the nine-millimeter he used to shoot the cop twice in the back of the head.

Chapter 27

AGNES HEARD THE gunshot through the phone. She gasped, buckled at the knees, and everything went black.

Agnes saw Jack's eyes open wide from the shock of the bullet entering his skull. She saw his head explode with brain fragments. She saw the brain matter splatter against an endless white wall as she tried to scream. She saw her mouth open wide, but there was no sound coming from it.

Agnes felt a sharp pain in her chest and couldn't move. She was paralyzed in darkness.

It had happened before. After she killed Kenneth Becker in

her friend's Las Vegas condo, the police had found Agnes sitting on a kitchen chair with a handgun in her lap. She couldn't see then either.

One psychiatrist had told her it was because her rage had been released through the firing of a gun and that her mind had acted as a filter, sorting out her consciousness to bring her back from where her rage had taken her. Another expert in the field of psychology agreed that the blindness was a defense mechanism in the form of a mental catharsis, but one that required she make it all a dream.

Yet another doctor, a general practitioner Agnes had gone to, suggested her blindness might be a way she hid from who she really was.

"Excuse me?" Agnes had asked him.

"Not everybody needs protection," he had said. "Perhaps there's a part of you that's comfortable with what happened. Killing your attacker, I mean."

"Are you calling me a predator?" Agnes had asked.

"Some might," he had said, "because of your line of work, at least. There might be some other underlying urge you have."

Agnes was upset at what the doctor had told her that day, but his words had never left her. There was only one man she hadn't been able to manipulate, and she was still comfortable attributing that single failure to her father's weakness rather than her own. If she was a predator, so be it.

The hysterical blindness she experienced after killing Kenneth Becker had lasted for hours. Now her vision returned much quicker. She was choking as she tried to breathe again.

When she was composed, Agnes saw herself in the mirror

across from the bed. She heard a persistent beeping sound and realized she was still holding her cell phone.

"What?" she said.

The Russian said, "You are there, Agnes?"

She thought he was playing with her. She didn't respond.

"Agnes?"

"You motherfucker," she growled.

"What you are mad for?" he asked.

She imagined him standing over Jack's body as he taunted her. He was making her pay for not being on the street last night instead of Lorelei; for not being in her apartment the afternoon they had kicked her door in; for managing to escape them for longer than she should have, and if she hadn't, maybe Jack and Lorelei would still be alive.

"I'll kill you myself," she said. "I swear to God. I will fucking kill you myself."

The Russian took his time. She continued holding the phone to her ear.

"Okay," he said. "Stay calm, lady."

"Fuck you," she said.

"Boyfriend is here. You want to say hello?"

Agnes's eyes opened wide. She couldn't speak.

"Agnes?" he said. "Hold."

She closed her eyes in anticipation of Jack's voice. She saw his face again. Then he was on the phone.

"Don't do it," he said. "Whatever they want, don't do it."

"Jack! Are you okay?"

She heard the Russian grumble something in his language. Then she heard a loud slap.

"Jack!" she yelled again.

"Boyfriend is fine," the Russian said. He was breathing hard as he spoke. "Is stupid man but is fine."

"Let me talk to him," Agnes said.

"You already talk. Enough for now, eh?"

"Please."

"You come see him," the Russian said. "You want to make trade, what you say. You come and we let boyfriend go."

"Don't do it!" she heard Jack yell in the background one more time. "Agnes, don't!"

The Russian mumbled something under his breath again. Then she heard a series of thuds. A long pause followed.

"Hello?" the Russian said. He was breathing harder.

"What happened?"

"He gets kick in stomach for big mouth."

"Leave him alone."

"He is fine."

"Bring him to a hospital and I'll come to you," she said.

"What you are talking, lady? You come to where we say. Then we let boyfriend go."

"No, I don't trust you. Leave him at an emergency room somewhere I can see, and I'll come to you."

"I give you address, you come see him."

"I'll do whatever you want, but you have to let Jack go first."

The Russian didn't respond.

"Hello?" she said.

"I call back in two hour," he said.

The connection was gone. Agnes thanked God Jack was still alive. She looked at her watch and saw it was nearly six thirty. It would take her an hour to get back to Brighton Beach. Then she would have another hour to find the boss of the Russian mob and either work out a deal to free Jack or kill Viktor Timkin herself.

•◆•

Lisa Russo had called the police in her attempt to reach Jack's ex-partner. She was told Jerry Klein was on vacation. She tried reporting Jack as a missing person and was frustrated when she learned he would have to be missing twenty-four hours before anything could be done.

That had been several hours ago. At six fifteen, a Detective Robert Moss found her in the waiting area on the floor where her son was recovering from his leg surgery. He introduced himself before expressing his regrets for her son's injury.

"Where's Jack?" Lisa asked.

The detective explained what had happened. Lisa shook from the news.

"His son is upstairs recovering," she said. "He's been asking for his father all day. What am I supposed to tell him?"

"We're doing our best to find him, ma'am," the detective said. "We need for you to remain calm, though. We need you to not contact anyone about this, not yet. Jack's life depends on us being able to move with stealth. If the media gets hold of this story, it could be dangerous for him. Right now the people we think might be holding Jack aren't aware that we know he's missing. If his abduction gets out, we're afraid they might panic."

Lisa shook her head. "I didn't call them," she said. "I called you guys. Jack had a partner he's still friendly with, Jerry Klein, but he's away on vacation. I tried to report Jack as a missing person, but they said he had to be missing twenty-four hours."

"Our department is aware of what's going on," the detective said. "I just came from headquarters with this. We'll be turning it over to the FBI tomorrow if we don't find him tonight."

"Jesus Christ."

"I understand, ma'am," Moss said. He took both her hands in his. "You have to be strong. Try to be strong."

Lisa collapsed into his chest. The detective held her while glancing up at the clock above the doorway leading to the elevators. Lisa spotted Paul coming back from the men's room and reached for him.

"What's going on?" Paul asked.

"It's Jack," she said.

Paul looked from Lisa to the detective. "What happened?"

"Jack's been abducted," the detective said. "We're trying to locate him now."

"Jesus," Paul said. He looked to Lisa. "Maybe it'll help then."

"What?" Lisa asked.

"I stopped off at the garage on my way back from the house before. I told the guy there works on the CBS vans about it. He said he'd give his friend a call, the guy drives the van for one of the reporters."

"Shit," the detective said.

"Paul, why?" Lisa said. "Why'd you do that?"

"I thought I was helping," Paul said. He pointed at Lisa. "You were all crazy before when you got that call. Jack this and Jack that again. Hey, I thought I was doing good."

The detective handed Paul his cell phone. "Call your friend back and tell him to squash it."

Paul turned to Lisa. "The fuck is going on?"

Lisa pointed to the cell phone. "Make the call," she said. "Now, Paul, please."

•◆•

"Michael Lyons is missing," Nance said. "He's the cop we think is dirty."

Vanya was sipping coffee from a Styrofoam container at the Canarsie Pier. He looked out over the choppy water and had to turn his back to a gust of cold wind.

"Where is your partner?" he asked.

"Trying to stop the local news from airing the story about Jack Russo being abducted," Nance said. She buried her hands inside her jacket pockets.

Vanya shook his head. "Oh, no, Anita," he said.

"I know, I know. It wasn't us, though. It was Russo's ex-wife. She has a boyfriend or something, and he said something to somebody with the news."

"He is dead when television shows his face."

"Bob is trying to stop it," Nance said.

"He has to, eh?"

"He's trying."

"Why he doesn't want to talk with me, your partner?"

"Because you're mob squad, and he assumes you won't share information with us."

"Is common belief. Sometimes is true. Why I'm not sharing?"

"Until this ex-cop was kidnapped, I was only concerned about one thing in this, the woman who was butchered. Now that an ex-cop is involved and there's another woman who might get herself killed . . . ."

Vanya said, "There is also an Arab involved."

"Huh? Who?"

"I don't know."

"Where'd you hear it?"

"Barber cuts woman's hair. Viktor Timkin doesn't know about him, or barber is dead, too. Then we find porn dealer in Brighton Beach contracts actors for Yuri Timkin. We find them in canal."

"This is all tied together. Can we arrest anyone? It sounds like we can."

"For what? Barber is dead man if we let him go. Porn dealer is same. They aren't there for woman's murder. They can talk, but nothing important."

Nance bit her lower lip. "Shit."

"We need Arab."

"Do you know anything about him?"

"Not yet, no. Just is close to Viktor Timkin. Maybe FBI knows who Arab is."

"But?"

"Maybe FBI protects, too. Maybe they watch him. My guys don't see Arab. They don't sit on Yuri Timkin crew last week. He's idiot, eh? He does something, everybody knows. No need to watch him. Why Viktor kills stepbrother's crew, all of them, so problem goes away."

"What did the Arab do with Rachel? Why were actors involved?"

Vanya sighed.

Nance grabbed his free arm. "Are we talking about a snuff film? Is that what happened?"

"Maybe," he said.

"Jesus Christ. And, what, the FBI has something going on and we have to back off?"

"I don't know this about FBI. Why we don't go to them first, though. If FBI knows Arab, investigation is over."

"What about the Italians? Those hits with the Corelli people."

"Viktor Timkin is friend to all, but only one really. He goes where strength is—Vignieri, not Corelli. If he helps Corelli, is with Vignieri blessing."

"Fuck me. How do we dance around the FBI?"

"People around this are dead," Vanya said. "Viktor Timkin cleans mess. Why?"

"Because he needs the Arab. For what?"

"Or because he doesn't need mess."

Nance was confused.

"What has happened, all the killing, is nothing compare it to snuff film is public."

"He's trying to keep his name clean?"

"Just from this, yes, I think so. Today is another shooting in Coney Island. I don't know details yet. I get call from one of my guys."

"Another Russian?"

"I don't know."

"I want to find this Arab," Nance said. "I have to."

"You are crusader."

"For this one I am, yeah."

Vanya smiled.

"Don't you patronize me now," Nance said.

"What this means?"

Nance said, "Look, I understand the rules need to be

stretched sometimes. I heard a few stories about you. I don't mind stretching the rules for this one."

Vanya chuckled. "What stories you hear? Bee hive? Rats? Dogs? Crabs?"

"Not the rats or dogs," Nance said.

"Alligator? You hear this one?"

"No."

Vanya waved at her to join him on a bench facing the water. Nance did so.

"Is no alligator," he told her. "I make joke."

Nance waited for more.

"I am from small town in Russia, near Moscow," he said. "Mother dies when I am born. Father is hard man. Working man. Raises me alone. Takes no one for himself, no women. I am thirteen, *Vors*, Russian mobsters, come to extort him. He refuses. They kill him. I go to live with uncle. Uncle is drunk and thief and whoremaster. Sleeps with his own daughter. I run away, pay for papers, and join army. I am fifteen. Army is dirty like government. I am sixteen in war in Chechnya. Friends I make I see die. Others are gangsters when they get out. I join police."

Nance waited for more.

"In Russia police is like government is like army, all corrupt," Vanya said. "Are good people, Russians, but poverty permits Mafiya there to run country. Officials, politicians, everybody. I survive there because I learn to ignore, to lose feeling." He touched his chest. "Here."

"When did you come here?"

"I have friend there," Vanya continued. "Detective friend is homosexual. Good man. He makes arrest of banker in Moscow is crook. Banker has powerful friends. My friend is exposed. He is found hanged, eh? They say he hangs himself, but he was murdered. I know who's does this and I find them."

Nance put up a hand. "No need to confess to me," she said.

"I come here," he said, "because I can do nothing there."

"Do you have family here?"

"None," Vanya said.

"Friends?"

"Police."

"Your squad?"

He nodded.

"You afraid to have family here?"

"I am alone, I can do job. I have family, I can't do job. Is most my squad. No family. No wives, no kids."

"Will you go after this Arab?" she asked.

"Yes, of course."

"I want to help."

"I know."

"I mean it."

"You are helping already. We helping each other."

She wrote down Agnes Lynn's cell phone number. She handed it to him.

"Maybe she'll answer if it's a new number, although we tried that a few times already. It's Agnes Lynn, the woman hiding from them."

"She hears my accent, she doesn't think I'm police."

"We have to try," Nance said. "Please."

"Okay. Now?"

"Soon as you get a chance," she said. "Can I ask you something else?"

"Of course," he said.

"Is it true about Russians and African Americans, that you don't care for us?"

"Is bullshit," Vanya said.

Nance smiled.

Chapter 28

Moss met up with Nance at the traffic circle at the Canarsie Pier. The two sat in Nance's car. Moss was cramped. He had to turn sideways on the passenger seat to accommodate his long legs.

"What happened?" Nance asked.

"They're gonna air it in a few minutes, they haven't already," Moss said. "They didn't care it might get the guy killed. What Pirella say?"

"Nothing useful. We shouldn't play with the Russo situation regarding reporting it, and he thought Vanya is a psycho sadist who gets away with stuff nobody else could, because he's going after the Russian mob."

"He mention anything about Vanya being on their payroll?"

"What?" Nance said. "Where'd you hear that?"

"I didn't," Moss said, "but it's a legitimate question. Suppose he is? Who would know? Maybe he beats up on some low-level muscle every now and then to make it look good."

"What is it with you and Pirella and these fucking pissing contests?"

"I don't want you clouding your judgment, partner, that's all. I know you like the man. I'm sure your ex-boyfriend figured that out, too."

"It has nothing to do with my judgment, Bob. I'm fucking fine. Okay? My judgment is fucking fine, too. Jesus Christ."

"Okay," Moss said. "In the meantime, what he say?"

"He thinks it was a snuff film they were shooting, that the older stepbrother is trying to clean the mess before it becomes public."

"That the reason he kept mentioning the day we met him?"

"I guess so."

"Well, Lyons has disappeared. If he was involved, it makes sense he took off. We're trying for a warrant to search his house now."

"You think Lyons is gone?"

"That or dead. If he was playing ball with the redfellas, he might be either."

"Vanya also said he thinks it has to do with some Arab, the snuff film."

"An Arab? That sounds federal to me."

"It might be, except Rachel Wilson is our case and Jack Russo was our connection, and now Agnes Lynn is all we have."

"He really thinks it was a snuff film? You know how many of those have been documented in the history of law enforcement? Something like zero."

"He thinks it might be because of how the Russian mob went after one of their own crews. He thinks it was probably unsanctioned, what happened to Rachel Wilson."

"That doesn't make it a snuff film."

"The two dead porn actors might. Plus the way she was found. The guy who shaved Rachel Wilson's hair said it was for the Arab, the haircut he gave Rachel."

"Koloff arrest the hairdresser?"

"I don't know. Isn't it enough what he found out already?"

"He torture anybody to get it?"

"I didn't ask him," Nance said.

They looked each other off. Nance tried calling Agnes Lynn again. She hung up when the answering machine picked up.

"She talked to me before," she said. "Now she won't."

"We may have to wait for her to call us."

"And if she doesn't?"

"I don't know," Moss said.

Nance's cell phone rang.

"Yeah," she answered.

"Woman shoots Igor Mahalov a couple hours ago," Vanya said.

"What? Who's Mahalov? Where?"

"Mahalov is Russian pimp. Handles prostitutes come from Russia. He's shot today and brought to private doctor in

Brighton for wound. Somebody calls it in, says woman shoots him and drives off. My guys just find out and call me."

"Jesus Christ, where are you?"

"Bay Ridge. Fourth Avenue, outside Tiffany Diner. My guys are wearing blue hats. They are to make an arrest. Don't get involved, eh?"

"What?"

"My guys are going to arrest someone at the diner. They are undercover wearing blue hats. Don't get involved."

"Okay, we're on our way."

"Don't forget, blue hats."

"Right," Nance said, then she killed the connection and turned to Moss. "Agnes Lynn shot a Russian gangster this afternoon."

Moss squinted. "What?"

"What Vanya just said. She apparently pulled up to some guy and shot him."

"Jesus. So she's armed and dangerous and taking on the Russian mob. What next?"

"I told Vanya we'd meet him in Bay Ridge."

"Why there?"

"We need to coordinate with him."

"And why's that?"

"He knows the Russian mob. He knows Brighton Beach."

Moss said, "I'll leave my car. Let's go."

Nance put the car into drive and drove around the circle, through the red light on Rockaway Parkway, and made the left onto the entrance for the Belt Parkway heading west.

"You okay?" she asked.

"Yeah," Moss said.

"You're worried about Russo, I know."

"Let's just hope Agnes Lynn doesn't get him killed."

·◆·

Agnes had put on tight black slacks and a matching top that hugged her chest. She used fire-red lipstick, red nail polish, and Obsession perfume. She wore black heels and wrapped herself with a shawl instead of wearing the new coat she stashed in a shopping bag. She fit the handgun in the black handbag in her purse.

She was cold when she first got in the car. She listened to traffic reports until the noise disturbed her ability to think. Agnes had a lot on her mind and wasn't quite sure what she could or would do.

She took the FDR Drive to the Brooklyn Battery Tunnel to the Prospect Expressway to Ocean Parkway. Agnes thought about Jack the entire trip. No other man, including her father, had ever been there for her the same way. Jack had come to help her with his son in the hospital. He had come knowing it was the Russian mob trying to kill her. He had come risking his own life, and now she had to save him.

If push came to shove, she would go wherever the Russians told her. The thought of surviving Jack was too much to contemplate.

When she could see the el a few lights ahead on Ocean Parkway, Agnes noticed that traffic was bunched up near the intersection. The closer she got to the water, the stronger the wind gusts. She felt the car being pushed by the wind. Then she saw the accident under the el; two cars had hit head on.

Sirens filled the air a few moments later. Agnes turned left off Ocean Parkway.

Her initial plan was to walk into a known Russian mob hangout called Club Kruschev. It was located at Brighton Beach Avenue and Brighton Seventh Street, but didn't open until nine o'clock. She knew there would be people setting up, though, and she hoped to approach one of them.

As she searched for Brighton Seventh Street, Agnes's cell phone rang. She didn't recognize the number, but answered the call anyway.

"What?" she said.

"Agnes?"

The Russian, except his voice didn't sound the same this time.

"What?" she repeated.

"This is Agnes Lynn?"

"Who's this?"

"I am Detective Vanya Koloff with organized crime unit."

"Yeah, right."

"I spoke with Detective Nance. You spoke with her, correct?"

Agnes pulled into an open spot alongside a fire hydrant.

"Keep talking," she said.

•◆•

The weird thing was how peaceful he felt immediately after Michael Lyons was killed. Jack had been expecting to die himself. When Lyons had first appeared in the room, Jack was sure it would be Lyons who'd perform the execution. Then the situation turned, and Jack knew that Lyons had become expendable to the Russian mob.

He had once been on a buy and bust when things went wrong and Jack was left on the middle floor of a dark stairway with drug thugs above and below him. Shots rang out and he was sure he would die then, too, until something triggered his anger enough to switch him from a defensive position to outright attack. He chose the bad guys above and raced up the stairway before they knew what was happening.

The two guys on the floor above were shocked that a gun was pointed at them before they were ready. They both dropped their weapons, a nine-millimeter and a sawed-off shotgun. Then they let Jack cuff them without incident.

Jack told them to call out to their friends below. When the thugs did as they were told, he could hear the men below scatter down the stairway. They ran out of the building and into the police backup out on the street. The criminals had been rounded up without a single shot fired.

He was given a meritorious citation for bravery for his actions that day, although Jack never thought it was more than a temporary loss of sanity that had sent him charging up a dark stairway with his department-issued Glock.

He briefly wondered whether it was shock he was experiencing now, because he still wasn't afraid of dying. After the cleanup crew arrived with buckets and saws and tarpaulins, they dragged the dead cop's body into the bathroom.

Jack felt his composure returning, and he thought about an escape.

The first thing he realized was that his hands were no longer cuffed. He had been pummeled pretty hard before Lyons arrived. He remembered the Russians had removed the cuffs and blindfold when he was first brought to the room.

He could feel his facial bruises when he swallowed. His right side ached when he tried to turn.

The guy in charge had left the room mumbling something about Coney Island. Then the other two guards stepped out a minute later.

The guys dismembering Michael Lyons were working in the bathroom. Jack was safe unless he backed into their line of sight. He saw that he could make it to the door undetected, but he didn't know if the guys with the guns were out there taking a break or if they had left thinking the guys in the bathroom would stand guard.

Jack glanced around the room to see what he might use as a weapon and did a double take when he saw what he guessed was Lyons's throwaway piece, the .380 Colt, on the corner of the bed. His eyes opened wide at the fortunate discovery.

The gun was half covered with Lyons's leather jacket. Jack forced himself to crawl across the floor to the bed. He grabbed the gun and did his best to stand. A sharp pain on his right side momentarily stopped him. He remained motionless until he heard an electric saw cutting through what he assumed were Michael Lyons's bones.

Then he racked the slide on the .380 to chamber a round.

Chapter 29

"Russian mob doesn't deal," the guy claiming to be a Russian detective said. "Don't waste time playing games."

"Fuck you," Agnes said. Her eyes darted from the side-view mirrors to the rearview. She had pulled over to hear what the Russian had to say.

"You can't shoot them all, eh? You shoot one today, but there are too many."

"What do you want?"

"You are going to find friend?"

"Maybe."

"He is kidnapped?"

"Yes."

"He is alive?"

"Who the fuck are you?"

"How you are helping him?"

"I'll give myself up. I want to trade. Straight up, Jack for me. But he has to be released at a hospital. I have to see him walk into a hospital before I'll show myself."

"I am not negotiator for mob. I am police."

"How do I know that? When Jack Russo is safe in a hospital emergency room, I'll come out."

"Why they are believe that?"

"Because they don't have a choice."

"They have friend?"

"Yes, damn it!"

"Then they have choice. Listen to me . . . ."

Agnes looked at her watch. It was seven fifteen.

"I'm listening," she said.

"Viktor Timkin."

"What about him?"

"Viktor Timkin is boss. He is who killed the men found in the water. The men in the water killed your friend."

"What do you know about that?"

"I am investigate case. Me and Nance and her partner."

"This Timkin killed the people that killed Rachel?"

"Not for justice. Viktor Timkin is piece of shit, too. But he doesn't kill your friend. The men in the water did that. And another man."

"Who?"

"An Arab. I don't know name."

Agnes was hopeful at his mention of the Arab. She tried not to show it. "What Arab?"

"The one hired your friend. Probably through Yuri Timkin and Harlem pimp, why they are dead, too."

"You know about the Arab?"

"I know about him, yes."

"You really legit?"

"I am real deal, lady. One hundred percent."

Agnes waited.

"I have idea, you want to help friend," the Russian said.

"What?"

"Timkin."

"What do you mean?"

"We kidnap him."

"Huh? How?"

"Is easy. I am law."

"And what about Jack Russo?"

"If he's still alive, Timkin is only one can save him."

Another moment of silence passed. Agnes looked at the digital clock in the dashboard.

"What you say, Agnes?" the Russian asked. "Time is running out."

•◆•

Lisa Russo turned off the television in her son's room before the cable news replayed the story about Jack's abduction. She maintained a fixed stare at her boyfriend. Two policemen were stationed in the hallway outside the room.

"Where's Dad?" Nicholas Russo asked.

"He had to help the police with a case," Lisa lied. "It was an emergency."

"He's retired."

"They needed him."

"Can't he call?"

"It's a surveillance case, Nick. He can't."

"Why are there police outside?"

"They're friends of Dad."

"Huh?"

"Daddy's friends," Lisa said. "They came to say hello. I asked them to wait outside."

"When's Dad get off?"

"Soon, honey."

Nicholas yawned. "I'm tired," he said.

"Then get some sleep, okay?"

Nicholas nodded.

"Love you," Lisa said.

"Love you," Nicholas said.

"I'll be right outside."

"Wake me when Dad calls."

"Of course," Lisa said. Then she covered her eyes so he couldn't see her tears.

•◆•

One of the men who had stood guard inside the room was standing across the hall and talking on a cell phone when Jack peeked out from behind the door. The man turned at the sound of the door opening, and Jack shot him in the forehead.

He looked both ways in the hallway and was surprised it

was empty. Jack ran toward the far end of the hall. He found the stairwell door and pushed it open.

He carefully looked over the edge of the stairwell. He saw it was clear below and started down the stairs. He checked the doorway leading to the second floor to make sure it was open, then continued down the stairs. When he reached the first floor, Jack looked through the small window in the door and saw a group of men in the lobby, near the lounge. All of them were armed.

Jack looked behind him and saw there was at least one more flight leading to a basement. He knew he'd be trapped, but he was sure the stairwells would be checked first. When he heard a doorway open a few floors above him, Jack raced down the last flight of stairs.

• ◆ •

Nance's passenger seat wouldn't adjust to Moss's long legs. He switched places and took over the wheel when they pulled off the Belt Parkway. When they arrived at the Tiffany Diner, a handcuffed man was being dragged through the parking lot by two men wearing blue baseball caps.

"The fuck is going on here?" Moss said.

"Blue hats," Nance said. "Vanya said his guys would be wearing blue hats."

"They're cops?"

"His guys, yeah."

"Who's the guy they just grabbed?"

"He didn't say."

"Doesn't look Russian."

"I don't know, Bob. How can you tell?"

Moss's cell phone rang. "Yeah," he answered.

Nance watched as the handcuffed man was shoved into the back of a dark sedan. The car pulled away from the curb and sped to the corner. It stopped before running the light to make a right turn.

Nance looked to Moss. His face seemed contorted.

"Damn it, what took so long?" he asked.

"What's up?" Nance asked.

Moss held up a hand. He let out a breath of frustration when he ended the call.

"What?" Nance said.

"Agnes Lynn rented a car from Hertz at three this afternoon."

"And it took this long to find out? It's four and a half hours."

"They're trying to track the car, but she took the most popular model, a navy blue Chevy Cabriolet. There are thousands of them. We can have an APB issued, but there's a chance it'll be picked up by the bad guys."

"You mean by a dirty cop or a scanner?"

"What's the difference?"

"Shit."

Moss reached for a cigarette. He said, "She keeps playing hide-and-seek with us, they're going to find her first."

"Vanya said to wait here."

Moss, fidgety, began cleaning his nails. "And do what?" he asked.

"Maybe he contacted Agnes Lynn."

"And maybe he's jerking us off."

Nance rubbed at her temples again. The pain was coming back.

Moss grabbed his lighter. "Well?" he said.

"We can't drive around the city looking for a Chevy Cabriolet."

Moss put fire to the cigarette. He took a hard drag and held the smoke in his lungs a long while before letting it go.

"Except we do know the Russian stronghold is Brighton Beach," Nance said.

Moss started the engine.

"What are you doing?" Nance asked.

"Heading for Brighton Beach," Moss said. "It's better than waiting around for phone calls."

Chapter 30

PASHA CHENKOV HAD left the hotel as soon as he learned Igor Mahalov had been shot. The private doctor administering medical treatment to Mahalov's wound was located in Sheepshead Bay. Chenkov was on his way there when he heard the story of Jack Russo's abduction over the radio. Chenkov called the hotel and learned Russo had killed one of his men during his escape.

Instead of continuing on to meet with Mahalov, Chenkov stopped in Brighton Beach and picked up his fourteen-year-old Ukrainian girlfriend. Chenkov knew it was best to manage this crisis from outside the perimeter. He instructed his men to conduct a room-to-room search and work their way down toward the basement. They were to keep the place sealed and make sure they found Russo. Chenkov would call the woman to give her an ultimatum. Either she showed up at the Sheepshead Bay exit along the Belt Parkway within the hour or they would kill her boyfriend.

Chenkov used one of the disposable cell phones he carried in the glove compartment. He dialed Agnes Lynn's number and was surprised to hear her voice after one ring.

"One hour, lady, that's it," he told her.

There was no response.

"Hello?" he said.

"Where do I go?" she finally said.

Chenkov gave her a cell number. "Wherever you are now, go to Sheepshead Bay," he said. "Call number I give you. They tell you where to go."

The woman remained silent. Chenkov opened his window and let a rush of cold air inside the car. He cocked his left hand and tossed the cell phone out the window. He let the cold air refresh him another few minutes before bringing the window back up.

•◆•

Several years ago, when he was dealing with a Libyan official, Aalam al Fahd was able to trade a case of Tech-9 semiautomatic weapons for two young Lebanese sisters, ages eleven and thirteen. Fahd had been assured that the girls were both orphans as well as virgins and that he could resell them when they were older if he desired.

Although he wasn't a pedophile, Fahd thought he would use the girls for future bartering with men he knew lusted after children. In the interim, he had let his bodyguards use them as sexual servants.

It was a few months later when Fahd first discovered that sexual violence excited him. The bodyguards had presented him with videotapes they had made of the girls being beaten and raped. Each of the bodyguards had taken turns filming their savage attacks on the two girls. Although one of the girls had committed suicide, Fahd decided to have his own excitement with her sister before she too might kill herself.

Now he negotiated the distribution and sale of the DVD he had made of the black woman's murder. Fahd was seeking assurances that he could relocate to Saudi Arabia if staying in the United States became a problem.

He had several influential friends in the Saudi government. He had procured films for a few of them in the past. He knew of two films made in South America that had been bought by executives working for the royal family.

"Can you provide safe passage?" Fahd wanted to know after explaining his situation to a Saudi diplomat with the United Nations on his cell phone.

"Of course," the diplomat assured him. "What makes you ask?"

"I'm being safe. I have to know for sure. I'm losing friends here."

"Just get me the disc. I'll take care of your situation personally."

"So long as it can be done quickly," Fahd said.

"It is done," the diplomat said. "Now, it's getting cold outside. I must go."

Fahd looked through the blinds from his stateroom out

across the marina. He could see the man he was speaking to standing alongside a stretch limousine. Fahd brought the blinds up and down twice.

The diplomat waved to him.

"Okay," Fahd said. "I shall have it for you tomorrow evening. Send someone we've dealt with in the past, please."

When he hung up, Fahd couldn't turn away from the window. He watched the man get back inside the limo. He watched the car pull away from the marina and head north. He was feeling nervous since Viktor Timkin's visit to the yacht.

Fahd had decided he was tired of America anyway. He would move back to the Middle East and live out the rest of his life there. Viktor Timkin could buy his weapons from somebody else in the future. Life was too short and the world was too big to have to worry about a single gangster's vengeance. Fahd could go anywhere he wanted. There would always be women he could find to feed his frenzy.

These were his thoughts before he lay back on his bed and used the remote to burn another disc of the black woman's torture and murder.

•◆•

Agnes was double-parked side by side with a car on Brighton Avenue. A tall broad man with white hair and blue eyes was holding up a police badge. Agnes showed him her gun as they continued to speak to each other through their cell phones.

"You can get that badge anywhere," she told him.

"True," he said, setting the badge down. "You should do

same with gun before somebody sees. Timkin has driver, armed bodyguard. He sees gun, he doesn't ask questions."

Agnes lowered the gun to her lap.

"He will come in five, ten minute," the Russian added. He thumbed over his shoulder. "From behind, eh?"

"How do you know that?"

"Surveillance. He comes to bakery two times every day."

"And?"

"They know who I am, Agnes."

"Me, too, apparently."

"They will ignore me."

"Not me."

"You have answer for everything, you don't hear what I'm saying."

Agnes glared at him. "Go ahead and explain, but do it quickly. One of them called a little while ago and said I had less than an hour to save Jack."

"Who calls?"

"I don't know. He fired a gun next to the phone before to scare me. I thought he killed Jack."

"They don't kill friend until they have you."

"Yeah, so?"

"You need proof I am cop, no?"

"It would help."

"I shoot bodyguard."

"Huh?"

"I shoot Timkin's bodyguard."

"How? Why?"

"You'll see. Just don't shoot me, okay?"

"How do I . . . what . . . how?"

He interrupted her to point over his shoulder. "They are here," he told her. "They coming now."

Agnes saw the Mercedes in her rearview mirror. The windshield was tinted black. She saw the man she was hoping was a cop pull into a space alongside the curb. She quickly pulled ahead into another space farther up the block.

The Mercedes slowed down before pulling into the small parking lot in front of a bakery. She saw the cop get out of his car with his weapon clearly visible in his left hand.

She nosed the front of her car out enough to take off if they came her way. She looked up ahead to make sure it wasn't a setup. When she turned in her seat again, she saw the driver was out of the Mercedes. Then she saw another man on the other side of the car, the big shot, she was thinking, because of the way he took his time.

She watched the cop approach the driver with his weapon drawn. The driver argued before finally turning around to be frisked. The cop found two weapons on the driver. The other man, the big shot, had come around the car and was yelling.

Agnes glanced around front again, in case it was a setup. As she turned back around, she heard the gunshot. Her eyes opened wide when the driver went down. Then she saw the cop handcuff the other man and pull him by an ear. She slipped the transmission into reverse and backed up to meet them.

•◆•

Jack was lucky to have made it down to the basement, but it was a matter of time before they looked for him there. He did his best to find another way out.

There were light switches along one wall, but Jack decided to leave the basement dark. He focused on the area around him until his eyes adjusted to the lack of light. He walked carefully around a skid of Sheetrock and managed to find a short stairway that led to a padlocked door.

Jack could see light under the door. He searched the area for something to break the lock, then gave up when he thought he heard voices outside in the stairwell. He could shoot the lock, but it would give away his location sooner than he liked.

He barricaded the door leading to the basement instead. It would hold long enough for him to shoot the lock if he had to. He stood waiting near the barricade and wondered if someone in the hotel had heard the gunshots and had called the police yet.

Chapter 31

VIKTOR TIMKIN KNEW there would be aggravation as soon as he saw Vanya Koloff approaching the car. He had even told his bodyguard to stay calm, because he had seen the Russian detective do something crazy once before.

It had happened two years earlier, after one of Pasha Chenkov's men had beaten a woman in her hallway for being late with an extortion payment. The detective happened to be visiting another tenant in the same building. Koloff dragged the gangster out to the street, where everyone could watch him use a two-by-four to beat the man. Timkin had just pulled up in his car when it happened.

It was brutal and quick and something Timkin could appreciate. A few days later he had one of his men approach the detective to try to put him on the Russian mob's payroll. Koloff broke the messenger's nose.

A few minutes ago, when Koloff was frisking his body-guard, Timkin was thinking it was harassment for the sake of breaking balls. Then the detective had spoken Russian and told the bodyguard, "I am going to shoot you in the leg. Use your belt to make a tourniquet before you call an ambulance."

Then, just like that, Koloff shot Misha in the leg.

It was humiliating for Timkin to let the detective handcuff him, then pull him by the ear, but it was something he could deal with at another time. Timkin wasn't sure what it was about until he saw the woman in the car. Somehow he knew it was Agnes Lynn.

•◆•

"Vanya, right?" Agnes asked the Russian detective after he shoved the mobster onto the backseat.

"Yes," he said, "my name is Vanya. Detective Vanya Koloff."

He sat in the back and held the barrel of his gun against the mobster's ribs.

Agnes drove a few blocks before she had to stop for a red light. She turned on her seat and looked the Russian mobster in the eyes.

"If anything happens to Jack Russo, I'll kill you myself," she said.

Timkin looked her off. He spoke to Vanya in Russian.

"What I hate about this country the most," he said, "their women."

"What he say?" Agnes asked Vanya.

Vanya answered Timkin in English. "Careful, piece of shit. She was willing to shoot me. She would enjoy shooting you."

Timkin looked away from both of them.

"Can he save Jack?" Agnes said.

Vanya turned to Timkin. "If you can, you better," he said.

"Who is Jack?" asked Timkin, without looking at either of them.

Agnes tossed her cell phone into Timkin's lap and pointed her gun at him. "Do it," she said. "Right now."

Timkin looked her off again. Agnes fired a shot into the backseat a few inches to the left of the mob boss's shoulder.

"Now!" she yelled.

Timkin picked up the cell phone.

• ◆ •

When he could hear them trying the basement door, Jack stood back from the padlock, took aim, and fired. The lock broke apart. He pushed his way into another stairway.

He could hear them banging against the barrier he had constructed in front of the basement door. Jack guessed he had a few minutes before they would break through.

He raced up the stairway and stopped when he reached the top. There were two push-doors that led to the loading dock. He stepped outside and stood behind a container filled with construction debris. A moment later he could hear a car pulling into the loading bay.

Jack was thinking he would be surrounded when the guys in the basement finally broke through the barricade. He would be in the middle of crossfire, and it would be his own fault.

•◆•

Chenkov picked up the young girl he had chosen as his sex slave six months earlier, when she was first smuggled into America. He needed an uninterrupted hour or two with her now and maybe a long nap afterward. He was still in a cranky mood when she sat in his car.

Olga Barsukov lived with an aunt and uncle in Brighton Beach. She was a tall, thin girl with pale skin, long blond hair, and bright blue eyes. Her mother's sister and husband had encouraged their niece's role in Pasha Chenkov's life. Keeping the powerful mobster happy had its rewards.

Chenkov was glad to have finally killed the big-mouth cop who had insulted him for more than two years, but now there was another problem he wasn't as anxious to resolve. The mess back at the Sheepshead Bay hotel seemed to be escalating. Chenkov decided he would take the girl with him to a hideaway apartment in Canarsie until the problem resolved itself.

He turned the radio on and listened to another report on 1010 WINS about the former NYPD detective who was believed to have been abducted near his home in Perth Amboy, New Jersey.

"Focking shit!" Chenkov yelled in broken English. "God damn shit!"

The young girl jumped in her seat. Chenkov swung an open backhand at her head. His hand caught her in the shoulder instead. She backed herself against the door.

"Fock!" he yelled again before glaring at her.

She tried to reach behind her for the door handle. Chenkov reached out and pinched her thigh hard. She shrieked, but it only encouraged him. He smiled as he reached across her to open the glove compartment. He grabbed the last disposable cell phone and quickly dialed one of his men back at the hotel.

"What's going on?" he asked.

He was told the boyfriend was trapped in the basement. Chenkov said, "Kill him," and then he broke the connection.

He handed the cell phone back to the girl. "Put back," he told her.

The girl looked into the glove compartment and saw a small handgun off to one side. She put the phone inside and was about to take the gun when Chenkov slammed the compartment door shut.

Olga jumped back in her seat again.

Chenkov reached over and pinched her higher up on her left thigh. This time he didn't let go. He applied pressure until she screamed at him to stop.

"Please, don't do this! Please!" she yelled.

Chenkov finally let go. Olga kept her hands folded rigidly on her lap. She watched the road straight ahead. She did her best to ignore the pain in her left thigh. Her skin throbbed where a bruise had already started to form.

Chenkov said, "I eat you, fock you, and bring you home in two days, eh?"

Olga silently swore that she would kill this pig one day. She would hide a knife under her clothes and stab him through the heart over and over until blood poured from his mouth and nose and his thick, ugly body was limp forever.

•◆•

Nance was on her cell phone with Vanya when the call came in about a shooting outside a pastry shop. Vanya told her that Jack Russo was being held at the Brooklyn Inn hotel in Sheepshead Bay.

"That's close," Moss said. "It's right off the Knapp Street exit on the Belt. It's on our way."

They had been on their way to Brighton Beach. Moss put his flashers on. He slapped the portable light onto the roof and hit the siren.

Nance said, "Lucky we didn't get off the Belt yet, or we might be stuck in street traffic."

"We're okay," Moss said. He was making time weaving in and out of the parkway traffic.

"We're close, right? Sheepshead isn't far."

"Two minutes."

"Vanya is sending his guys, too."

"The blue hats?"

"Yeah."

Moss pulled into the left lane and leaned on his horn until an SUV moved over.

"There's something else," Nance said.

"What's that?"

"Agnes Lynn has a gun, and she's not afraid to use it."

"Huh?"

"Vanya said she almost shot the head of the Russian mob."

Chapter 32

JACK HAD DUCKED behind the container along the left wall of the loading dock platform and waited until the car engine cut before he leaned out enough to aim his weapon. The two men sat in the car smoking. Jack waited in silence.

When he heard footsteps coming from the stairwell to his left, he fired a shot at the wall to keep the men from coming up. The gunshot alerted the men in the car. Both got out, brandishing weapons of their own.

Jack fired again, this time blowing out the driver's side window of the car. The return fire was immediate. He flattened out on the ground and hoped the bullets wouldn't ricochet off the garbage bin.

When a second set of shots came from somewhere outside the loading dock, Jack used the opportunity to jump off the platform down to the truck bay. He dropped to his chest again and tried to locate the shooters behind the car's tires. He spotted a set of feet, took aim, and fired one shot through an ankle. The man groaned as he went down a few feet from the car. Jack was still on his chest. He saw the wounded man had located him.

"Drop it!" Jack yelled.

The wounded man didn't flinch.

"Drop it!" Jack repeated.

The wounded man leveled his weapon.

Jack lined up a second shot at the same time sirens filled the air.

The wounded man fired first and missed. Jack shot him in the chest.

•◆•

They arrived at the hotel in time to see two of Vanya's squad running armed through the parking lot toward the hotel. Moss drove around to the back of the hotel, where two more of Vanya's men were already engaged in a shootout. He stopped just inside the parking lot entrance and drew his weapon. Nance was already out of the car.

Moss hustled in a crouch toward a parked car closer to the opening of the loading dock. He could see Vanya's men returning fire into the loading dock from behind an SUV. He signaled to them by waving his arm. Both undercover cops acknowledged him. Moss hustled to the back wall of the hotel twenty yards from the loading dock entrance. He saw Nance taking a firing stance a moment before she went down.

·◆·

Jack figured the guys in the basement would be out on the loading dock any second. Crawling on his stomach along the bottom of the platform's left wall, he made his way to the entrance and peeked around the corner. He could hear shots being fired from behind. He looked over his shoulder and saw the muzzle flash of a shotgun. The boom was deafening inside the loading dock. Jack felt a burn in the back of his right leg. He rolled onto his side and then scrambled around the corner to safety.

Once outside the loading dock, someone yelled at him to stay low. Jack continued to crawl. He heard another barrage of gunfire from inside the loading dock and looked to his left. He saw a black woman in the parking lot go down clutching her stomach.

Jack stood up to run. Gunfire echoed around him. Someone yelled at him to stay down, and he dove to the pavement and covered up. When he looked up again, a man wearing a blue baseball cap was dragging the wounded black woman behind the cover of an SUV. Jack could see her stomach was bloody. He heard footsteps behind him and tried to run again. As he got to his feet, he felt a kick in the back of his right leg and fell forward. He watched as his weapon bounced a few feet ahead.

Jack lay flat on his stomach waiting to be hit again as sirens blared on Knapp Street. He felt someone grab one of his arms and pull.

"You're okay, Russo," the cop said. "Just stay down."

Another series of gunshots rang out. Jack was pulled behind a police cruiser where a half dozen uniformed cops were crouched with their weapons drawn.

The cop who had pulled him to safety was a tall black man. Jack looked for him to thank, but the cop was running across the lot where the black woman lay behind the SUV.

Suddenly the shooting stopped. A series of shouts came from inside the loading dock.

"Don't shoot!" Jack heard. "Don't shoot!"

•◆•

Agnes had raced through the streets back to the Belt Parkway heading east toward Sheepshead Bay. When she pulled into the hotel parking lot, it was already crowded with police cars and ambulances.

Viktor Timkin's call to the men holding Jack Russo had come too late. Russo had already escaped. A gun battle had erupted at the motel, and now several Russian mobsters were being corralled for arrest by members of Vanya's mob squad and uniformed officers of the NYPD.

Vanya had called one of his men and learned about the woman detective. She had been shot in the stomach during the gunfight. He told Agnes to drive around the back of the hotel.

"You know her?" Agnes asked.

"She is friend, yes. Anita Nance."

"The one I spoke to?"

"Yes."

"Is she bad?"

"Stomach wound is always bad."

Vanya had allowed himself to get close to one woman since coming to America. It was an intimate relationship that had lasted just under six months before Islamic fundamentalist terrorists crashed two commercial airliners into the World Trade Center on September 11, 2001. Marta Gruber was one of more than three thousand innocents killed that day.

He drank for two weeks afterward and was eventually forced into treatment by NYPD brass. One month later he was back on the streets doing his job. He knew it had nothing to do with the alcohol treatment. He knew it was work that would save him. He had learned the lesson well in Russia. People died; life went on.

Now he was trying to convince himself that what he had started to feel for Anita Nance was something else to get beyond. Nance was the first woman he'd felt something for since Marta. It had felt good to think about her.

They arrived around the back of the hotel in time for him to see Nance being lifted by an EMS team onto a gurney. He got out of the car and ran to her. He could see she was still conscious. A group of uniformed officers blocked his path until he showed them his badge. He tried his best to get her attention before the gurney was pushed inside the ambulance, but was too late. The rear doors closed and the ambulance took off.

He spent the next few minutes talking with two men from his squad before returning to the car he had come in.

When he saw Viktor Timkin being helped out of the back by a uniformed officer, Vanya scanned the area for Agnes Lynn.

She was gone.

•◆•

Once she saw Jack being helped into one of the ambulances at the back of the hotel, Agnes had pointed her weapon at Viktor Timkin's chest one more time.

"Who killed my friend?" she asked.

Timkin had hesitated a moment, then said, "They are dead already."

"Who's the Arab?"

"Pervert," he said. "Rich pervert."

"What's his name?"

"I don't know his name."

She aimed the gun at his head. "You have two seconds."

"Fahd," Timkin said. "I don't know what else he's called."

"Why did he do that to my friend?"

"He pays for it."

"What do you mean?"

"He makes film."

"What kind of film?"

"Bad film. I don't approve."

Agnes felt her jaw clenching tightly.

"Is pervert, eh?" he said.

"How much did he pay?"

"I don't know."

"You know."

"I don't. Is not something I want. I leave people responsible in water. I kill one myself."

Agnes wanted more. She moved the gun closer to Timkin's face.

"Arab is on boat," he said. "Has bodyguards. You can't touch. I try already."

"He has the film?"

"I don't know what he has except for bodyguards."

"He does, doesn't he?"

"Is not my business."

Agnes saw there were more police cars gathering in the parking lot. She jammed the gun in her bag and slid off the front seat.

"Hey!" Timkin yelled. "Let me go handcuffs!"

Agnes never heard him.

Chapter 33

WHAT SHE DID was make her way back to Manhattan by bus and then train. Before returning to her room, Agnes headed to St. Mark's Place, where she bought an outfit and boots she intended to use to board the yacht. On Third Avenue she found a cutlery store, where she purchased a Sabatier five-inch boning knife.

When she was back at the hotel, she immediately began to dress. She wore black thong bikini underwear under a red leather miniskirt. She wore a tight white top without a bra. She used sheer nylons to keep her legs warm and then pulled on red leather thigh-high boots with three-inch heels. She paced around the room a few times before she was comfortable. Then she jerry-rigged a sheath made of cardboard inside the right boot and practiced pulling the knife out from different angles.

Agnes called the hospital for an update on Jack and felt relieved when she was told he was recovering. He had suffered a bullet wound in one of his legs. She watched the local news and learned he had been credited with killing two of his captors. Then they showed a picture of him in his dress blues as a former member of the NYPD. Agnes smiled at the picture of a much younger man.

She was upset when she learned that the woman detective remained in critical condition. Agnes had no way of knowing the detective had been honest with her until after she was shot. She hoped the best for Anita Nance.

She spent the next few minutes looking over a street map of the East Side. When she was confident she knew the area well enough, Agnes reapplied her lipstick, combed her hair, and spent a long moment looking at the tiny mirror above the bathroom sink.

She was thirty-five years old and had never made love or been made love to, not really. She had spent ten years of her life as a sexual zombie trading herself for money.

Agnes had hoped that Jack would be the man to help her break free of the emotional restraints of her past life, but she had almost cost him his life. She couldn't imagine facing him again after what had happened.

Next Agnes wondered about the only other man she had ever been close to, her father, and she began to sob. She wondered what he was doing at that exact same moment and could picture it clearly. Francis Lynn was probably petting his dogs the way he always did after taking them for an after-dinner walk.

Agnes reached for her cell phone. She dialed her parents' home number. A man answered, but Agnes wasn't sure if it was her father. She asked for Francis Lynn.

"He doesn't live here anymore," the man said.

"Did he move?" she asked.

"Divorced," the man said. "Who's calling, please?"

Agnes heard a woman ask who it was in the background. She recognized her mother's voice and hung up.

She saw her tears in the mirror and quickly wiped her eyes. She remembered crying in her room on her fourteenth birthday after discovering her mother with another man. Here it was twenty years later and nothing had changed. Her mother was with another man, and her father wasn't there for Agnes.

She stared at her image in the mirror until her anger returned. Maybe she was comfortable playing the role of a predator. She shifted her weight to one leg and pushed her hip out in a seductive pose. Instead of disgust, Agnes felt confident.

Not everybody needs protection.

Agnes thought about her friend Rachel, and her jaw tightened. She was filled with anger and determination. She took one last look at herself in the mirror before going after the man who had paid to watch her best friend die.

•◆•

The way Vanya had figured it, the woman was going after the Arab, and Viktor Timkin couldn't care less. Agnes Lynn had mentioned the yacht docked somewhere on the East Side. Vanya knew there was only one place it could be and parked nearby.

He knew she would head there as soon as she had disappeared from the hotel parking lot back in Brooklyn. He had stayed in contact with his men and learned that Anita Nance was still in critical condition. She had hemorrhaged a lot of blood. A surgical team was desperately trying to save her. Vanya said silent prayers for her while driving into the city.

When one of his men told him he was being requested to report back to police department officials, Vanya did not say where he was headed.

He spent the next hour and a half hiding under the FDR Drive north of the South Street Seaport. He knew Agnes Lynn would come to the yacht. It was only a matter of time.

Vanya could see the marina clearly from where he was parked. The lights on the boat flying the Saudi flag were bright. He tried to guess at the number of crew on the boat. He figured at least a dozen. He guessed the Arab had bodyguards as well and that they would be armed. So might the rest of the crew.

At ten o'clock he saw a woman approach the guard booth. At first he didn't recognize Agnes Lynn. It was after she seemed to negotiate her way inside the marina when Vanya realized who she was and that it was time to move.

•◆•

Agnes squinted at the black man sitting inside the booth at the marina entrance gate.

"Jeffrey?"

It took a long moment before he recognized her. "You the investigator?" he said.

Agnes flashed a smile. "On the job," she said. "He up there?"

"Who up there?"

"My client's husband?"

"I wouldn't know. There hasn't been anybody else up there tonight, and the limo is in the back, so the man hasn't gone out either."

"The man being Mr. Fahd?"

Jeffrey shrugged. "Arab dude owns the yacht," he said. "Don't know his name. You going undercover or what? You dressed like one of the girls now."

Agnes pulled out a fifty-dollar bill. "Why I'd appreciate it if you didn't announce me," she said.

"I can't lose my job for fifty bucks, lady."

"I have more."

"You don't have enough. This job is how I pay my bills. You want to go up, I have to announce you."

"Well, can you tell them I'm here as a gift?"

"You mean lie?"

"Exaggerate."

Jeffrey hesitated. "I guess I can do that, but I'll deny it if anything happens, I get called to testify."

"You won't be called to testify, I promise."

Jeffrey's forehead wrinkled as he thought about it some more.

"And I would feel better if you took the money," Agnes said.

"I wouldn't," he said. "Just go 'head up."

"Can you hold something for me down here?"

"What?"

Agnes pulled the gun from her purse.

"Jesus, lady," Jeffrey said.

"Please?"

"Give it here," he said.

She could see lights on throughout the yacht as she went through the turnstile. The yacht was long. Agnes wondered where the sick fuck who owned it watched the snuff film he had made of her best friend. She wondered if he invited other sick fucks to watch it with him.

She stepped up onto the gangway leading to the main deck. It was a long walk in the spiked heels. She used the handrails to steady herself. She knocked on a locked gate a few times before a thin Arab man in a white uniform responded.

"I'm here for Mr. Fahd," Agnes said.

The Arab was confused.

"I'm a surprise from Mr. Timkin," she added. "Viktor Timkin."

The Arab seemed to recognize the name. "Come," he said, and proceeded to unlock then open the gate for her.

She was led into a lounge facing the rear of the yacht. She was offered a drink that she declined before the uniformed Arab left her alone. She could hear Middle Eastern music from the deck above. She wondered if she had interrupted a party. She looked up at a clock on the wall and saw it was nearly ten thirty.

After five minutes she felt nervous waiting there. When the music stopped, Agnes began to sweat.

•◆•

Holding out his police identification, Vanya approached the guard in the booth. His weapon was drawn. He asked the guard who the woman was he had just let inside the turnstile.

"Don't know her," the guard said. "She here for the dude owns the yacht."

Vanya motioned for the guard to take off.

"I leave, I lose my job."

"Then stay out of way," Vanya told him. "And don't call police, eh? I am police."

The guard stood silent. Vanya jumped the turnstile and walked in the shadows of the Arab's yacht. He was up the gangway when he spotted the locked gate. He used a lock pick to get inside.

He was close to the rear of the yacht when footsteps on the deck above forced him to hide in the shadow of a stairway. Vanya stood still for what seemed like forever as two men held a conversation directly above him. When they finally walked away, he made it the rest of the way to the rear of the yacht. He was surprised when he spotted Agnes Lynn through a window. She was removing her clothes.

Vanya racked the slide on his Glock.

Chapter 34

AALAM AL FAHD scratched Kasib's neck while two of his men took the woman's clothing. She was down to black thong panties, the white top, and her boots. He pointed a finger and motioned for her to turn around.

She did as she was told.

"What are you doing here, miss?" he asked.

"I'm a gift," she said.

"Really? From whom and for what?"

"For a Mr. Fahd from a Mr. Timkin. Viktor Timkin."

"Really?"

"It's what the agency told me."

"I see," he said.

"I don't have to stay if you don't want," she said. "It's no problem for me. I'll get paid either way."

"You're a hooker then?"

The woman shifted her weight onto one foot. "What else did you think?"

Fahd tugged on the dog's collar. It growled. The woman gasped before stepping back. Fahd's men laughed.

"That isn't funny," she said.

Fahd looked to his men. He spoke to them in their language and asked if they had frisked her for a weapon. They both nodded.

"What about the boots?" the woman asked. "Should I take them off, too?"

Fahd looked up and down her body. "I rather like the boots."

"Keep them on?"

Fahd turned to his men. One of them reached out and slid a hand on the woman's right shoulder. She spun and slapped his hand away.

"What's wrong?" Fahd said. "You don't like Muhammed?"

"No touching," she said.

Fahd chuckled. "A whore who doesn't want to be touched," he said. "That's a new one."

The woman pulled her top off. She handed it to Muhammed.

"Very nice," Fahd said. He was leering at her now. "Are they real, your breasts?"

The woman covered them with her hands.

"Ah, a shy one," Fahd said.

She slowly let her hands down.

"How you are going to make love without touching?" Fahd asked.

"I'm not here to make love," she said. "No kissing, no touching."

Fahd spoke to his men in their language again. The three of them laughed.

"I doubt they want to kiss you," Fahd said.

The woman crossed her arms over her chest.

"Now show us your pussy," Fahd said.

"In front of them?" she asked.

"Why not? You're for them. You're my present to them."

She held up both hands. "Oh, no, we don't," she said. "That's not what I was told."

"What's the problem now, dear? You are a whore, are you not?"

She was waving her hands now. "I don't do gang bangs, hon. Sorry."

Fahd tugged on the leash. The dog growled again. The woman gasped one more time.

Fahd said, "Show us your pussy."

•◆•

Agnes wondered if this was what the slob had done to Rachel to humiliate her. She wondered if the dog had been there, too, and if the two bodyguards had helped film her murder.

When the dog growled the second time, Agnes was already thinking she needed to get the knife before it was too late. She had played them just right by offering to take her boots off, but now things were progressing in ways she hadn't considered. If the two bodyguards were going to take her, she'd never get to the fat Arab responsible for killing her friend.

She tried to stall for a better opportunity.

"Can I at least have a drink first?" she asked.

Fahd motioned at one of his men. The one holding her top went to a bar across the room.

"Vodka tonic, if you have it," she said.

"When did you speak with Viktor?" Fahd asked.

"I didn't," Agnes said. "A service I work for told me to come here. They told me to tell whoever asked that Viktor Timkin sent me as a gift. I never met the man."

"When was this?"

"I got the call this afternoon, but I don't know when it was arranged."

The drink was handed to her. She took it and motioned at her top. "You want me to autograph that?"

The one named Muhammed tossed her top on the floor.

"Viktor Timkin was arrested two hours ago," Fahd said. "Do you know who he is?"

Agnes shook her head. "I have no clue."

Fahd took a seat on a large stool near the bar. The dog remained on the leash. Agnes took her time sipping the drink.

"How much would you charge us to film you?" he asked.

"Film what?" Agnes asked. She motioned toward his men. "Me with them?"

"Why not?" Fahd said.

"Ten thousand," she said.

"Very amusing. You must have a golden pussy, love."

"Something like that."

She felt a hand on her ass and reacted instantly. She smacked it. "I told you no touching," she said.

Muhammed was smiling at her.

"How much for them to go through the back door?" Fahd asked.

Agnes felt her heart racing. Her sense of panic was surging. She wasn't sure she could fight it off.

"How much?" Muhammed asked.

Agnes focused on his eyes. "No anal," she said. "Sorry."

"Come now, love," Fahd said. "There must be a price. How much?"

"I don't do it," Agnes said. She could feel adrenaline overtaking her panic. She set her drink on a cabinet and arched her back.

"Your pussy," Fahd said.

She pulled down her thong underwear enough to step out of them. Muhammed took a step toward her. She tossed him the underwear. He slapped them away and reached for her.

"Hold it," she said, pointing a finger at him.

Muhammed stopped. He looked to his boss.

Fahd tugged on the leash one more time. The dog growled on cue.

"No more bullshit," Fahd said, "or Kasib rips you to fucking pieces."

•◆•

Vanya watched from a window along the wall and waited for an opportunity to enter the cabin. His first concern was the dog and the damage it might do to Agnes Lynn if he didn't kill it with the first shot. He could see both bodyguards had weapons in holsters around their waists. He was pretty sure he could take them both out before they reacted, but the dog and the fat guy were another story. A pit bull that size could do a lot of damage to a big man in a very short amount of time. Agnes Lynn might be dead before he could help her.

He could hear footsteps on the deck above him again. There was a stairway twenty or so feet directly behind him. If the footsteps started down the stairs, he would have to make his move whether the timing was right or not. He would have to neutralize the situation in the cabin before he could defend Agnes from whoever else was on board.

Vanya suddenly wished he had told his men where he was.

He could see Agnes was naked except for her boots now. The fat guy had taken a seat. The other two were standing off to one side. One of them was holding her underwear up to his nose. The other was opening his pants.

Vanya saw her flinch and then noticed the dog was showing its teeth. He took a step closer to the door that he hoped was unlocked so he wouldn't have to waste a bullet.

Chapter 35

HER ONLY CHANCE to get the knife was if the dog was tied. She might have to start things with the two guys wearing guns on their hips, but she was willing to take care of them if it meant getting Fahd. She asked Fahd to tie the dog up before they began.

He sat on a short leather stool. "Why?" he asked.

"He makes me nervous," Agnes said. She picked up her drink again. "I'll give you a show and a half if that's what you want, but that dog will definitely keep me from getting into it."

Fahd draped the leash around a cabinet handle alongside him. "Now finish your drink," he said.

Agnes downed the drink. "Who's doing the filming?"

"Start with Muhammed, please," he said. "Suck him off."

She turned and saw that Muhammed was stepping out of his pants.

"Can I at least have some pillows?" she said.

The Arab motioned at the other man with his hand. He went to the couch on the far side of the room and tossed two throw pillows where Agnes stood. Muhammed was naked below the waist now. He pulled off his shirt.

"Now, please, start the show," Fahd said. "How do you say, action?"

Agnes felt her teeth clench at what he'd just said.

Muhammed took a step toward her.

Agnes pointed at him without breaking eye contact with Fahd. "Don't you fucking touch me," she said.

The dog began to growl a moment before there was a loud metallic sound followed by a gunshot.

Fahd reached for the dog's leash.

•◆•

Vanya didn't see the guy behind him until it was too late. He ducked when he saw the shadow against the wall and just missed getting hit in the head with a pipe.

He spun away and could see a tall man wearing a kufi was holding the pipe. The man swung again, and this time Vanya couldn't avoid the blow. His left forearm was broken. He cursed through clenched teeth before firing his weapon.

The tall man was thrown backward onto the deck from the force of the bullet. A moment later Vanya could hear a commotion inside the cabin. He pointed his gun at the door when it suddenly opened, and the dog was there showing teeth.

Vanya took aim as the dog began to charge. The bullet found the dog's throat. The wounded pit bull slammed against the wall and then scrambled to its feet, choking on its own blood. One of the bodyguards in the doorway had a gun, but Vanya shot first. The bodyguard fell back inside the cabin.

Vanya could see the dog was still choking. He couldn't watch it suffer. He killed it with another shot, this time in the head. Then Vanya felt a jolt in his left shoulder and spun with the force of the bullet that had come from somewhere inside the cabin.

•◆•

Fahd hadn't trusted the woman when she said she was there as a present from Viktor Timkin, nor did he believe her story about working for an escort service. He had his security guards frisk her before calling up to make sure his men on the deck above hadn't spotted police in or around the marina. When he was sure it was safe, Fahd decided he would let his men have some fun with the bitch, whoever she was.

They were just about to start when the gunshot outside the cabin changed things.

The first thing he did was set the dog loose to find the intruder. Kasib had ripped apart two stowaways in the past: a man in Morocco the dog had found hiding inside the galley, and a Brazilian whore who had bit Fahd on the penis for tugging too hard on her hair. Both were dead within minutes of the dog's attack.

When he heard the dog choking after the gunshot, Fahd reached inside the cabinet drawer for a handgun he kept there. He turned it toward the door and fired a single shot before turning it on the woman as she reached for something inside her boot. He was about to shoot her when one of his bodyguards landed at his feet with a bullet hole in his chest.

Fahd looked for the woman again. Muhammed had her from behind and was choking her with his forearm.

"Kill her!" Fahd yelled.

The woman was holding something with tape around one end. He saw it was a knife a moment before she swung her arm down behind her and stabbed Muhammed behind his knee.

Another gunshot launched Muhammed forward into the woman. Fahd had taken aim at her. He fired, but the bullet struck Muhammed in the neck instead.

"Fucking bitch," Fahd yelled a moment before another series of shots were fired.

•◆•

Agnes saw Fahd turn toward the door after shooting his bodyguard by accident. She charged him with the knife.

He was surprised by her attack and fired a wild shot into the man at his feet. She grabbed his right wrist with her left hand, then kicked him in the stomach with a knee. Fahd lost his wind and fired another wild shot, this time into the ceiling.

Agnes stepped back and kicked him in his crotch.

Fahd's mouth opened wide. The growl he emitted came from deep in his throat. The gun fell from his hand as he slowly dropped to his knees. He reached back with one hand to steady himself and inadvertently grabbed the television remote off the cabinet. The television above the bar clicked on. Agnes looked up and saw Rachel on the screen. She was on her stomach. A man with a knife sat on her back as Rachel kicked her legs wildly.

Agnes cringed when she heard Rachel's bloodcurdling scream. Then she felt a hand grab her ankle. She was calm this time and didn't pull away. She had already picked up Fahd's gun. She aimed it at his face.

Another scream from the television forced her to look up. Someone had held a camera directly over Rachel and the man cutting her. Agnes grabbed the remote from the floor and killed the power.

Fahd let go of Agnes's ankle and rolled onto his right side before looking up to beg for his life.

"Don't shoot," he pleaded. "I have money. I have a lot of money. I can make you rich. Don't shoot me, please."

Agnes glanced to her right, saw the knife on the floor, and said, "Deal, I won't shoot you."

•◆•

Vanya took another shot from somewhere up the stairway before he killed the shooter. The first bullet had caught him in the left shoulder and spun him. The second bullet tore off a piece of his left ear.

It was reflex when he fired up the stairway. It was luck when he placed two shots in the center of the second shooter's chest.

Vanya heard someone yell something in Arabic before a

floodlight illuminated the yacht from bow to stern. He waited with his gun trained at the top of the stairway until he heard another shot from inside the cabin.

He made his way across the deck to the cabin door when a shot whistled past his right ear. Vanya dropped to the floor, rolled, and returned fire. His shots struck the shooter in the face. The force of the bullets sent the shooter over the railing into the water. Another shot from the deck above forced Vanya to return fire in that direction.

He heard a grunt a few seconds before a gun bounced at his feet. Vanya rolled out onto the deck with his weapon pointed up at the stairway. There was nobody there. He took quick glances around him before making his way back to the cabin door. He stepped inside and saw the two men he had shot lying on the floor. He took another few steps inside and saw Agnes Lynn was dressing herself. Vanya saw a blood-soaked towel on the floor at her feet.

"You okay?" he asked.

Agnes didn't answer.

He looked from her to a pair of feet to her left. It was the fat guy lying dead on his back. Vanya stepped closer and saw that a knife was buried to the handle in the middle of the fat guy's throat.

Epilogue

DETECTIVE ANITA NANCE was moved from the intensive care unit to a private room after two days of blood transfusions. On the third day of her recovery, Vanya Koloff returned to see how she was doing. She smiled at him when he walked into the room; he was carrying a potted plant in his free hand. His left arm was in a sling. His left ear was heavily bandaged as well.

"Did you really shoot that guy in the leg?" she asked him.

"Hello, how are you, too?" Vanya said.

"I'm sorry," she said. "How is your arm?"

"You forget shoulder and ear. I am fine." He set the plant

on the windowsill. "This is Russian olive tree. Is beautiful when is full."

"That thing will become a tree?"

"Why you need backyard. You have?"

"No, I don't."

"Okay, we fix."

He moved a chair alongside her bed and sat.

"Thanks for coming," she said.

"I'm here twice already but you are not out of ICU," he said. "I pray for you, Anita. You give me great scare."

She reached out and took one of his hands. "I was worried about you, too," she said. "I still am. Now, did you?"

Vanya was under investigation for allegedly shooting Viktor Timkin's bodyguard in the leg. There were several other alleged charges pending, including failing to respond to emergency calls. He had been suspended pending the investigation.

"Was very confusing," he said. "I don't remember."

Nance gave him an exaggerated frown.

"I was big hurry," he said, "everything goes fast." He waved off the issue. "Forget nonsense. What doctors say? When you are coming home?"

"Moss said they're giving you a hard time."

"I am suspended. Big deal."

"He said they're looking to get rid of you."

"Then I have life, eh? I can have family. They do me favor."

Nance squeezed his hand. "Do you know what happened to the woman?"

"I'm there on boat in shootout. I find Arab is dead. I find film he has of Rachel Wilson. Woman is gone."

"Vanya, Moss said they're considering criminal charges."

"Viktor Timkin is out on bail in less than twenty-four hour, eh? What they say here is true. Is good country, America."

"They can't hold him?"

"Unless they find Pasha Chenkov and to flip him," Vanya said. "Timkin stays Timkin. Is still boss."

"That's crazy," Nance said. She tried to sit up and coughed.

"Go easy," Vanya said. "Is what happens in organized crime. Igor Mahalov and Tevya Bartnev are found in car trunks this morning in Brighton Beach. One of my guys calls to tell me."

"Executed by Timkin?"

"His orders, sure."

Nance closed her eyes in disbelief.

Vanya said, "Is what happens, eh? Boss stays boss. His day comes another day."

Nance was still upset. "You might be arrested, but the head of the Russian mob won't be?" she said. "That's fucking crazy."

Vanya patted his stomach. "I get arrested, I go away and lose twenty pound. I'm not worry what they do. You are okay, that is what matters."

Nance sighed.

Vanya poured himself a cup of ice water from her plastic pitcher. He drank it fast, then refilled the cup.

"I am thirsty," he said.

"What was the story with that guy at the Tiffany Diner?" Nance asked.

"You are full of questions, today," Vanya said.

"Well?"

"I do that for friend with organized crime task force, okay? Now he has snitch with LaRocca people."

Nance eyeballed him. Vanya stuck his tongue out at her.

"I hope you're not going to keep secrets from me in the future," she said.

"Depends I am cop or no," Vanya said. "Hopefully no."

"You don't want to be a cop anymore?"

"I want to have family, eh? Is time."

Nance chuckled. "Is this, like, a proposal for a date?"

Vanya kissed her hand. "I don't waste time with date, lady. I have backyard."

•◆•

Pasha Chenkov decided to temporarily hide at the apartment where his young girlfriend lived with her aunt and uncle. It was a location where he was sure he would be safe for at least a few days before he left New York for Israel.

Olga's aunt was anxious to please the Russian gangster and offered to cook whatever Chenkov desired. The uncle stayed to himself and was mostly nervous whenever Chenkov was in the same room.

It was a small two-bedroom apartment. Chenkov took over the master bedroom and moved the aunt and uncle into Olga's room.

The girl had gone out to shop for groceries and wasn't home when Chenkov woke from a nap. The aunt complained that Olga sometimes stopped at a bar to visit with friends when she should come straight home.

When she finally returned, Olga argued with her aunt a few minutes before the woman slapped her face. The sound of the smack brought Chenkov out of the master bedroom. He was holding an empty cup of coffee. He handed it to the woman and told her to make a fresh pot.

He looked Olga up and down before asking, "Where were you?"

"Shopping," said Olga defiantly.

"Your aunt said that was long ago. Where were you now?"

"Bar."

Chenkov chuckled. "Bar? What bar? You're too young. You want to drink?"

Olga slowly shook her head. "No," she said. "No drink."

"What bar?" Chenkov asked again.

"Nicholas."

Chenkov was about to light a cigarette. He stopped when Olga named the bar. It was a local hot spot for black market guns.

"Nicholas bar," she repeated, then pulled a revolver from her bag.

Her aunt gasped at the sight of the gun.

"Easy, woman," Chenkov told the aunt. "Olga knows better than this. She is upset. Leave her alone."

Olga remained silent.

"Give me gun," Chenkov said. He offered his right hand. "Come."

Olga shot him three times in the middle of his chest.

•◆•

It was the first time Jack and Lisa Russo were alone since he was shot five days ago. She had brought Nicholas to spend the day with his father. Jack was resting on the couch in his living room. His face and ribs were still badly bruised.

"He came across the country to see me, but he's downstairs with some broad now?" Jack asked.

"He's on the phone with her," Lisa said. "He probably doesn't want you grilling him about it either."

"He could talk to her anytime. Why didn't you stop him?"

"You're gonna start now?" Lisa said. "I took the morning off to make this trip."

"It's the first time, please. What is it, a big thirty miles?"

"You make it feel like a lot more than that, buddy."

Jack lit a cigarette. "Sorry," he said. "Where's Paul?"

"None of your business."

"I'm not being nosey, Lee."

"You're not being polite either."

"Actually I was."

Lisa took one of Jack's cigarettes and lit up.

"I thought you quit," he said.

"We broke up," she said. "I broke it off."

"I'm sorry."

"No, you're not."

"You're right, I'm not."

Jack smiled. Lisa gave him the finger.

"When's he getting off the phone?" Jack said. He turned to the digital clock in the cable box.

"It's the girl he's been hot for the last six months. She pushes him home in the wheelchair. Your son thinks it's the greatest thing in the world."

"Crystal?" Jack asked.

"Crystal Dawn Lawson," said Lisa, mocking the name. "Can you believe it?"

Jack smiled again. "That the green-eyed monster I detect?"

Lisa flipped him the bird again. "Detect this, Jack."

He chuckled.

"She's probably cutting class to make this call," Lisa said. "I should tell her mother."

There was a noise at the front door. Jack looked at his watch.

"That's the mail," he said. "I'm greasing the super a few bucks a week to slip it under the door until I can get around."

Lisa got up to retrieve the mail. When she came back, she was looking through it.

"Isn't that against the law?" Jack said.

Lisa stopped halfway through the pile.

"You know an Agnes?" she asked.

Jack looked up open-eyed. "Yeah," he said with a bit too much enthusiasm.

"Jesus, I guess you do," Lisa said. She walked the postcard over and handed it to him.

Jack looked at the picture before turning the postcard over to read.

"You never mentioned her," Lisa said. "Since when?"

"Huh?" Jack said. He was reading Agnes's tiny scripted message.

Lisa saw he was preoccupied and went through the rest of his mail.

Jack read:

Dear Jack,
Sorry for all I put you through. I hope to meet you again someday. I can't say when, so please don't ask or look for me. I'll contact you when I'm ready. I promise.
Thank you for being there. It means a lot to me.
I hope you and your son heal quickly,
Agnes

Lisa set his mail on the coffee table and waited for his attention. He was squinting at the postcard.

"Christ, Jack, you look jilted," she said.

"Huh?"

"You lose your ability to speak or something?"

"I'm sorry," Jack said. "What?"

"Wow, I guess I should be jealous," she said. "I've never seen you react that way for me."

Jack didn't hear her. He turned the postcard over again and stared at the road sign picture. It read: *Welcome to Fabulous Las Vegas.*

Special thanks to Rose Benvie (the fastest word processor in the big leagues), Jim Nyland (my official gun man), Brian Riccioni, Steven Sidor, Craig McDonald, Dave Greshman and Ann Marie.